Praise

An audacious literary achievemen ~~and Timbuktu, Sophy Burnham's~~ *cat's eye view of love, betrayal, high* ~~charming and deeply wise.~~ *is at once charming and deeply wise.*

—C.M. Mayo, author of *The Last Prince of the Mexican Empire*

The delicious appeal of **Love Alba** *has largely to do with the extraordinary voice of its cat-narrator. This voice grows more and more endearing with every page. Alba's openhearted generosity toward the stumbling emotional antics of her humans leads a captivated reader on a charmed journey to the last sentence. I intended to read the first few chapters yesterday and didn't raise my head until I was halfway through. What a writer!*

—Margaret Dulaney, author of the play *The Hummingbird's Tour*

Leave it to literary shape-shifter Sophy Burnham to riff on the feline novel vein of Rita Mae Brown, Don Marquis, Natsume Soseki, and Robert Michie, as told by a snarky cat with a spiritual streak. Burnham possesses a fearless acrobatic imagination, which makes for a magical ate-a-canary smile of a novel.

—Richard Peabody, editor, *Gargoyle Magazine*; author of *Richard Peabody Reader*

Love, Alba *is a charming, romantic cat's tale that will leave you purring. . .and mewing for more! I hope it's the first in a series.*

—Anne Simpkinson, former managing editor at *Guideposts.com*, contributor to Love Dem Cats! blog

In this comedy of manners, human foibles and feline nature combine in delightful, ingenious storytelling. Alba, the cat, is as memorably wise, funny, observant and vulnerable as any great character—yet always believably a cat. With humor and grace Burnham extends a generosity of spirit to all characters and suggests that we humans are lucky, indeed, to be looked after by these divine creatures. We don't quite measure up, but they love us poor souls anyway.

—Maureen McCoy, author of the novel *Junebug*

Love, ♥
Alba

For Hope Childs
a long lost friend
Love ♥ Sophy Burnham

Also by Sophy Burnham

Nonfiction

Novels

Plays

Children's Radio Plays (NPR)

Love, ♥
Alba

Sophy Burnham

Love, Alba

ISBN 978-1-935914-47-1

eBook ISBN 978-1-935914-60-0

Cover design by Lissie Fein and Peter King *sweetandfizzy.com*
Author photo by Erin Kellaher *erinkelleherphotography.com*
Interior design by River Sanctuary Graphic Arts

This is a work of fiction. Names, characters, places and incidents are the product of the author's imagination and any relation to actual events, locales, or persons (living or dead) is purely coincidental.

Printed in the United States of America

To order additional copies please visit:

www.sophyburnham.com

Library of Congress Catalog Number: 2015931134

Cats are intended to teach us that not everything in nature has a purpose.

—Garrison Keillor

When a man loves cats, I am his friend and comrade, without further introduction.

—Mark Twain

1

Love is a nail that pierces your heart, leaving you sighing, heartsick, yet never willing for it to stop. Who would have thought that at her age Lorna would fall in love? Or hide it at such cost? But it began with her fancy, newly painted, orange toenail nudging me aside.

"Out of my way. Move." Lorna pushed me. "Scat."

Such a disagreeable word. You'd think a lady wouldn't use such language to a cat.

I slid out the door and up the stairwell to a pretty little balcony I'd spotted earlier and stopped short. A huge black male rose from the floor, muscles rippling. He hissed at me, lips drawn back in a snarl. I felt the hair rise on my neck. But sometimes the best thing to do when you're scared is to pretend you're not. I sniffed the fresh, warm, balmy air, with its scent of lilacs and new-mown grass, and settled cautiously in the sun, my back half-turned to him.

Everyone says I'm beautiful with my gold highlights and smoky tones. I was wearing my blue necklace with diamonds that Lorna says makes my eyes even bigger and bluer.

He stretched luxuriantly, darkness like thunder, and lay down facing me.

==You must be new.

I stared into the distance, ignoring him.

==You moved into 2.

I washed my shoulder.

==Cat got your tongue?

Males can be so. . . vulgar. I looked down my nose at him and sniffed.

==Well, aren't you going to talk? Too proud? Stuck up?

1

He stood up then, enormous, and started toward me. I shot to my feet. My goodness! He was the size of a raccoon. I gave a swish of my tail and ran, heart pounding, into the building and down the stairs—skittering through the doorway toward Lorna, no pretense at being brave.

"Oh, there you are." She picked me up and snuggled her cheek in my fur, while I clawed up onto her shoulder in distress. Lorna is beautiful, with short tousled curls, and no one smells as good as she. But it's not only her scent that you notice. It's her calm and quiet energy. You just feel good when you're next to her. This morning she was dressed in jeans and a white tee shirt while she unpacked. She spilled me to the floor. We'd been doing this (moving, I mean) for the past two days, and I was tired of it, and I guess Lorna was, too, because she had already remarked to me acidly how in novels the heroines were never caught vacuuming or doing the ironing but only led exciting lives chasing spies or catching criminals, and how banal it was to find ourselves in Washington, District of Columbia, our nation's Capitol, with the biggest problem being unpacking books and music or going to market to buy food.

"Now for the couch."

She put her shoulder to the tattered sofa (tattered because I prefer its upholstered legs to my scratch post) and pushed.

==Lorna! Stop!

I jumped to the windowsill and curled up beside the bitter-scented geranium, spiking red against the thin white curtains.

==Sit! Relax!

Sometimes I think the 2-leggeds are deaf. But then I remember they aren't as smart as cats.

What else could I do? The planter was so big that I had to shift my whole weight against it. It fell with a CRASH and broke into a dozen shards, scattering dirt, leaves and roots across the floor and rugs.

==Oh, I said daintily.

"Oh, Alba!" Lorna wailed, and then, to my surprise, she burst into tears. I felt awful. She swiveled on her pretty feet, turning in helpless circles. "I don't even know where the dustpan is!" Just then the front door banged open against the wall, and we both turned in surprise.

He was dressed in khakis, barefoot, unshaven, his hair tousled, and his eyes half-closed in sleep, and in his arms lounged the huge black male.

He hissed. The next moment he shot to the floor. I jumped for the curtains.

Lorna screamed.

My claws ripped through the fabric. I twisted round, hit the floor with a thud, and threw myself behind the chair, every hair on end. Then I took a stand, tail lashing, ears back, and lips drawn into a frightened snarl. He was twice my size. His fur bristled, his tail turned into a bottlebrush, his green eyes snapped. Did he know he was in the wrong—invading my apartment? On *my* territory? I rushed him, scattering books and papers underfoot.

"Alba!" Lorna flung herself at me.

"Goliath!" shouted the intruder.

I slithered through her fingers as the black cat dashed to the table-top, with me right behind, slipping on the geranium dirt. A lamp fell and shattered. Lorna lunged to catch me. The man leapt for Goliath, and both 2-leggeds collided and fell amidst the boxes, dirt, stems, and broken terra cotta. Goliath dashed behind the sofa and out the door.

I chased him as he whipped into the hallway, down the stairs, and into the apartment below ours. Then I ran back upstairs to prowl my perimeter. I was a ball of electricity, every hair alight. Being attacked is frightening for a poor little thing like me. His scent was everywhere. I wasn't sure if I hated it or not.

Meanwhile the 2-leggeds had untangled themselves with apologies, and the man was brushing Lorna off. He suddenly stopped, embarrassed, and the next thing I knew my sensitive, kind, sweet Lorna, who wouldn't hurt a spider, Lorna who always catches flies under tumblers of glass and carries them carefully outside rather than

swat them dead, who eats vegetarian so she won't harm an animal—
had turned on him. Her eyes flashed.

"What do you think you're doing, barging in like that?"

"I came to stop the noise."

"Noise? Of course there's noise. I'm moving in." Her eyes filled
with helpless guilty tears.

"As anyone can see." He gestured to the room. "But it's Sunday.
I'm trying to sleep."

"Oh, I'm so sorry," she said with open sarcasm. But she was
shaken. His dark eyes and broken nose gave his face a rugged charm.
The problem was, she really was apologetic and didn't want to admit
it. "I'm so sorry to have woken you up." She tossed her chin. "And I'm
especially sorry at your revenge. Look at this place."

I crept under the couch to hide. She flicked off the CD. The silence
hit like thunder. The place was a wreck.

He looked about a moment, picked up a toppled lamp and put
it on a table.

"And how dare you bring a cat into someone else's apartment!"
she challenged.

==And a male, I called out, who might spray.

"And a male. I'm lucky he didn't spray!" she continued.

His jaw clenched. "And you're lucky I didn't call the police," he
said in a voice dangerously contained. "I came up merely to ask you to
be quieter. Or maybe to offer you a hand later, like a good neighbor,
if you would stop moving furniture right this minute, right on top of
my head." He picked up an overturned chair and set it right side up.

"Oh," she said.

He stared at her.

"I'll try to be quieter." Her reluctant apology.

"I'd like that. I worked all night. I'm trying to sleep."

"Oh. Do you work every night?" she asked in a tiny voice, and I could hear the thought whirling through her mind: that buying this apartment on the floor above him was a bad idea.

"I'm a lawyer. I've got a big case coming up."

"Oh. Well. I'm sorry." She shot out her hand. "I'm Lorna Stanford."

"David Scott." There was an embarrassed pause as they shook hands. "David Campbell Scott."

"Ah," she deadpanned. "Lithuanian, I presume."

He blinked, then laughed, to her delight. Her face lit up as she joined him.

After he left, she flung herself onto the sofa. She was shaken. "Oh, dear, I shouldn't have shouted at him. Whatever will he think of me? And we're neighbors." A moment later she rolled over on her stomach to hang over the edge and peer at me hiding under the couch.

"Come out, Alba. I'm sorry. I didn't mean to scare you. Come on out, kitty-kitty."

But I huddled in the dark, flaring with nerves. Once I saw two ducks get into a fight. They reared up on the water angrily, quacking at each other and beating their wings. The fight was over as soon as it started. Then each duck stood on the water and flapped as hard as possible to rid itself of excess energy. Being a cat, I groom my fur. The 2-leggeds think we're washing, but actually we're licking our light into place. The 2-leggeds aren't even taught how to comb their energy down their arms and sides or pat their auras into place. Instead, they walk around all day, bristling and boiling, with no idea how to rid themselves of the residue of their distress.

Lorna, for example, walked into the kitchen for a cup of tea. She broke out laughing, and the next second kicked a box in irritation. That was how she released her energy. Then she reached for the phone to call her friend Nicole, whom we all call Nikki.

Only she didn't tell the whole story. She didn't reveal why she thought the situation so funny that she told it twice, not forgetting to repeat his name: David Campbell Scott. Nikki listened politely, but what she wanted to talk about was her boyfriend's birthday coming up next week and the marriage proposal she expected on that day.

3

When she put down the phone, Lorna stood in the middle of the room, staring at the chaos around her. She was exhausted. She threw herself onto the ancient sofa that still occupied the middle of the floor. Unpacking had suddenly grown too much for her.

"Those boys." She meant the college students who claimed to operate a moving company and had agreed to move her for half the price of the professionals; and they had done it, sure, if you like the chest of drawers left in the bedroom aslant against the wrong wall or the bed not put together and boxes higgledy-piggledy all over the apartment. They had not arrived to load the van until late, and by the time they unloaded their truck, it was almost midnight. Lorna had already paid two-thirds of the money in advance, and when they announced that the job was done, all the furniture inside, and they wanted the final payment, she had bristled.

"No. You haven't finished. You can't leave things like that!"

"We have exams tomorrow. If you want us to come back in a few days, we can unpack for you. It'll cost more."

"Sue me." Through gritted teeth.

They had stormed out, leaving us to spend the night, forlorn and lonely on the mattress on the floor. "I'm too old for this," she complained as she settled down, but she was laughing, too. She gathered me into the crook of her knees. "Are you ok? You'll be all right? I put your litter box in the bathroom, if you need it." That's the kind of person Lorna is, always thinking of others.

But the fact remains, neither of us slept well. I was awake, prowling the place, while Lorna rocked with restless dreams. Which is why she sank down on the sofa now in discouragement.

"This is what comes of having a husband die without a will, his finances in disarray." She ducked her head.

"It makes me so mad," she snarled. "I'd kill him if he were still alive."

I never knew her husband, but I think the marriage had ended long before he quit his life. Later I heard of his lingering illness and the death that wiped her out, as she explained, rubbing the little gold cross she wore at her throat. The medical bills alone! It turned out that for years he'd been secretly gambling, dipping into their Retirement—in the end leaving her scrabbling for money. She'd sold their house to pay the bills, and then she'd found Nikki's ad for a roommate, and despite their difference in age (Lorna being old enough to be Nikki's mother), the two became great friends. They could not be more different: Nikki small and dark, with thick Italian hair that rolls down her back. "Thy hair is as a flock of goats, that appear from Mount Gilead," Lorna quoted from the *Song of Solomon.* "Have you ever seen a flock of curly goats jumping off the hillocks?"

"And the buttocks of a bear," Nikki would shout back—the two of them laughing—as she stomped in her bare feet, heels smashing against the hardwood floors of our little clapboard house in Arlington, Virginia, which is a commuter's suburb of Washington, D.C., and a bit snooty about those who live as well as work in the city. Nikki is impulsive, impetuous. In contrast, Lorna, older, more mature, gives off a radiant, quiet dignity. She is easy in her skin. Every gesture is mindful and graceful with none of Nikki's bumptious passion.

Now she sank into the sofa, and feeling her despondency, I leapt into her lap and began to knead her belly to comfort her.

"What have I gotten us into?" she whispered, stroking me. I agreed. I liked living with Nikki in the Virginia suburbs. I liked Puma, and the outdoor deck overlooking the garden, and the good bird hunting, and the dust under the porch to roll in. Also, I liked that Nikki worked at home with her paints and smelly chemicals, so I always had company when Lorna went off to her job.

"I'm too old for this," she muttered, and then she pushed me off and rose to her feet. "Okay, a cup of tea and then I can unpack the kitchen boxes; they won't make any noise. Things are good, Alba," she continued bravely. "We're here. We have a place of our own. I have my job, my health, and if I'm frugal. . . "

She left the thought unfinished, indulging in a favorite reverse daydream—how if she weren't prudent she'd end up a bag lady, sleeping on the grates, with two shopping bags at her feet (some clothes, a hairbrush, a change of underwear), myself in the crook of her arm, and shoes so worn they'd probably split open, exposing her toes like teeth to the constancy of bitter snow and rain—a life of penury and poverty, begging, old, abandoned, lonely, weary, and lost. . . .

Having taken curious comfort in these sad thoughts while drinking tea, she rose eventually and bravely attacked the tape on a nearby box with a butcher knife.

4

I should say a few words about Lorna. I think Lorna is a lovely name, don't you? It has dignity, but it flickers with humor and inner happiness. It's water running over rocks in a stream with fish. Nikki is a nice name, too, but it's full of fence spikes and you have to be careful when you jump on them. Lorna is pretty and slender with short hair the color of moonbeams in summer. Taller than short, plump Nikki, she's strong and fit. She had a husband once, and one little girl who died of leukemia, and another daughter, Nancy, who lives in New York with her husband and who calls her mother on the phone to complain about the tensions of her life. She also has a mother in Santa Fe, and a sister, and various friends whom she talks to on the phone. But at heart she's not as social as Nikki. She likes to be alone sometimes, and then I think she's purring in her own human way.

Lorna works at the Smithsonian Institution, which is a sort of College of Higher Learning, with research branches and many free museums. She works in Development, whatever that is; I only know that it's Important and involves Bringing In Money. Right now she is totally occupied (when she's not busy with moving house or caring for me) with the opening of the new Hall of Physics. The Vice President of the United States is scheduled to open the ceremonies, and famous physicists from around the world will give speeches at the formal dinner, all of which Lorna is helping to organize under the supervision of a difficult and irascible boss, and she is utterly distraught, as she explains to her mother, which is why she can't possibly come visit her in Santa Fe until it's all over.

I think Lorna had managed to unpack two boxes when we heard a faint knock at the door.

"Nikki?" She called out in delight as she turned the knob.

But it was the handsome neighbor from downstairs. He was fully dressed this time. In his teeth he clutched a paper bag that he thrust at her with a motion of his chin, both hands being occupied by white paper to-go cups of coffee. I trotted over to sniff his ankles. They smelled of tomcat.

"I'm sorry," he said as she relieved him of the paper bag. "I've brought croissants and lattes. To make up for my bad manners."

"Oh." She was taken aback. "Oh no. I'm the one who should apologize. First, the movers didn't even *arrive* to load their truck until eight o'clock last night, so we were bumping over your head at ten and eleven-thirty at night, and then this morning. . . I'm sorry I woke you up, I really am."

"Well, I can't go back to sleep." He cast an eye around the room, taking in the mess. "So, I thought I'd help you settle in."

"Oh, I couldn't ask you—"

"No, but you didn't, did you?" He grinned at her. He had barged fully into the apartment now. "Would you like to drink your coffee? Or shall we go right to work? What do you want to do first? The living room? The bedroom?"

I don't think I've ever seen Lorna fussing before. She seemed unnerved, picking up objects and putting them back down. She admitted that she didn't drink coffee, but only tea, and it was thoughtful of him, but she already had a mug right here at hand, black English Breakfast was her favorite. I think these last were almost her only stumbling words. She couldn't lift her eyes to David's face, but snatched quick, furtive glances as he sipped his coffee, and, to avoid looking at him, she pushed at the boxes or stared with fascination at the floor. He leaned one shoulder on the door jamb, meanwhile, and had no trouble at all taking in Lorna, in her white tee shirt and jeans and flaming orange toenails. I realized I'd never seen her with a man before—only Jeremy, who was Nikki's boyfriend after all, and didn't count.

"We should take care of the bed first," he decided, smiling down at her. "In case you want to take a nap later." He seemed perfectly at ease.

After a while they got down to business and put the bed together, then heaved the mattress onto the slats, and Lorna found the box with sheets, which allowed them to make the bed together, and then they pushed the chest of drawers in place and straightened the rugs, and in a short time the bedroom looked quite pretty. It would take days for the pictures to rise up from the floors.

While they worked, I drifted out the door that they'd left open and padded downstairs to sniff at the door to the apartment below. A few black hairs had caught in a hinge. It took a while to examine them. Then I explored the building. It wasn't big: in the spacious high-ceilinged entry hall a bicycle, smelling of oil and dust, leaned against the stairwell; behind the stairs a closed door led to a basement that smelled (sniffing under the door) of cold air, cobwebs, hornet's nest, mushrooms, and a different kind of oil. David's apartment with access to the garden took up the whole big rambling first floor, while ours occupied the floor above. Above ours, a small half-landing opened on one side to a storage attic and on the other to the balcony where I'd encountered the black cat. The balcony also belonged to us. In other words, this entire enormous stucco Victorian house counted only three floors (or four with basement and attic), which had been separated, upgraded, and converted into two respectable condos. Lorna says the housing market is really tight in Washington and prices are beyond belief. After my inspection I trotted up to the balcony and settled in a splash of sunlight to wash my ears. From below me the low rumble of voices floated up, broken by bursts of laughter or grunts and heaving of furniture. They were working hard. I lay in the sun and thought how little the 2-leggeds understand.

For instance, how rest is not idleness, and to lie in the sun on a warm spring day, listening to the rustle of the wind in the trees or watching the clouds float across the sky is by no means a waste of time.

5

I don't remember how Lorna first found me, but I've heard her tell the story many times, and it explains why I love her so much and also why I don't like being caught in tight places.

Lorna had recently lost her husband, or maybe he'd been dead some months, I'm not sure, but she found herself alone and also nearly destitute because he'd spent all their money as well as his retirement. On his death she discovered that he'd even taken a second mortgage on their house, which she didn't discover until after his death. She was scared. Moreover, all this took place during a financial crash, so that even selling her house was tough.

One morning she set off to market, counting her money and talking to herself about how she had to keep her chin up, don't despair, trust in God, admonitions that carried little weight because all the time she could hear the booted footsteps of fear crunching toward her up the basement steps. She reminded herself to "get a grip on herself." Which I find odd. As if she could carry herself by the scruff of her own neck.

In the grocery store parking lot, a little boy and his sister ran over to pull on her sleeve. "Wanna buy a kitten?" For some unknown reason, she paused to peer into their cardboard box, and what she saw made her reach in and pick up the tiny stumbling smoky gray kitten (me!). I rested in the palm of one hand. The children told her how they had rescued me from the drainpipe in their new housing development. I was only two or three weeks old, scared, scruffy, starving, calling for my mother. The children didn't know what to do, since their parents said they couldn't keep me. In desperation they had brought me to the public parking lot, looking for someone to adopt me. They said Lorna could buy me for only ten dollars.

In a flash, all of Lorna's troubles fled.

"Oh, you poor thing." She stroked my ears, and I mewed and curled against her shoulder. "Aren't you beautiful?" And she kissed me, dirty as I was.

"Can you take her?" asked the little girl. Lorna says there was something so winning in her pleading big eyes that she couldn't imagine saying no.

"Our dad says we have to drown her if no one takes her. We've been here an hour, and no one's stopped."

"Drown her! No!" She put me back in the box. "Listen, I'll take her, but right now I have to go in the market to buy some things. Can you wait for me? I'll be right out. Don't let anyone else take her. She's mine."

"We're selling her for ten dollars."

Lorna huffed. "I'll give you five. That's all."

The children looked at each other, then nodded. "Okay. Five."

"Wait for me. I'll pay you when I come back."

She hurried off and bought her orange juice and cottage cheese and who knows what all, and when she returned to the parking lot she paid and carried me to the car. Before going home she drove to the nearest pet store and bought formula and two small baby bottles, thinking all the time how crazy she was to take on a kitten when she hardly had enough money for herself. But I clung to her. I mewed when she left the room and tottered after her. I slept in the crook of her arm. I kneaded her belly and crawled up to her throat. I wouldn't let her go.

The vet told Lorna I would likely die, having developed no immune system whatever yet. Moreover, I was too young to receive shots or deworming. Yet miraculously, I lived, and soon afterwards Lorna was offered her job at the Smithsonian. She named me Alba, because of my smoky color and gold tipped ears and because the word means *dawn*, which she says I represented: the dawn of her new life.

One of Lorna's requirements for moving in with Nikki was that she could bring me along. Nikki was delighted.

"Your relationship with a cat is special," said Nikki. "I don't know what I'd do without Puma. I found him when I was in college, just a back-alley stray, and look at us all these years later."

Puma, the ancient king, stalked stiffly up to sniff me, and after I scratched his nose and ran away, we became friends right off.

Puma's jaw has caved in and his muzzle gone grey, but even moving with arthritic dignity he taught me how to climb a fence and hunt a bird. He taught me cleanliness and proper cat manners.

Lorna always took the bus to work, but Nikki worked from home, conserving paintings, and I loved the company. Her studio smells of varnish and oils, rags, brushes, and other art supplies. I especially admired one white plastic tray with a glory of ground powders: orange, gold, azure blue, emerald green, turquoise, red, ochre, punk, and pink. Some are made of semi-precious minerals that Nikki is always shooing me away from, in case I sneeze. Which I don't. I like to sit on a shelf high above the hot table and watch her mix the powders with tinctures to make her paints.

Sometimes in the evenings the two friends went out to dinner, sometimes they cooked at home. Sometimes they sat up late, each with a cat on her lap, and talked. Sometimes Nikki would go out to a party while Lorna stayed home.

And then one day Jeremy Bell came into our lives and everything changed. Sooner than you can catch a bird, he was in Nikki's bed.

That first morning Puma kept a disdainful distance, but I was young and curious. The autumn light streamed through the window. It was already late in the morning. I sprang up on the bed and began to wash myself so they wouldn't be embarrassed at lying in bed at that hour, and that's how I heard the whole conversation that first morning after Jeremy spent the night.

He peered at me, the covers tucked to his chin.

"There's a cat on the bed."

"Can anyone keep a cat off a bed?"

"Will we have cats on the bed when we marry?"

"Oh, are we going to get married?" asked Nikki, choking with pleased laughter at the idea.

"I think so. Don't you?"

"No."

"Well, that's a refreshing response. Why not? You think I won't want you all my life?

"Well, it is a little sudden. But that's not the only reason."

"No?"

"It's because my mother died four months ago."

"Yes, you told me. I'm sorry." There was a pause while he kissed her and considered the next move.

"So you're saying that because your mother died, you can't think about making a commitment?"

"Oh, I can make a commitment. I just can't get married."

"Is there something I'm missing here? Why do I think that's a *non sequitur*?"

"I promised."

"Who?"

"Claire Boisson, my godmother. She lives in Paris but keeps a house across the river in Washington, in Georgetown." Georgetown is a fashionable neighborhood in Washington, District of Columbia. I think the word means money.

"And?" he prompted. By now he was propped on one elbow looking down at her, and you could feel the professional newsman taking over, the investigator digging out secrets, looking for a story.

"She was my mother's best friend. When my mother died, Claire was in Paris with a broken hip and couldn't come to the funeral, but she phoned to warn me that the first few years after the death of a parent, especially a mother, are dangerous."

"Dangerous." Jeremy rolled the word on his tongue.

"She says it's life-changing, and you don't think clearly. She made me promise not to marry anyone until I'd known him for at least a year. Two is better. She said—" and here Nikki blushed, "she said there's too much money at stake."

"Oh, money." Jeremy made a face. "The old bugaboo. So can we be engaged?"

"No, she's right, you know. Look at us."

"Right." He lifted the covers to peer at her body under the sheets. "I like the way that looks." Then, seeing her expression: "Okay, I'll be serious. You're an heiress. But what's to examine? You don't like me? It's not your money I want."

I stopped washing now and stared discreetly at the wall. I was shocked, but then I was only a young thing at the time, not much more than a kitten. Even though I'm very pretty, I wouldn't want anyone to look at me like that.

"Of course I like you. But here we are in bed! Way too soon! I don't do things like that."

"You just did."

"I know! I know! That's what I'm saying!" she wailed and hid her face in the pillow. "It's because my mother died, and I'm lonely, and now I've lost my head."

"Your heart," he murmured, kissing her neck and then moving on to her breasts. "Listen, I won't hurt you. I would never hurt you."

"And now I'm in bed with practically a total stranger."

"I'm not a stranger. I've been waiting for you all my life. Don't you feel it?'

"No." She snuggled closer. "I think you're crazy."

"I'm not talking about thinking."

Another long silence followed. I licked and licked myself, a jumble of electricity and nerves.

After a while she said, "I think you should go home."

The silence this time was even longer, and I felt so uncomfortable that I stopped washing my upraised hind leg to listen. Then I jumped off the bed with a *thunk* and went to find Puma.

They took a long time to get up.

At the door, Jeremy twisted a strand of her hair between his fingers. "Shall I call you later?"

She nodded.

He kissed her on the brow. "I can wait a year or two."

It gave me a lot to think about. I asked Puma what was going on, but he was so jealous that he refused to speak to Nikki or even talk to me about Jeremy, he was that upset. What was worse, Nikki didn't notice. She stared at herself in the mirror or admired the flowers he sent the next day. She moved the vase from room to room. She could do that because she works at home all day.

It should be noted that Lorna was more cautious than Nikki, because that's her nature. But then Lorna wasn't going to bed with the man, as she was quick to point out. It wasn't that she didn't *like* Jeremy, she confessed over dinner; rather, she was concerned that he'd come on so fast that in the end he would hurt Nikki. Nonetheless, the months passed, and the house was filled with male laughter and heavy footsteps, the rattle of newspapers and click of computer keys, and eventually he even won Lorna over with his indignation over Congress and politics and his open support of Nikki and her work.

"Why are you a conservator?" he asked Nikki at breakfast one day. (I don't remember all their conversations, but he'd given me a piece of chicken sausage, and out of courtesy I felt obliged to sit on his lap and listen in case he had more on his plate.) "I mean, you could be a serious painter."

"No, I couldn't. I'm an excellent conservator. I can restore a torn canvas and do the in-painting so well you can't see the strokes without ultra-violet light. But I'm not good enough to create great art, and since I see it all the time, anything less would be a disappointment."

"You'd have to practice. Develop a style."

"What, you want me to die in poverty, a starving artist?"

"Let's see: Rothko, Klee, Picasso, Georgia O'Keefe. How many millions are enough for you?" They were laughing in each other's eyes.

"You didn't notice they're all dead? Most artists barely scratch out a living. I have a trust fund and enough income to live on if I'm careful and keep working all my life, but frankly I don't care to live in a garret with no heat and the chance to contract TB. Better to do what I do well, I say, and leave the celebrity to others."

"Nah, take the dare," he said. "You can leave a fortune to your children."

"Maybe you didn't notice. I don't have any children." Teasing each other. There were a lot of overtones and subtext unexpressed.

"Not yet."

At which I saw her melt. "And if I don't?" she laughed, glancing at him out of the corner of her eyes.

"Well, you can name me in your will. I'll be happy to collect your millions. I'll spend my remaining years cataloging your work and making you posthumously famous."

"I thought I'd leave everything to a foundation for cats." I looked up. This showed uncommon good sense, but the subject changed (the 2-leggeds have such short attention spans). Just then Lorna burst in from her run, and I jumped down from Jeremy's lap and scooted over to brush against her leg. She plunked down at the breakfast table, pushing the newspapers aside, and picked me up.

"What are you two talking about? Hello, Alba, did you miss me?" Which is silly, since she hadn't been gone long enough for a good nap.

6

On that first day in our new place when Lorna went off to work, it was these happy days I remembered, and I roamed our apartment mournfully. I felt cooped up. The air conditioning repairman had still not come yet to fix the broken unit, and Lorna had left the screened windows open to catch the early spring breeze for me. Outside I could hear the birds twittering and traffic swishing past. Early that morning I'd heard the love-gurgles of a pair of mourning doves, which brought to mind the call of springtime wildness, of things deep in the earth gnawing toward the light, of blooms bursting into life. I love that. It fills me with ecstasy. I wanted to see the landscape drenched with color and hear the air resonant with the hum of bees. Instead I was trapped, scratching at the window screens, meowing in loneliness at the free-flying birds and in longing for the surge of thrusting life that I could see outside.

In only a few hours, though, I managed to scrape a hole in one of the living room screens, and in another day (day two of my confinement) I'd widened it enough to climb out onto the cement window ledge. From there to the next windowsill was an easy hop. That window, unblocked by screens, was fully open. I landed in the hallway outside our upstairs apartment.

I pattered down the stairs and sniffed outside Goliath's door. It drove him wild. I centered myself neatly on the ugly green doormat, paws under my chest, and dozed. I could hear him sniffing and snuffling on his side of the door. It gave me pleasure to bring interest into his boring life. Some of us have a giving nature.

When I came back the next day, I smelled his scent right there on the green mat, where he'd walked outside to see what he could find. I was careful to rub my fragrance along the hallway baseboards, knowing he couldn't get out or attack me. And that was how I spent my first few days until the terrible night that Nikki telephoned in tears.

An hour later, she ran up the stairs and flung herself into Lorna's arms.

"Oh, Lorna!"

I brushed against her leg in greeting.

But she ignored me, stunning us with her impassioned announcement.

"It's over. Finished. I'm never marrying that man. Lorna, I want you to come back home and live with us again."

"Nikki!"

"I'll help you pack."

"Nikki, I've just bought the apartment."

"You can rent it. We want you home. I need you."

Lorna was anything but impulsive. "Sit down. Tell me what's going on."

The story came out in fits and starts, like a kitten chasing its tail, sometimes turning back on itself and sometimes sputtering forward in jerks and stops. All week she had planned an intimate dinner for Jeremy's birthday. For the last few weeks he had been working so hard she'd hardly seen him, she said, and when they met, he'd been preoccupied. At first he'd claimed he didn't want a birthday party, and a few days later he'd offered to take her out.

"And you know how he hates restaurants, it's so weird. But I wanted to make something special. He knew our waiting year was up. I talked about it. I told him I wanted a small wedding, nothing fancy, just our closest friends—maybe no more than one or two hundred people, and he'd smiled and punched my cheek to tell me everything was fine. He said I could have any wedding I wanted, and this night, his birthday, was going to be the night when he would—but you know this," she wailed, "—when he would make it official with the proposal and the ring. We've gone over it already—that's why you bought this condo, to be out of my house when we married."

"He's changed his mind?" Lorna was nothing if not quick. But then she'd half-expected something like this. She couldn't put her finger on it, but she was suspicious of Jeremy. She attributed it to jealousy—herself uncoupled, like the derelict caboose left on the siding while the young, clean, high-speed trains roared past in a swirl of wind and upswept leaves: herself unable to escape the happy couple as they lounged for hours in bed, always reaching out to touch or kiss. Sometimes being in company with the two lovers (even when they included her) had seeded pangs of loneliness in Lorna that she pushed down with work and friends and volunteer projects—the loneliness that also made her sometimes flee counter-intuitively into isolation, before getting a grip on herself and remembering to phone a friend.

"He's changed his mind?" she repeated in a gentle voice, at which Nikki broke down totally and wept and sobbed, balling up one Kleenex after another in the trash, as Lorna made her a cup of tea and settled her on the sofa under a light throw. Nikki could hardly speak, but neither could she stop, her voice cracked and croaking. Lorna listened quietly, saying nothing.

"I hate him! I hate him! How could I have been so stupid? I tried so hard." Nikki choked. "The flowers, the candles, the gourmet birthday meal. I spent two days, if you can imagine" (and here she laughed, self-deprecating, struggling to lighten up in ways that only made things worse), just *cooking*! I bought champagne. I talked to Puma, 'He's going to ask me to marry him tonight. Tonight we fix the date. Tonight he's giving me a ring.' Why did I think he would give me a ring?"

For weeks Jeremy had alternated between sudden shifting moods, one moment silent, withdrawn, mentally absent, and the next moment waltzing her round the house in a sudden burst of animation. He'd started reading poetry.

"I thought it was romantic," Nikki said. "I should have known something was wrong. And then he'd go into this distant brooding, the silent Lord Byron mood."

That evening he'd shown up at the house, kissed her lightly and handed her flowers, but his conversation was all about the story he was working on. Which was horrible.

"Horrible. I mean, I couldn't blame him for being low," sobbed Nikki. "It's horrible." In a foster home two little girls were found, no more than two or three years old, naked and bound to an iron bedstead: chained to the bed, starving. A third child, age five, had broken free, jumped out the second story window, and dragging her broken foot had run across the yard to pound on the neighbor's door for help. The police broke into the house to find the two infants chained to a bed and covered with feces, their hands and faces smeared with snot and dirt. Jeremy shook with indignation, describing the scene.

"Their foster mother had tied them up to keep them safe, while she passed out on drugs. This government!" He hit the table with one hand for emphasis, making Nikki jump. "They gave her three foster children, and she chained them up. Forgot to feed them. And no one to supervise! It's unconscionable!"

"And his eyes," reported Nikki, "—those sad dark eyes. He'd glance over at me with this ghastly look, as if he were revisiting the scene all over again. And I suppose he was, but I didn't want that, Lorna. Not then. I know I'm selfish. I'm self-centered. A silly goose, he called me once. At the time I thought it sounded affectionate. Okay, so I'm awful, I know, I'm shallow and silly, but for just that one night

I wanted it to be him and me together, being happy, without cruelty and suffering breaking over us; and here we were on this warm night, these huge stars hanging over us like lanterns, like glittering jewels. I'd put clean sheets on the bed. He was going to give me a ring. We were going to plan the wedding. And children. I wanted to have his children."

This set her off again. "Oh God, my heart hurts, Lorna. Lorna, it's a physical pain. I can feel my heart is breaking inside me, tearing itself in half."

"Nikki." Lorna's voice was soothing, defending him. "He'd just seen this horrible thing only a few hours earlier. He loves you. I'm glad to hear he was affected by it. It's in his favor. Would you want a man who didn't feel things deeply?"

Nikki lifted her haunted eyes to Lorna's, her mouth working, her hands shaking. "But that's not all. I can't forgive him. I won't ever, ever, ever forgive him. So you see why you have to come back home with us."

"What else?" asked Lorna quietly.

That evening Jeremy had written the story about the three little children after which (the good news) the editor had put him in charge of an entire five-part investigative series into children's issues: abandonment, poverty, neglect, foster care, government policies, childcare, and orphanages—a huge assignment, front page, above the center fold.

"He was rubbing his hands together in anticipation. Lorna, all he could think about was the story. 'It's a Pulitzer, if I can bring it off,' he said. 'This is big, Nikki.'

"You'd have been proud of me. I was supportive, even if I thought him awful to gloat about the Pulitzer.

"Dessert came," she continued. "I put candles on his cake, and I kept waiting for him to get off the orphans and foster homes and to say something—*anything*, so I could bring out the champagne, and all the time I'm reminding myself that he didn't *have* to propose this night, on his birthday, just because I'd wanted it. I'd gotten it in my head he would, that's all."

Instead Jeremy had suddenly lapsed into silence, twisting his fork.

Finally, Nikki reached across the table and took his hand. "Sweetheart, what's wrong. What's going on?"

He pressed her fingers. "Nikki, you're wonderful," he said. She flashed him a big smile.

"This isn't easy," he went on. "Help me out. You're my best friend."

("Best friend?" murmured Lorna. "I know, but it was *something*," answered Nikki, "I hugged it to my heart.")

"He said, 'I need advice. I'm a wreck.' He shot to his feet then and circled the table, running both hands through his hair. He pulled his beard and then he said the magic words, Lorna. He said, 'I've fallen in love. What do you think I should do?'

"Well, finally! So I gave a gorgeous smile. I thought it was one of his games, his playfulness. 'I think you should ask her to marry you,' I said.

" 'You do?' he said.

" 'Of course it depends. Do you think she cares for you?' I asked— Oh God, I was so saucy!

"He reached for the wineglass and gulped the last of his wine, and then it all came pouring out—how he hadn't known this woman long, ten days, two weeks. She's new at the paper, but when she passes his desk his heart pounds. He can't breathe. His legs go weak. His stomach twists. He can't work. Except now he's got the orphanage-foster-children story, and she's helping him with that, and she's smart and sexy. They make a great team. He's *alive* in ways he's never been before. He said that. 'We talk for hours,' he informed me. 'I talk about anything, and she's right there with me. When she's away I'm insane. I can't wait to hear her voice or see her again.'

"Lorna, I sat there with my jaw dropped open. 'Penelope?' I squeaked. 'The woman you mentioned once? Lorna, it took all my courage just to say that much, and my voice came out like the croak of a frog.

"He said, 'Oh God.' Reaching for my hand. 'I'm sorry,' he said. 'I know what this night means, but I can't ask you to marry me, can I?'

"I could hardly speak, I was so astonished. I asked if this was why he'd wanted to go out to a restaurant instead of eating at home, and he'd said yes.

"And all the time I sat there numb as a tomb, with Puma in my lap, thinking how happy I'd been that he'd brought me flowers. The tulips were on the table in front of me. I couldn't stop looking at them, the way they thrust out of the vase like proud little soldiers. Saluting. Like soldiers. And I had to be a soldier."

"He saw me looking at them. 'I know they're nothing,' he said, 'not good enough for you, but I'm confused right now. I don't know what I'm doing. Remember my telling you how dreadful my father was to my mother? Sometimes he wouldn't talk to her for days, or else he'd put her down. Ridicule and belittle her, even in public. Or else, when he was angry, he'd shout in her face. When I was little, my mother made me promise I'd never hurt a woman. *Promise me, Jerry, you'll never hurt a woman the way your father hurts me.*' I was just a kid. I promised. Every time. And here I am hurting you. But it would be worse, Nikki, if I lied. I'd hurt you worse. These have been the worst ten days of my life.'

"You know what I did?" asked Nikki, who was curled up under the blanket on the sofa. "I stared at my coffee cup. 'Oh, don't be silly.' I said, and I actually laughed. I laughed, because otherwise I would have burst into tears." She raised her eyes to Lorna. "And I wouldn't give him that satisfaction. But I began to shake. I had to hold my hands under the tablecloth, so he wouldn't see me shaking. Then I threw up my head, the royal princess, very proud. 'I think you should ask her to marry you.'

" 'You do? I haven't known her long. What if she doesn't want me?'

"Lorna, I could have killed him. If I'd had a knife in my hand—he was saved by the absence of a kitchen cleaver.

" 'Oh, well, you'll find out, won't you?' I said. Oh, I was so cheerful! 'But sometimes love hits like that. Like a sledgehammer. Eros. Horns of fire, and vine leaves in her hair, but it was his hair, wasn't it? Lövoborg's. In *Hedda Gabbler*, I mean, vine leaves in his hair, but I'm gabbling, aren't I?. . . Have you slept with her?'

"He opened his mouth. But I raised my hand.

" 'Actually, I don't want to know.' I picked up my dessert plate, but I was on automatic pilot. I had no idea what I was doing.

"He said he'd help with the dishes, and he started round the table toward me.

" 'No, no, really. This will only take a few minutes.' I gave him this brilliant smile. He reached out for me, but I lunged back. I didn't want him to touch me.

" 'I can do them. You know what you should do?' I said. (And Lorna, I meant it. At that moment I meant every word.)

"I think you should run straight over to Penelope's and take her to bed and ask her to marry you. She's probably waiting for you."

"Oh, Nikki."

I jumped off Lorna's lap and up onto Nikki's to knead her belly. There's nothing like a cat to soothe a hurt.

She was weeping, red-eyed, and with her nose running and the rain running down her cheeks and onto my fur in quite an irritating way. The blood had drained from her face. Her skin was white as milk, no color in her lips.

"I wanted to mush the leftover cake in his face. Or thrust a knife into his throat. Instead, all I did was see him to the door, as if we didn't have a relationship—*best friends*! He *dared* to call me his best friend? But I wouldn't show him I was hurt. 'No no, I'll clean up,' I said, bright as a penny. 'You run along. I think you should propose to her. Right away. Before you lose your courage.' Because I remembered how he'd proposed to me the very first time that we—that I—that— She threw another Kleenex onto the pile on the table next to her and tossed her chin up bravely.

"He looked terrified. He stood in the doorway. I think he would have kissed me, but I shut the door in his face.

"And then I phoned you. Lorna, I thought I was going to vomit. I wanted to throw up. I was shaking all over. I could hardly see to drive over here."

We three sat up well past midnight. "How could I have misjudged him so? We've been together all this time, and one day he meets another woman, and *Pow*! He's gone."

"*Coup de foudre*," murmured Lorna in French. "I know all about it. Didn't Harry do that with me?"

"And he's *slept* with her when we—" She sat up with a struggling attempt at a collapsing smile. "Except we weren't sleeping together much, were we, in the last few weeks? Because he had some story he was working on. So it's all very honorable of him. I tell you, if I ever see him, I will kill him with my own two hands! A knife, or a gun. He's lucky to be away. And now, tra-la, I'm free. I think the first man I like—I'll seduce and marry him."

"Nikki, stop it," said Lorna, as her friend began to tremble again. "Breathe, breathe." She held her by the forearms. "Breathe."

"I'm breathing. There." She lifted her head bravely. "Well, it's not the end of the world, is it? Imagine, if I'd married him, and then he'd— My god, that happens. It's the old, old story. You can say that

I was saved." But she hugged her elbows with both hands. "It was actually very ethical of him, wasn't it? Buddhist Right Action. So, why does it hurt so much?"

I put my front paws on her shoulder and purred into her ear.

"Alba knows I'm hurting. Don't you, sweetheart? Are you trying to comfort me?"

Which shows how off–the-mark the 2-leggeds can be, because what I was telling her was to stop with the drama and go to bed. You'd never find a cat paying so much attention to rejection. We'd stalk away with our tail in the air, and let the other live with his regret.

7

It was a long night. In the morning Nikki had a new concern. She wanted to rush back home to Puma.

"Because he's eighteen, and he's been so sick," she explained at breakfast. "He was at the vet's twice last week. What will I do when he goes? What will I do when my cat dies? Believe me, there were times in the last few years when I was sure he wouldn't make it. One day you think he doesn't have the strength to do anything except sleep and pick at his food, and then he'll hear a bird fight outside the window, his ears set, and his tail starts thumping on the radiator, and the next thing you know he's dashed upstairs to get a better view." She chewed her Cheerios sadly. "He's my best friend. I thought it was Jerry, but it's my cat. And you, of course," she added quickly. "I love you most of all. I want you to come back and live with us again. I need you, Lorna. You're the wise one."

"Not wise. Older, that's all. I've had more experience."

"I'm thirty-six." Nikki shuddered. "I'm thirty-six years old. I don't suppose I'll ever have children now," she said, doleful in her self-pity.

"Oh, really, Nikki!" Lorna was impatient.

"No. By the time I meet someone else it will be too late." She looked up at Lorna with lost and empty eyes. "All my life I've wanted children. How did I get to be thirty-six and never married? You've been married, and had God knows how many boyfriends. And children."

"Yes."

"No children," repeated Nikki, captive to her own self-pity. "I'll be one of those old women, hobbling on my cane. A shawl around my shoulders. I'll look at the little children playing on the swings at the playground. I do it already, I go down the street, and if I see a baby or a two-year-old—any age, really, but especially the little ones—my head swivels round like an owl's. I wanted Jerry's children," she finished in a whisper.

She was picking a piece of toast apart as if it contained maggots.

"I can't believe I didn't see the signs," she said. "I mean, how could I have been so blind? So stupid?"

"You're not stupid. Really, you must not talk to yourself like that."

Nikki said nothing.

"Listen." Lorna reached one hand across the table. 'This isn't even all that unusual."

"It's not?"

"Of course not. I heard of a woman only last week who was married to a diplomat. Children. Money. Assignments abroad. The whole Kit 'n Kaboodle," she said (a word that made me prick my ears—I liked it almost as much as 'delicate'). "They were living in Prague. One day he calls from the office and says, 'I'll be home for dinner, I have some news.' His wife thinks maybe he's been offered Paris or Rome. 'I'll make something special,' she says. She spends all day cooking this fantastic gourmet dinner. They eat it with the candlelight gleaming on the polished silver. He doesn't tell her. . . doesn't tell her. Finally, over coffee, she smiles across the table at him. 'Well, what's the news?'

" 'I've fallen in love with my secretary, he says. I'm divorcing you to marry her.'"

Nikki blinked. "You made that up."

"Swear to God," said Lorna, raising one paw. "Moreover, he's monumentally rich and she got *nothing, no-thing* in the divorce. She's nearly destitute. We removed her name from the Explorer roll. It's sad. But I simply can't imagine asking her for a $5,000 pledge. You want another story? How about this? A politician this time, and I forget his name. He was in the Senate. His wife of forty years worked to get him there. His sixtieth birthday comes along, and she says to him, 'I want to give you something special, something you really want. What do you want?'

"He says, 'A divorce. I've fallen in love.' My god! I mean, Jeremy is a treasure compared to those. Jerry's charming, sexy, handsome. He's fun. He's smart. He's honest and idealistic. But face it, he's just demonstrated he has the emotional depth of a duck."

"Not a duck," said Nikki miserably. "Don't ducks mate for life?"

"That's swans," said Lorna in a crisp voice. "Actually mallards will gang up and rape and sometimes even drown the female. They only pair up once she's hatching eggs."

Nikki glanced over at her. "What odd things you learn at the Smithsonian." Then, with another weak attempt at a smile. "You certainly know how to cheer up a girl."

"Come on, Nikki," said Lorna. "I'll go back to your place with you. Help clean up the dinner dishes."

"Oh, Lorna, you don't need to."

"I know, but it's Saturday. That's what friends do for each other."

And indeed Nikki looked forlorn and pale. She twisted her fingers together and smiled the brave smile that never quite reached her eyes.

"Listen, Nikki, it's not too late for children," Lorna continued as she dug in her purse for keys. "Maybe you don't want to hear this now, but soon you'll meet someone else who rings your bells. In fact, I'm sure someone wonderful is right now waiting in the wings. And when he enters, just go after him."

It was only later that I remembered these portentous words and thought how it might have been better if Lorna had never said a thing.

"Shall we bring Alba? Puma would love to see her. It'll be like old times."

"Good idea. Come on, Alba," said Lorna, scooping me up in her arms. "You don't need a carrier today." Lorna knows how much I like cars. I like to sit on the headrest behind her, watching the land roll past, and I'm careful not to jump about or put my paws on the steering wheel. My tail switched, I was that thrilled: not only a drive in the car, but soon to see Puma again! What I didn't expect was the tale Puma would recount when we got to Nikki's house. And anyone who loves a cat, anyone with a paw-lick of compassion, will understand how I had to go away and lick my trembling fur and clamber into Lorna's arms for comfort. I'll repeat it for you now. I warn you, it's very sad, and if you don't like sad tales, then skip ahead to more about Lorna and Nikki's love affairs.

8

When we got to Nikki's, Puma was sunning himself on the deck. He came arthritically to his feet and struggled to a wider patch of sunlight, where we could both bathe in golden warmth. That's an example of his generosity. I hadn't seen him in a week or more, and I was shocked to see how old he looked in only the few days I'd been gone.

It was scary. I decided right then that I would never get old like him. I'm too pretty to grow gaunt and grey.

==You've gotten old, I blurted. At his hurt expression, I could have bit my tongue. I mean, what's it like? I asked to cover my *faux pas*. What's it like being old?

Puma merely raised his mild muzzle and took the question seriously. I knew he slept much of the time now, and though I missed our earlier bird hunts, the pleasure of curling up beside a warm body to sleep cannot be underestimated, nor the reassurance of someone snoring in your ear. Now he lifted his bony, scruffy, grey head and smiled at me gently.

==When I was young, I moved faster than the 2-leggeds. If I could walk, I ran. I jumped for no reason other than for fun. I batted at bugs. Everything I saw or smelled or heard provided fodder for curiosity, and everything was bathed in golden light.

I've always admired the way Puma speaks, which he says every kitten learnt in his day, and no one does anymore. He says the younger generation know nothing of manners anymore.

== I think the world has dulled, he went on. I notice things approach me now through a white mist, and sounds are muffled. Insects don't scream as loud as they used to, and people mumble more.

== Can you hear me? I asked in concern.

== Oh, yes. But we speak mind-to-mind. I hear the thought-pictures of animals—dogs, birds, you. But the outer world has lost its voice, just as food has lost its taste.

== Food? Lost its taste? What an appalling thought!

== Cat food used to have more... *spark*, he said.

I groomed myself nervously. Aging is serious.

== I've slowed, he continued. My joints hurt. But as a result, Time lives now in my head, as does Place. I can go to any Place or Period I want, and I can live it all over again, but better, for everything is bathed in golden light. I know more now than I did as a kitten, and I accept most things without fighting and resisting them. They simply *are*.

== So, you don't care anymore?

== I care more, the old cat said after a thoughtful pause to consider. There's nothing I can do about most problems, but my heart aches in ways I don't remember it doing as a kitten. For example, take what happened when I was at the vet's last week.

Then he told this story so disturbing that when he finished I had to trot into the other room and leap on Lorna's lap just to calm down.

==It was on my first night there, he said. The cat in the next cage could not stop talking. He was an orange tiger-stripe with a blunt, brutal nose. Restless, anxious, bristling with indignation. Late into the night he prowled, keeping me awake.

You're lucky, he said. *You'll only be here a short time, but I've been here for weeks. Two nights ago a cat died. Right in the cage you're in. His name was MacDuff. He was a Siamese. A Blue Point.*

==I didn't want to know about the cat. Not when he'd died in the very cage I lay in, but the orange tabby could not stop.

What happened, he growled, *MacDuff was alone in his house while his 2-legged went on a trip with her children. She left a window open in the children's bedroom so he could walk in and out, and because the sash cord was broken, she'd propped the window open with a stick. Such a stupid thing to do! MacDuff went out the window that morning, but in the afternoon when he jumped back in, he accidentally hit the stick. The window slammed down on his right front leg. He was caught, hanging against the wall, unable either to scramble back up to the sill or pull himself free. He dangled in the air, his shoulder dislocated. It was awful.*

Here at the hospital, they cut off his leg. That's not serious. I've seen lots of cats run around on three legs. What he couldn't do was rally from the trauma. I tell you, the orange tiger cat continued, while pacing up and down, *I tell you, seeing him when his person-mother came to visit would tear your heart out. Sometimes she came two and three times a day; but the last time was the worst.*

She approached the cage, her face working, and MacDuff stood up, wobbling from his surgery and heavy with drugs. He hobbled to the door of his cage with a broken wail, and when she unhinged the lock, he threw himself into her arms. Then the two of them clung to each other, and the tears poured down her face as he struggled to get closer and closer to her. If he could have crawled under her clothes and right into her skin, he would have done it. He hid his head beneath her chin, while she covered him with her scarf; and he told her over and over what had happened to him, and how he had hung there, in the vise of the window. Once he mewed—a bitter sound—and reminded her never to prop up a window with a stick if you have an animal in the house. The same could happen to a dog, he said, a child. Meanwhile, he wanted to come home. He asked her please to take him home. He wanted to go home.

She rocked him in her arms and petted him. She told him how in one more day she'd bring him home.

When she put him back in the cage, he strained against the bars, wailing to her, "No, no," and "Take me home, don't leave me here." She poked her fingers through the bars and whispered to him not to worry.

"Tomorrow," she said. One more day in the doctor's care, and then he'd lie on the sofa again and sleep on her bed beside her. He'd be fine with only three legs, she said, and by the end of summer he'd be hunting birds, she was sure of it, but right now, she wanted him to stay one more night to help himself get well.

"I love you, I love you," she kept repeating, and then she opened the cage again and almost crawled inside herself as she said one more good-bye.

'That night he died.

I think he knew it was coming. I think he wanted to die at home.

During this long recitation I sat stunned. Cats rarely talk so long, but Puma fixed me with his aged, milky eye and held me prisoner. I could not move. I've never been in a hospital, and I listened, eyes wide and both ears flattened in horror. From the kitchen I could hear the voices of Lorna and Nikki rising and falling as they cleared the table, did the dishes. But Puma lashed his tail. His story wasn't finished yet.

We were all upset, the orange tabby said, his voice grating in the dark night. *All us cats were silent in our separate cages in the dark. Would you believe,* he said, *I saw his spirit leave? It had four good legs, and it came up and peered into my cage in the dark of night to say good-bye, because we'd been hospital buddies by then for quite a while. Then I saw it drift slowly up toward the ceiling and trot off to see his human mother, who was probably lying fast asleep in bed and would never know MacDuff had come to say good-bye. Or if she saw, she'd likely think it just a dream.*

The next morning she arrived to pick him up. When they told her he had died, she let loose a howl of despair. They said they'd dispose of the body for her. But she said, No, she would bury him in her back garden, even if it was against the law—and she wasn't going to ask: she wanted him in the garden where he'd hunted and sunned himself and where she'd have him always near.

So, they gave her his body in a pillowcase, and also the amputated leg, and she staggered away with her sack. She could hardly walk. I thought she was going to be sick. Her shoulders were bowed and her head down, and she was sobbing as she cradled the burden of his body against her chest.

And all because she'd propped up a window with a stick.'

==The room was silent then, said Puma. I could hear the big tiger in the next cage prowling nervously, and the other cats who had been listening (some of them familiar with the story) shuffled or coughed in the darkness.

'I'm sorry,' I told the orange tabby. *'It's sad.'*

Oh, yessss. His hiss a snarl of anger. *But he had a person-mother, didn't he? She loved him and he loved her. She didn't just leave him here.*

I said nothing. I knew there was more. I wasn't going to be spared.

==Puma, I don't like this story, I interrupted. Don't go on.

==No, there are things you need to know, said Puma. He stared my protests down, and I curled into a ball, my shoulders hunched, ears pinned.

Not like me, the cat muttered under his breath.

==Alba, you're small, svelte, sinuous, Puma said. People stop to exclaim how pretty you are with your blue eyes and gold-tipped ears and pink nose. But this old tiger was ugly. Scruffy. Dirty. As if he didn't clean himself. As if his human never washed or brushed his coat. Or didn't care. He was called Pie for Pirate, and with his torn ear it wasn't inappropriate. He prowled his cage as he talked.

Not like me, he said again. So I knew I had to ask.

'And you?' I whispered politely. 'What are you in for?'

Hmm Hmm. He hummed deep in his throat, a thrumming, a drumming, the purr of a tiger if tigers purred (but tigers are the only cats that don't). By the time he answered, I'd almost forgotten the question.

I scratched my human.

'What?'

He scared me.

==This time the pause extended for so long I thought he'd finished, and I relaxed against the back of my cage, ready finally to go to sleep, if I could only forget the poor Siamese who'd died there only days or maybe only hours earlier.

I didn't mean to! the orange tiger shouted. *I was asleep in the closet. He picked up the dirty clothes I was lying on, and I slashed out in surprise.*

'For that he sent you to the vet?'

It could have been worse. He could have sent me. . . there.

'I don't understand.'

I scratched him! he shouted, his voice lifting in annoyance. *Just a tiny scratch. It was an accident. But it got infected. He's in the hospital. He nearly died.*

'Oh.'

Because of me, he grumbled to himself, and I could hear him still pacing in his cage. *I'm being boarded,* he said, then continued his prowling with that rumbling, thrumming in his throat, not a purr, nor yet a growl.

'How long have you been here?' I asked.

Who knows? Long, long. I live in Now.

==I nodded and licked myself vigorously. We cats know about living in the present moment. It's the 2-leggeds who make themselves unhappy by playing in the garden of fearful futures or lollygagging in the past, when only awareness of the present moment brings you peace. Nonetheless, his words—'*I live in Now*'—were spat out with such intensity that I recoiled. Hadn't he just been remembering and recounting the past?

==We said nothing for so long a time that I started to doze. Purring away the images of pain, the scent of grief and fear and death.

They're coming for me, though. Hmmm hmmm.

'Your 2-legged?'

No. Then hardly more than a whisper: *They.*

'Who, they?'

They! They! he shouted. And he beat against the bars and meowed. *Remember me,* he rasped. *Promise. Promise to remember me? I didn't mean to scratch him. It was an accident.* Then turning on me viciously— *I didn't hear you promise.*

'Promise what?' I curled at the back of my cage, panting.

Remember me. It was a pathetic plea.

'Of course.'

They're coming tomorrow.

'I don't understand.'

I have to spell it out? he cried angrily. **Put down! Put down!**

==I flinched. What cat or dog doesn't know those dreadful words?

'You don't know that.' I mewed to comfort him, but in my heart I knew he did.

==We were silent then for a long time. After a few minutes, he spoke again, low in his throat, barely audible. *They say it doesn't hurt.*

==The next morning a man in white opened his cage. He wore gloves, though the old orange tabby was careful to sheathe his claws as the man hauled him out, pulling him by the scruff of his neck, as if he were a kitten.

"Come on, old boy." His voice was gentle, and he stood a moment at the cage, stroking that delicious spot behind his ears. "Don't be afraid. Aren't you a beautiful, big guy. Big as a coon cat."

Remember me, he mewed, and I won't forget the look he cast behind at me.

When he finished, Puma fell silent.

I couldn't think of what to say. That's when I left to rub against Lorna. I thought I could never be happy again after hearing such sadness. I hadn't known before that the 2-leggeds would kill a cat. Why would they do that? But maybe the tiger cat wasn't put down. We don't know. We don't know what happened to him, as I told Puma. Why assume the worst? Maybe his owner came back and took him home and fed him gourmet chicken out of a tiny tin and played with him using a strand of yarn. Or maybe another family adopted him.

==He sits on my heart, that poor, ugly cat. All he wanted was the chance to love, be loved. Isn't that what any of us want? Now the only thing I can do for his memory is to try to be the best cat that I can—to do no harm; help others.

== Help others? I asked in surprise. Do you mean the 2-leggeds? The idea had never crossed my mind. After all, it's up to *them* to care for *me*.

9

All this time we could hear Lorna and Nikki murmuring softly at the back of the house as they cleaned up the kitchen and the debris of the dining room: the dirty plates, encrusted forks, the crumbs on the tablecloth, the centerpiece of pink and yellow tulips (already sagging as if in echo of Nikki's despair). When that was done, Lorna started gently to put away reminders of Jeremy in the house. Methodically, she went through the rooms, picking up his toothbrush, the books on his side of the bed, his odd socks and clothing. She stuffed them in a big paper bag. She plucked two silver-framed photos from the shelves, and raised her eyebrows in question at Nikki, who stared in defeat at the bare spaces where the pictures had stood.

"Do you want me to leave them?" Lorna weighed the photos in her hand. One showed Jeremy and Nikki in black tie before a dance, and the other showed the two of them with triumphant grins on a mountaintop, dressed in hiking boots and woolen caps and heavy parkas against the cold.

Nikki shook her head. "No."

"You look like Napoleon." Lorna put one arm around her friend. "Riding back from Russia, silent in his carriage. On that whole, long journey home, they say he never spoke."

"Meaning?" said Nikki without even attempting a smile.

"He led an army of 500,000 men into Russia—the largest military force ever before assembled in Europe. It was June, 1812, and five months later, in October, when he left Moscow and began his disastrous retreat, he took back a straggling, starving army harassed by winter and the marauding Russians. Three hundred eighty thousand men died, 100,000 were captured. He came back with something like 27,000 men."

"And?"

"You look like that."

"Silent in my carriage."

"Yes."

"Shut into myself."

"Yes."

"What is there to say? I feel like Napoleon. Utter defeat." Two tears seeped down her cheeks.

"Of course you do," said Lorna. "Go ahead. Grieve. Mourn. Weep. It's absolutely appropriate."

"Right now I can't imagine how the sun can come up," said Nikki, struggling to smile. "How can it be so oblivious?"

"I know. And you don't want to hear that in a few weeks you'll feel better, and in a few months you'll even maybe want to meet another man. But it will happen. I know. I've been there. We all have. Every woman alive. Probably every man."

"Not every woman," said Nikki with doleful exactitude. "My cousin met his wife when they were twelve, and they've been married for forty-two years. And they're still in love, and he's never thought of anyone but her."

"And one day one or the other will feel as you do right now. When the other one dies."

"Oh, Lorna."

"I'm just saying—"

"Give them to me," said Nikki, holding out her hand for the photographs in their silver frames. "I'm not ready to take them down yet." She set them back on the shelf.

"We ought to go," said Lorna. "Will you be all right?"

"I'll be fine."

I noticed that Nikki didn't press her friend to stay but walked deliberately to the door and opened it wide. I guess she'd had enough of Lorna's sympathy.

10

They say a cat is always content, but there's another saying, that Curiosity killed it. Every day I slipped through the hole I'd made in the window screen, having no idea that my adventures would have an impact on all the 2-leggeds around us. In fact, if it were not for me, they would not be leading the lives they do right now! But you'll see what I mean. A cat is not to be dismissed.

A week or so after we took possession of the apartment, when Lorna had gone to work as usual, I settled on the cement window ledge, tail lashing, and watched the birds twittering in the bushes below, teasing and taunting me, *ta-witt-tit*, or *cheep-cheep*. It's more than a cat can bear. Opposite me grew a ragged pine tree. I gauged the distance, crouched (the birds cheeping and chirruping, tweaking their tantalizing tails), and launched! My claws dug into the rough bark. I hung there, a half-mile above the ground, peeking over my shoulder at the planet below. My heart thudded in my breast. I could hardly catch my breath. But I was so proud of myself! I'd *done* it!

I inched backwards. When I was roughly the height of a man from the ground, I let go, twisted in mid-air, and landed perfectly on my four-square feet. Instantly I was the hunter, crawling, belly to the earth, and only the flick of my tail giving me away as I crept up on two sparrows fluttering in a dust bath. I inched forward, sprang—and the flock flew off, leaving me with nothing.

I was mortified.

The next moment I realized I was free. Wow! Free! I trotted about. I sniffed the bushes, leaving my scent on the bricks, the grass, the dirt under the azalea bushes. A wooden fence surrounded the garden. I hopped easily onto the top plank and jumped into the adjacent yard. Oh my. Above me I saw Goliath's face pressed against his window. I swung my tail, waving my banner, and then I stretched my back and extended my claws and rolled in the warm, dry dust. He watched.

Beauty is so beguiling.

The difficulty came when I wanted to go home. Distant thunder rumbled along the black clouds gathering overhead. I returned to the tree, jumped as high as I could and began to climb. I was surprised at how far above the ground our window had grown. I'm an indoor cat, and for all my bravado I felt weak in the knees. I was really high!

The wind had come up, too, as the storm swept in, howling like wild dogs, and shaking the tree in their teeth so that it swayed and swung, and I clung there, lashed back and forth. I hugged the tree trunk with all twenty claws. I crawled out along one branch toward my window. From this angle, the cement ledge looked too narrow to land on, and the leap from tree to the half-open screened window... oh goodness, it was tricky. Especially in the fading light. Even if I landed on the sill, I could smash my nose against the half-open glass pane and fall. It was a very small landing field.

Carefully, I crawled back along the branch to the relative safety of the tree trunk and then clambered up to a higher branch, for every cat knows it's easier to jump downward, beginning from a higher slope. From this angle I could leap to the open hallway window, the one next to ours that had neither screen nor glass to block my jump. But now I was perched on an even smaller, thinner limb. It tossed and swayed in the rising wind, one moment pouring far over the left, the next whipping to the right; or else it shook up and down, as if determined to dislodge me. I dug in my claws. I was still wondering how to jump, when who should I see blinking at me through the hallway window but Goliath. How he'd gotten out of his apartment I don't know.

== Jump! He shouted at me.

I clung to the swaying branch. I felt a bit ill at being up so high and on so thin a branch. The summer storm raced in hard now, with peals of thunder overhead. Lightning flashed. The black clouds tumbled wildly over each other, chased by winds that tossed and tore at the tree. I held on tight, eyes closed. I felt queasy.

==Jump! He shouted again. He was running back and forth on the ledge right where I would land if I were stupid enough to take his advice. Imagine! I'd barrel into him and get thrown off. Didn't he see that?

Just then I heard Lorna's open-hearted laugh, the kind where she throws back her head and lets go joyously. How can you help but love someone who can laugh like that? I looked down. She was running up the sidewalk with Nikki, her purse held over her head against a windswept scattering of rain. I mewed:

"Meee-!" And again, louder: "Look at meee."

"Was that Alba?" Both friends stopped to look around.

"I thought I heard Alba." She had her key in her hand and started to poke it in the lock of the white front door.

I mewed again: "MEeeeeeeee—."

She looked up. "Oh my god! Nikki! Look!"

I flattened on my swaying branch, relieved that she'd seen me!

==Jump! Goliath called again. You can do it!

Down below me, Lorna put her purse on the wet step and held up both hands. "Come here, kitty-kitty." I stared at her in disbelief.

What did she think? That I would leap into her arms? I was twenty, thirty feet—good grief, who knows how high?—up a tree with the rain pelting down hard as nails and the darkening sky casting a greenish light over everything. The rain spurted, stopped, squirted, waffling, undecided whether to drizzle or let loose the slanting, steady sheets it threatened to release.

Nikki said, "We need to call the fire department."

"Oh Alba, how did you get up there?" cried Lorna in distress.

"Firemen are always getting cats out of trees."

"I think that's a myth," said Lorna, practical as cactus. "I don't think they do that anymore."

"They don't." The male voice came from behind her, and she turned to see our neighbor approaching with another man.

"Hello."

"Oh, David, my cat's in the tree."

"Treed."

So then they shook hands, all around. "David Scott. . . Charlie Pace."

They stood bareheaded with the rain dripping down on me. "Lorna Stanford. Nikki Petrelli."

"David has the apartment below me," Lorna needlessly explained. Charlie pulled out his card case and passed his card around despite the wet.

"It says Chandler," murmured Lorna.

"I'm Charlie, though."

And then they all stood in the pale rain and stared up the tree at me. David wore a striped, Oxford cotton shirt with jeans, and he looked athletic enough to climb up the tree after me despite the grey in his hair; but his friend was dressed with city elegance in a lightweight suit and tie. His shoes gleamed with polish. In one hand he carried a leather briefcase embossed with initials. None of them seemed to mind the wet.

"Well, David," Charlie said, amiably. "You're the wildlife expert. What's your counsel?"

David grimaced in self-deprecation.

"I thought you were a lawyer." Lorna flashed him a glance.

"When I was a kid I wanted to be a wildlife vet and take care of rhinos and elephants in the veldt."

"He used to collect all the stray, sick animals in the neighborhood," said Charlie, and I could hear the hint of admiration for his friend—"birds, dogs, rabbits, trying to heal them. An opossum once, remember? It was playing dead. You bandaged up its head. Then it walked away."

"True," David admitted with a rueful laugh. "And I thought my doctoring had made it well. I was only six."

"I think we should call the fire department," said Nikki, hugging her elbows. "I don't have my cell. Who has a phone?"

David stared up at me. "You know," he said thoughtfully, "usually a cat will find its own way down." I was aghast. But the next minute he recovered my respect. "I'm going upstairs to look at the problem from the window there."

I shot my eyes at Goliath, pleased that in a minute he'd be punished. For having threatened poor, lost, frightened, pretty, little me.

David grazed Lorna's elbow with two fingers. "Keep holding out your arms. See if you can talk her down."

Lorna started at his touch. I watched her light-body stream after him, caught in his gravitational pull, and snap back into her like a rubber band.

Few of the 2-leggeds can see the shield of energy that envelops them (not to mention trees, cats, grass, dogs—*even dogs!*). It's easiest to see with soft-focused eyes. Most don't know this, but when they say, *I'm beside myself,* of course they really are. *"I'm out of sorts,"* they say without even hearing their own words. Puma says we're all connected, every living thing, by this universal light field and our own electrical energy, the kind that makes the fur on the back of your neck rise up when you are scared.

Lorna's energy heaved after David. But I had no time to pursue the implications, because a moment later he appeared at the hallway window. Goliath jumped inside with a *thunk*! (Whoever says "silent as a cat" has never met Goliath.)

"Hello, you." David spoke gently. "How did you get out? Is that why Alba's out there trapped in the tree?" Goliath flinched at the charge. I could see him from my branch. He cataloged his innocence, presenting his defense: that he was only encouraging me, a fraidy-cat, to jump. *He called me fraidy-cat.*

If I'd been a 2-legged, I think water would have spurted from my eyes. I didn't want to be a fraidy-cat. But I had no time to listen, for just then a gust of wind hit my tree. I clung to the bucking, plunging branch, my heart in my throat. It was velvet-dark. The light from the hallway cast yellow pools across the purple grass below. The rain-fresh air smelled rich with grass and clover, roses, lilacs, tree bark and pine, and motor oil from the streets, and if I hadn't been so cold and wet and scared, I might have appreciated the scents and also the attention. I closed my eyes to push away my fear.

"Come on, Goliath. Inside with you." David gathered his cat in his arms and disappeared from view. A few moments later, devoid of cat, he rejoined the others in the little circle below the tree. He'd swung a raincoat over his shoulders and carried an umbrella that he opened with a smile over Lorna.

"She never goes outside," Lorna explained in anguish. "What if something happens to her ?"

"Like what?" asked Charlie.

"I don't know. An owl. Or she could fall. What if she catches her collar on a branch and is strangled?" I was surprised. The way her mind rushed to disaster sounded more like Nikki than my gentle and cool-headed Lorna.

"Why not call the Fire Department?" Nikki murmured, despite the futility of the suggestion. She didn't expect anyone to listen. But oddly, both Charlie and Lorna turned to her, discussing the possibility and how or who or where to call, and whether 911 was suitable for a cat in a tree.

Meanwhile, David gazed off into the middle distance; and seeing him emptying his mind, I told him how in fact she was wrong: how I *always* went outside, how I'd seen the sparrows twittering in the bush, how I'd leapt from the window into the tree and clambered down, how I'd hunted with the patience of a panther, and pounced and almost caught a sparrow—its terror as my claws raked its back, its sudden beat of wings, its upward flash and heart-stopped *cheep*, leaving me with two feathers at my disgusted nose, and how I'd explored the backyards and sunbathed until dinner time, when I'd climbed the tree under the darkening, beautiful glowing sunset, the wind-driven clouds—and found Goliath blocking the window, and also my caution about making the dangerous leap in the rain-swept green light off the bucking violence of the tree.

When I finished, I blinked to indicate full stop.

The rain settled into a steady downpour. The two women crouched under the umbrella. Charlie looked dismally unhappy. He smoothed his wet hair with one strong hand.

I don't know how much David got of my story, but he was better at listening than Lorna.

"Oh, how did you get up there?" she called, as if I hadn't just described it all.

"I think she went birding," said David, "and then she couldn't get back inside. Come on, it's raining. Let's go inside. We'll have a drink and think this through."

"Just leave her there?"

"Good idea. We need a drink." With one hand at her back, Charlie guided Lorna toward the door. "Don't worry. We'll get her down for you. I promise you."

I was stunned: What was he thinking? That he'd climb up to rescue me?

"You promise?" she teased, smiling.

"I do."

"I like your English accent."

He laughed, pleased. "My mother was English. I do a lot of business in London. I can't seem to lose it," he finished happily. Of course not, I wanted to shout; it's his trademark.

"Investment banking," interjected David, anticipating Lorna's question.

All this time Nikki had been subdued. I hadn't seen her in a few days, and she seemed different, withdrawn. Mute and disconsolate, she followed the two men, as if she had to remind herself what to do, while her thoughts were occupied with circling elsewhere.

David held the door for her: "Are you coming? It's raining." Then, suddenly protective, "Are you all right?"

She smiled weakly at him, so fragile and vulnerable that he put a comforting arm around her shoulder.

The door closed, and I was left alone, with the rain running in ribbons down the tree, down my fur. I was miserable. I settled tighter on the branch, digging in my claws. The bark was slippery. People say cats have nine lives, but we're simply very, very careful. Thunder rumbled in the distance. The greenish light had turned to black night, cut only by the angled shafts of yellow that spilled from the open windows of our apartment block. I backed up closer to the trunk. The rain poured down, soaking my fur.

A cat's hearing is acute—except that of blue-eyed, white cats, who are often deaf, poor things. But with the blowing wind, the rain, the passing cars swishing through the puddles on the nearby street and with my unhappy ears pinned back against the wet, you'd think I could hear nothing. David's voice was loud, though, as he passed drinks and food to his guests. He was holding court.

"A cat is a perfect predator," he was saying. "Designed to kill."

"Da-vid!" That was Lorna protesting.

"What an awful thing to say!" This time Nikki.

"No, it's not," he defended himself. "It's a compliment. Look, a cat is the only animal whose hips allow him to put all four feet in a straight line. That's why he can walk a fence. A cat can leap six or eight feet in the air. I saw Goliath once jump to the top of that door there and land comfortably on a quarter-inch ledge. Can you jump straight up in the air as high as four times your height? Its tongue is barbed for grooming its fur. Its ears swivel almost 180 degrees, and its eyes have double lenses for seeing at night—infra-red vision, as it were. And consider its patience. A cat will wait for hours stalking its prey, a bird, a chipmunk. Patient. Controlled."

I began to admire how exceptional I was.

"It always lands on its feet," said Nikki. "It turns over so fast."

"That's due to the balance in its ears."

"It can squeeze into any space big enough for its head," Lorna piped up. "Its whiskers measure the width, so the cat always knows whether it can get through."

"And more important," said David in approval, "whether it can get back out. A cat is a killing machine."

I tucked my feet under me on my branch, dropped my chin and flattened my swivel ears to keep the water out. I was a killing machine, the perfect predator, and if I hadn't been so wet and lonely, I might have felt more than simply miserable.

I think I must have slept, for the next thing I heard was David's voice below me.

"Alba? Are you all right?"

I peered down.

"I can't see you," he called up, "but in case you're there, I've brought you a treat."

The next minute he had gone. The rain had stopped and only isolated drops fell on my wet fur: drop... drip...plop....

The moon was shining like a tin bowl, peeping through the scudding clouds: clouds rolling over each other like romping kittens. A warm breeze brushed the tree, mingling with music from David's apartment. The next moment an aroma filled my nostrils: Fish!

My stomach twisted.

I was hungry.

And tired.

And cold.

And lonely.

And wet.

The scent made my tail twitch. I stared down at the ground. The next thought clobbered me: *What if another animal eats my dinner?*

Slowly I began to back down the rain-soaked tree, one careful claw at a time. Creeping.

I hung vertically on the tree trunk, looking over my shoulder at the grass below.

The smell of salmon.

I jumped.

The salmon was delicious. Then I curled on the doorstep waiting to be let inside. Inside I could hear them laughing and talking animatedly (if I can use that word) above the soft Blue Grass banjo and fiddle. I felt very sorry for myself. They'd already forgotten about poor little me, the perfect predator.

11

It took a long time for the party to break up. When the door opened, Charlie almost fell as I flung myself between his legs. He caught me with two heavy hands on my back, squashing me to the floor.

"Look what I found!" He smelled of wine and cheese, salmon and onion and a curious lemony scent from his after-shave. I wanted to jump away, but he picked me up in two extended hands, holding me as far away from his good suit as possible. "One wet cat."

"Alba!" Lorna raced to take me in her arms. "Oh, honey. You're all wet."

"Didn't I tell you we'd get her down for you?" He winked at her. "I'm happy to accept all kudos."

Imagine! It was David who got me down, and here was Charlie taking credit! I felt offended, but Lorna's eyes were shining: "How did you do that?"

"My secret." He lifted one triumphant thumb.

I was too tired to care. I snuggled against Lorna, grateful to be with her again.

"Here. You need a towel." That was David lunging forward with his offering, and the next moment I was being dried and wrapped in lovely warmth.

The group had already divided into surprising pairs. Nikki clung to David, hovering at his side.

"That's so thoughtful." She glanced up, her brown eyes large and innocent. I think Lorna turned away, unable to bear the view.

Goliath ran along the wall, the hackles raised high on his back, and I drew back my lips to hiss at him. But Lorna was kissing and toweling me and hiding her face in my wet fur, and to tell the truth I hadn't the heart to make a fuss about him just then. It was enough to be enveloped in her sweet scent.

Nikki came over to pet me ("Poor Alba, were you scared up there?"), and even Charlie dared to poke at me with two fingers, once he saw the others do it. He patted my back, then wiped his wet palm on a handkerchief, and then he didn't know what to do with the handkerchief because it had wet cat fur on it, but finally he folded it carefully a few times and tucked it in his breast pocket.

"Well, all's well that ends well," Nikki purred. "I'm so glad."

"I have to be going," said Lorna. She suddenly felt rigid, reserved. "David, I can't thank you enough." For a moment their eyes met. What had gone on in my absence? I never knew, but Charlie opened the door for us, and David watched us climb the steps, while Nikki, laughing a little too loudly, proclaimed that she wasn't at all in the mood to leave, and she'd accept another drink if David offered it, and later she'd drive herself back home. I felt Lorna's back stiffen.

"Goodnight then, everyone," she called from the floor above, and so we climbed the stairs to our apartment.

"I'll call you in the morning," Nikki shouted after us.

That night, after brushing her teeth, Lorna stood in her blue cotton bunny-rabbit pajamas. She stared at herself for a long time in the bathroom mirror: her level gaze, the short-cropped, curly hair. I crouched down to drink from the water running from the faucet. I like drinking from the faucet. This is our bedtime ritual, and Lorna always waits for me to finish before turning off the water. I wouldn't dream of drinking from a bowl on the floor, like Puma.

"He's nice," she said out loud to her reflection, followed a moment later by a critical snarl: "Look at you. You're sixty-one years old. Who do you think you are?"

I looked up in surprise. Lorna is beautiful. It always surprises me when the 2-leggeds dislike themselves, and now Lorna had suddenly caught the infection. It defied comprehension.

Who would you like if not yourself?

12

The next day I didn't feel well. I was logy. Listless. By the time Lorna came home from work my eyes were seeping fluid, my nose ran. I sneezed and sneezed. I didn't care for food, all I wanted was to sleep.

"Oh dear, if you don't get better," she murmured as she wiped goo out of my eyes and nose, "I'll have to take you to the vet." I pricked my ears in horror. *Go to the vet*?! Not after what I'd heard from Puma! *You wouldn't catch me going to the vet!*

But three days later, there we were, driving in the car to the animal hospital. I prowled the back seat, hopped to the back window, jumped to the front seat, pressed myself in Lorna's lap and stared out the windows at the passing trees (it's so curious the way the landscape runs past the car—and stops—and moves again). I tried everything I could to tell her I felt fine, that I didn't need the vet.

It did no good. She held me down on her lap with one hand, her fingers hooked into my blue diamond-studded necklace and wouldn't let me prowl. I mewed. I complained. I was scared. I didn't want to meet the white-jacketed ones or listen to an orange alley cat. I tried to jump out of her grasp.

Thankfully, the vet was so unlike Puma's that I wondered if he'd made his story up. This is what I remember: my claws scrabbling against the cold metal table, her strong hands holding me down, a pole pushed up my bottom, and fingers kneading my belly and neck, a stick poked in my ears, a light in my eyes, and hands forcing open my mouth to push a vile-tasting substance down my throat; also the fur on my butt pulled high followed by a sharp prick; and this: Indignity! Humiliation! Mockery! Disrespect!

Then the doctor was petting me and admiring my pretty nose and gold-tipped ears. She gave me a treat, which I licked off her fingers, courteously. And then she stood there, talking to Lorna, smiling and petting me with luxurious fingers that knew just where I like to be touched. She had beautiful, warm hands.

So I calmed down.

She held and petted me some more and kissed the top of my head, and I thought what a loving woman she was, her energy pouring over me like brilliant light.

What a fuss for nothing.

Lorna pushed me back in the car and turned on the engine. "Now we're going to the car wash and then to see Mrs. Pullet," she said. "She's waiting for you, remember?"

Mrs. Pullet is ninety-four years old. We visit her almost every week. My job is to jump into her lap, purring, and look up at her with my blue eyes while she exclaims over me, and then I let her stroke me with her arthritic old hands, while the love rises up in her, melting over me so that my heart opens, too. When I leave, I stand up and put my paws around her neck and kiss her cheek.

Once when I did this she burst into tears.

Lorna makes tea sandwiches in Mrs. Pullet's tiny kitchen, and they play Scrabble for an hour, while I sit on Mrs. Pullet's lap. They make fun of politicians and Congress and the latest sex scandal and the pretentions of the Other Party, laughing all the time.

Mrs. Pullet lives on one floor of her big house and never goes outside anymore. She has a bed in the living room, with a small bathroom off to one side and the linoleum-floored kitchen on the other. Every morning she struggles out of bed and puts on underclothes and garter belt and stockings, a slip, and over it a dress, and on her feet a pair of low-heeled shoes. She clips on the pearl choker that covers the wattles on her neck. She combs her reddish hair and adds blush and lipstick and then she staggers to the kitchen, using the doorjamb and backs of chairs to support her wobbly self. She eats one-half a small yoghurt and drinks a cup of coffee, and then she weaves back to the living room, balancing herself on the furniture, and sinks into her chair. On one side are her books, and on the other the TV and telephone. Sometimes no one calls her telephone all day long. Sometimes no one visits. In the evening she undresses and goes back to bed. She says she's ready to pass over anytime, life's such a trial.

"I wish the good Lord would take me," she proclaims. "Sometimes the pain is almost unbearable." But every morning, to her disappointment, she's still here, and then she gets up valiantly and dresses herself for a new day. I lick her fingers in sympathy, but I can't imagine not wanting to leap awake to a brightening sky, it's all so interesting.

"Of course you can't give in, but oh, my dear, getting old is not for the faint of heart." She rolls her eyes when she says this, to underscore the joke.

Her table is covered with magazines like *National Geographic* and *O* and *The New Yorker, Vanity Fair, Rolling Stone* and *Vogue*. She keeps up.

It was Mrs. Pullet who had told Lorna, when approaching a dreaded birthday, "Oh, your sixties!" She waved one dismissive hand. "You won't even notice your sixties. I had wonderful times in my sixties. Now at ninety," she said thoughtfully, "you begin to slow down." She'd then leaned back to examine Lorna critically. "Anyway, I don't know what you're worried about. In my day women looked their age."

They talk of everything.

"Do you still feel sexual desire?" Lorna blushed as she asked the question, but Mrs. Pullet wasn't the least offended.

"Oh dear me, yes. No one would dare ask that but you, dear Lorna.

Thank you. Just the other night I had a dream that this man was making love to me. It was... delicious. I still feel it. Isn't that strange? I guess sexual urge never stops. Until you're dead," she concluded. "And then you're finished, all the life-force gone."

"I like that." Lorna laughed with her.

"Well, I'll tell you a secret." Mrs. Pullet leaned forward, her watery eyes shining.

"What?"

"I have a boyfriend."

"No!"

"I met him at the Senior Center. He's younger than I am, but then everyone is these days. We hold hands and always sit beside each other at Crafts, and sometimes we go outside, if it's a nice day, and he puts his arm around my waist. Of course he can't come home with me, and I can't spend the night at his place, but we love each other. It never ends, does it?" she finished dreamily.

And another time:

"Oh, Lorna! I've learned so much since I was ninety." Mrs. Pullet beamed at Lorna with excitement. "I've learned more since I was ninety than in my whole life!" I peered up at the courageous old lady, wondering what she could possibly have learnt when she lived all alone like a hermit in a Himalayan cave, with all her children dead and grandchildren on the other side of the country and no one coming to visit from one day to the next. Moreover, she'd led a wild and wicked life. What could she possibly have left to learn?

"Oh, there's always something to think about," she said. "I think about my life and all the mistakes I've made. Right now I'm thinking about how I might have handled things better. So much remorse. Regret. But you didn't come here to hear all that. Please, get yourself a cup of tea and come back and tell me what you young things are doing. That's what I want to know about, real life!" Lorna saved up tidbits to tell Mrs. Pullet.

This day Lorna told the whole story of Nikki and Jeremy. "She's crushed," said Lorna. "All she does is cry."

Mrs. Pullet was quiet for a long time.

"She was abused as a child? By whom? Her mother? Her father?"

"Her father. How did you know?"

"Well, someone taught her to curl up in her own inadequacy. The old, old victim story. You must help her to get angry," she said with a firm nod.

"Angry?"

"Anger is much underrated. Either that or she must meet another man right away."

Lorna laughed. "You advocate the rebound?"

"Nothing wrong with a good rebound. But unfortunately, in that case the same thing will probably happen to her all over again. Life has a way of repeating events until we learn the lesson. Think of it all as a series of lessons. But why is she taking this lying down? Why doesn't she go after him?"

"I don't understand," said Lorna.

"Heart!" Mrs. Pullet beat her chest with one hand. "*Courage.* The word comes from the French, *coeur*, for heart. En-*courage* her! She must *take heart*. Did I ever tell you what happened when my husband fell in love?"

A long story followed. Jimmy, Mrs. Pullet's husband, was fifty-one when he met a younger woman, only thirty-three. He fell madly, head over heels in love. He asked his wife for a divorce.

"I wouldn't hear of it. He was MY husband," she said, and my fur prickled at the force of her indignation which even after all these years rose up. "The father of two children—I wasn't about to hand him over to some tramp. I knew the girl. She was a floozy. A sex-pot, that's what she was. They met at a white-tie ball. She took one look at Jimmy and went after him."

"But how could you refuse the divorce?"

"I just didn't hear him." Mrs. Pullet tossed her red-dyed head. "I remember once I was sitting at my dressing table when he came in. He stood in the doorway and announced that he was leaving me. 'Now what have I done with my lipstick?' I said. 'Will you hand me my gloves?' I just wouldn't hear him, and I remember Caroline coming in, my daughter, and saying, "Oh grow up, Daddy. We're a family. You don't just divorce and start over."

"My goodness!" Lorna was taken aback.

"Well, I'm not saying it was easy. At one point the company transferred him to New Orleans. He told me he was going with HER, and he did. He just walked out and rented a house in New Orleans and set up housekeeping with HER. That hurt. It really hurt."

"What did you do?"

"I packed up our house in San Francisco and drove to New Orleans with the two children and the dog. Jane and Caroline were in their teens at the time. I bought a house in the same neighborhood where he was staying with his mistress, and I told him, 'THIS is your house. Not that other one. THIS one! Then I sent out cards and made sure all invitations and mail for him came to *our* house, my house."

"What happened?"

"They broke up," she said thoughtfully. She twisted her hands in her lap. "Eventually. It took a while. He couldn't stand the strain. I insisted on going to every social event with him or without, to every dance, every dinner party. Even if SHE was going to be there, too, he took me on his arm and met her there. In the end it was too much for them both. She left. He came crawling back to me."

Her soft hands stroked my ears. With one finger she traced the line of my jaw and pulled my whiskers absently.

"Once, at one of the balls, they had a raffle. The prize was a sterling silver wine bucket, and I had a premonition I was going to win it. I wanted it. I bought five tickets. When the master of ceremonies read out the numbers, SHE stood up and started to walk up to the dais for her prize. I was aghast. But then the master of ceremonies stopped her. 'Oh. I'm sorry. I've made a mistake. It's number— He read out another number, and it was *mine*! So I rose from my seat and walked to the front like a queen to accept my prize. It was at that moment that I knew I'd won. That Jimmy was mine, I mean."

"So you got him back."

"Of course you always pay a price. Our relationship was never the same. I couldn't forgive him. He couldn't forget. Later, when he had his stroke, I took care of him for eight years. Eight years, and that was no joke. He couldn't speak— 'Uugh! Oogh!' he'd say, and sometimes he'd let loose a whole paragraph of gobbledygook that must have meant something to him. Oh, it was tragic. Words. Sounds. They made no sense. I had to interpret for him. He'd get furious when I didn't understand. He'd beat his cane on the floor, or lift it up as if to strike me. It was dreadful. Many a time I wondered if I'd made the right choice, holding on to him. But SHE would have left him." Mrs. Pullet lifted her wobbly chins, eyes flashing. "SHE wouldn't have taken care of him once he'd gotten old or had a stroke."

A moment later a wet tear fell on me. I looked up at the pale, crepey skin of her wrinkled face. "It was hard," she said. "I don't deny it, but if your little friend wants her man, she should go after him. After all, she has a history with him, though that can work against her, too. Men can be so stupid," she added. "They always want the unfamiliar. Anyway, encourage her to get angry. Very satisfying."

Lorna rubbed her hands, laughing. "All right, are you ready for Scrabble?"

She took the advice to heart, though. I think this conversation led directly to what happened next.

13

When we got home Nikki was sitting on the front stoop, her arms wrapped around her knees. She stood up as we drove in and brushed the twigs off her skirt. Lorna gathered me in her arms, hooking a loving thumb in my necklace lest I should leap out in the street and be squashed by a car.

"Hi, Nikki. What are you doing here?"

"I just had to see you." They kissed and walked up to the steps together.

I was dismayed. I'd had enough emotion for one day, we all had, what with going to the vet and the car wash and visiting Mrs. Pullet. I hadn't even had time to reflect on all these—and now here came Nikki, who is high-maintenance, giving us more to absorb. Suddenly I envied the cows I've seen in fields, who every day lie down in green pastures to chew their pacific cud and muse slow thoughts as they gaze with huge and gentle eyes over the quiet landscape. I know that Lorna felt the same: a little shiver of disappointment fell over her, even as she welcomed Nikki. She would have liked a quiet evening at home alone with me. But she wouldn't be a good friend if she didn't accommodate the younger woman in her pain.

"Are you all right?" she asked, adjusting me higher in her arms to fumble for her keys. "Come inside." There followed the usual bustle of keys in the latch and feet clomping up the bare wood stairs, of more keys for our apartment door, and then I was spilled down onto the floor while Lorna moved to the kitchen.

"Will you stay for dinner?" It was already past 6:00 p.m. "Pasta and tomato sauce? With mushrooms?" Her voice lifted in questions, as if the dinner might not be to Nikki's taste.

Nikki perched on a high kitchen stool and watched Lorna move efficiently round the small kitchen. It was the first time I'd noticed how much Nikki depended on Lorna, or how completely my kind-hearted 2-legged accepted the role of mother to her friend.

Sniffing the alluring scent of Lorna's cooking, I jumped up on the kitchen counter and proceeded to walk delicately along the edge of the granite to remind my darling of myself. She swatted me to the floor.

"Feed Alba for me, will you? You'll find a can on that shelf." Both were busy then, and my stomach churned and my ears tingled with happiness. I forgave her for pushing me down, for what is nicer than the sound of a can opener crunching open a tiny tin of gourmet kidney stew?

At dinner, poking her salad with a disinterested fork, Nikki finally came to the reason for her visit.

"I have a confession to make." She pushed a walnut over to one side on her plate, isolated and alone. "Last night I drove over to his house. I had this insane idea that if we could just talk that maybe.... I don't know what I was thinking. It was late. I parked outside. The curtains were open. Oh, Lorna. He was with *her*. I saw her."

"Penelope?"

"I don't know what I was thinking." She fumbled with her fork. "That's not true. I knew exactly what I was thinking."

In a flash, I saw the pictures flickering in her mind: how he'd be home and how she'd ring the doorbell and hand him (her excuse) some photos. He'd be surprised and pleased to see her. He'd invite her in. They'd have a drink. They'd talk, and then... but she stopped at this point, because maybe he wouldn't want to kiss her and do all the rest of the stuff she liked.

"The thing is, I really care for him," Nikki said, breaking the silence. "Isn't that awful? When you love someone, you want him to be happy, don't you? I hope he'll be very happy."

Lorna rocked back in her seat. "Do you?" she said, head cocked with interest. "Aren't you angry?"

"Yes—no— I don't know. Sometimes I wake up in the middle of the night and just lie in the dark. I can't stop crying. But then I think how we wouldn't have been happy together anyway, would we? You can't *make* someone love you. He wanted someone more, more. . . I'm not—" she shrugged, disconsolate.

"Nikki, you're brilliant, beautiful, kind, artistic. You're—"

"No, no, don't. Please. You're so sweet to me. Well, let me tell you what happened. I sat in the car. I was stunned. I don't know what I'd been thinking, driving over there, but I certainly hadn't expected to find them together."

"What did you do?"

"Nothing. I sat in the car with the lights out, terrified that he'd see me. A peeping Tom. She's tall—taller than he is—leggy. Dripping with jewelry. At one point she stood on one foot with the other foot crossed up at her hip, like one of those statues of the dancing Shiva. I could no more do that, I'd fall over. She has thin thighs. Not like me. Of course she was barefoot, so I could see her sparkly ankle bracelet. Oh God! An ankle bracelet! When did that go out of fashion?"

"Where was Jeremy all this time?"

"He lay stretched out on the couch, his back to the window, fortunately, so he didn't see me. She reached out to pull him to his feet. To dance with him, I suppose. She put her arms around his waist."

"Oh, save me," Lorna muttered.

"I couldn't stand it. I thought I'd drive the car *smash!* into the plate glass window! That would surprise them. I thought of sneaking up and pounding on the window—or else I'd overturn his stupid birdbath and tromp through the flowerbeds, so that when he came out next morning he'd find his front yard trashed, and my footprints everywhere."

"What did you do?"

"Nothing." She covered her face with her hands. "Nothing. I'm such a coward. I let out the brakes and drifted down the hill past his house and past the next one before I even dared to turn the motor on and drive away. But I was furious. Hell hath no fury!" She tossed her head. "Dido. Circe. I understand Medea killing her children, Jason's children, weaving a magic cloak that would stick to his skin and burn him alive. I could have—" She stopped, embarrassed at herself. But her energy had collapsed again. Lorna watched in silent concern.

"I drove away, and all I could think of was my Nonna, what she would have done."

"What would she have done?"

"My father's mother. She was a kind of witch, my grandmother. She was tiny, not even five feet. She always dressed in black. This fierce, fiery, little Sicilian lady. 'Men are goats,' she used to say." Nikki gave a laugh, remembering. "She had contempt for pretty much all men, including her own sons."

"What would she have done?" Lorna asked again, pleased to see her friend rising out of her despairing impotence, no matter the reason why.

"First, she would have put her statue of St. Anthony upside down in a dark closet until he did what she wanted— a punishment, you see—and she would have prayed to St. Jude of Lost Causes; only her prayers weren't kindly requests, none of this 'Thy Will be Done,' but raging, fist-shaking, trumpeted demands, and she didn't hesitate to give exact instructions on how the saint was supposed to work it, or in what time-frame! And then she'd move on to the Holy Mother, because nothing is as powerful as a Mother, she used to say. Even God has to listen to the Mother. She would have got on St. Anthony's case, even if he didn't particularly mind being upside down in a cobwebbed closet in the dark. Or maybe, she would have taken some toenail clippings and a twist of hair round her finger, and she'd have cast a spell against the person who offended her."

"You should do it." Lorna leaned forward, eyes sparkling. She was remembering Mrs. Pullet's counsel. But the hackles rose on the back of my neck at the electricity in the room.

"What?"

"What would you ask for? That he come back to you? That he be miserable with Penelope forever? How about this? That whenever he's making love to Penelope he remembers you, loses his erection and regrets to his dying day that he lost you, and he longs for you all his long, miserable, unhappy life, chained to a nagging, ugly, greedy, nasty wife."

Nikki looked away. "But I don't have any toenail clippings, do I? Or a lock of hair."

"Ah." To Lorna all this was merely an intellectual exercise. "I suppose you could clean out the shower drain."

"What?"

"You know how hair gets caught in the drains? What else do you need?"

"Anything personal. A ring. A letter. A key. I have a letter."

"Oh, you have lots of things of his. Don't you need something from Penelope, too?"

"I don't even know her last name!"

"You'd need her full name, I imagine," said Lorna amiably, still intent on cheering up her friend. And indeed Nikki had perked up.

"It's Penelope I want to kill."

Just speaking those words aloud brought Nikki to a lighter mood. She looked up and smiled her dazzling, brilliant smile, and I thought how odd that plotting against your enemy would bring you happiness, or heightened energy at least, but there you are—the power of revenge; and then because they needed a last name, it blew into their hands, like a wind at the door, her guardian angel descending, trumpet in hand.

14

First came a hiss and muted *plonk* as the metal outside door closed downstairs. At the same time our apartment door, improperly locked, fell open. Lorna stepped to the door to shut it. "David?" she called into the hallway.

"Hi, it's me." His voice.

The next thing I knew Nikki had flown past Lorna out the door and down the stairs in a ripple of clattering footsteps. "Oh David!" she called. "Wait." A murmuring of voices followed, and soon she reappeared, one arm linked in his, her eyes shining up at him.

She missed the look that Lorna flung at them as they pushed past her to the table.

Could rebound come so quickly on the heels of hate?

"Hello, Lorna." David turned back to Lorna, still standing at the door, and kissed her on the cheek.

"Alba, how are you?" He bent down to scratch my ears, then picked me up. "Have you recovered from your night in the rain?" I sniffed his coffee breath, his pinesoap hands. He was taut as braided wire and covered in the odor of male cat.

"Coffee? Can I offer you a glass of wine?" Lorna remembered her manners. For some reason she had flushed bright red. Her voice came out odd.

"I'd take a glass of wine." He glanced at the two women. "But I don't want to intrude on you—"

"It's no intrusion," cried Nikki, grabbing his arm. "We want you. We need you. We're just sitting here. Two old maids being doleful."

Old maids? I couldn't believe my ears.

When David chuckled in response, I realized Nikki had made a joke, though I'm not sure Lorna got it, for she was fumbling, half-hidden behind the open kitchen cabinets.

"But while I'm here, listen, I'm giving a party in a few weeks. The 27th." He drew up a chair with a kick of his heel. "I'd love to have you come."

He smiled in his crooked, charming way, but I felt an edge in his voice. Things sharp and wicked left unsaid. The 2-leggeds are so complex, it's hard sometimes for me to know what's going on.

Lorna set a glass in front of him.

"Informal," he said as he picked up the wine. "I'll cook outside on the grill. Charlie will be there. I think he's coming down from New York just to see you two."

"He is?" Nikki sat up straighter.

"Do you always rinse the dishes before putting them in the dishwasher?" David teased Lorna.

"I do. It comes from not trusting machinery as much as people."

"Be careful with Charlie." David turned to his wine glass. "He's vulnerable just now. He's passionately in love. And just been jilted."

"He's in love with someone?"

"Charlie gets smitten. And when he falls, it's a skydiver without a parachute. I've seen it before. Right now he's in love with a woman who moved a few months ago to Washington. She wants to get into politics. She's put him through the wringer. Ruthless."

"He told me," Lorna murmured

"When?" David looked up in surprise.

"He called one night. He wanted to talk about being dumped." She sat at the table with the others. I was surprised. Where was I when she talked to Charlie? I'd missed the whole thing, and why did everyone want to tell Lorna about their latest rejection?

"Who is she?" Nikki pushed. "Anyone we know?"

"I doubt it. Penelope Smith-Hampstead."

Nikki gave a yelp.

"Penelope? Does she work at the *Post*? Tall? Dyed blond? Lots of jewelry? Fringes? Shawls??"

"She dyes her hair? I didn't know."

"You know her then? Will she be at your party too?"

Her excitement was spurting and spraying round the room. I jumped up on the table to defuse the situation.

"Hello, Beauty," David said, stroking my chin in my special sweet spot. "We're not paying enough attention to you, are we?" It's annoying when a man can read your mind. "No." He smiled at Nikki. "I wouldn't have her at my place."

"You wouldn't? Why? What's she like?" Lorna twisted the stem of her glass to make the red wine slosh in tornado circles.

"Well, she's sexy," he answered thoughtfully. "Smart. Manipulative. She's always got an adoring crowd around her. Like you, Alba," he continued, and I blinked at him in surprise. "She likes to be adored, like you, and she gathers admirers. She's Aphrodite. Irresistible."

Oh. What a nice compliment.

"I gather you're not an admirer?"

For a moment he held Lorna's eyes. "No. Mind you," he said with a nod, "She's sexy as hell, but frankly I've never found narcissism appealing."

"At least you're not judgmental." She laughed at him.

"I don't like those games. I don't play games."

Which made Lorna grow quiet, staring with profound intent at the swirling red wine in her glass.

Nikki's mind turned, though, on its private wheels. "Does she fall in love, too?"

David smiled across the table at her. "I imagine so. Doesn't everyone?"

"I just wondered. From what you said about her needing to be adored."

"Yes, but she also likes a challenge."

"And Charlie wasn't one?" asked Nikki carefully.

He stroked me quietly. "Charlie. . . I shouldn't say anything. Look, I've known Charlie all my life. We were kids together. He's a high-powered investment banker, travels all over the world—Paris, London, Tokyo. But—"

"But what?" Lorna challenged. "He loves deeply? You'd think that would be in his favor."

"It is. I think it is. But it depends on whom you choose to love. Charlie loves with the devotion of a dachshund. That time you met, when Alba was up in the tree, maybe you don't know, but he'd come to Washington on purpose to see Penelope. Oh, he had business, but it could just as easily have been done long distance. That's what computers are for. But when he called to ask her to dinner—very casually, spur of the moment— spontaneous invitation, because he found himself unexpectedly here in town— she was. . . well, she said she didn't care to see him. She said she's found someone more exciting. She didn't need to say that. Oh look, Charlie's a grown man, he'll recover. But her behavior was completely gratuitous."

"And Penelope?" Nikki asked in a small, wistful voice.

He laughed. "Oh, Penelope knows exactly what she wants. Someday she'll find the right man and marry him and move to the country, and they'll have five or six children all in pony club, and she'll be on the board of the local hospital, and her children will go to Stanford or Harvard. It happens all the time. I gather she's already found him."

Nikki stared at him.

"Anyway." He pushed himself to his feet, both hands flat on the table. "I'll send you a reminder closer to the date. The 27th. Will you come?" He was looking at Lorna as he spoke, but with her head down she didn't notice.

"I need to use the bathroom," murmured Nikki, jumping off her stool.

Lorna saw him to the door, where he paused as if about to speak, then clomped downstairs; but I slipped out at his feet, drawn by the odor of Goliath, and padded down beside him. He caught me in his arms and brought me back to Lorna.

"Your cat." He smiled. "I've two tickets to the opera Friday. Would you like to go? Tosca."

Lorna could only stare in astonishment. Then, as he turned, "Yes. Yes, I'd love to."

"I'll call you."

When she closed the door behind him with a click, she was shaken. But Nikki, entering from the bedroom and still drying her hands on her blouse, had come alive.

"Lorna! Do you realize what just happened? We have her name! And I'm damned if I'll let her have five children with Jeremy and a country house. And be on the hospital board. And send her kids to pony club."

Lorna looked up in surprise, for her mind was plowing far-off fields. She sat on the sofa in the living room, holding me in her lap.

"I wish I had something of Penelope's," Nikki exclaimed. "I wish I had an earring, a fingernail, all ten fingers, her tongue and eyes and ears."

Lorna pressed her thumb into the soft tissue of my paw, watching my claws extend.

Nikki watched intently. "Claw clippings!" she whispered. "From a cat."

"What?"

"That's so brilliant. My god, Lorna, you are so brilliant. I can do it by proxy, can't I? But it should be Puma's." Nikki was ferocious, fierce. "Because Jerry liked Puma. I'll clip his claws tonight." She stared down at me curled on Lorna's lap. "I hate Penelope," she said. "I hate that she encouraged Charlie and jilted him."

"You don't know she encouraged him."

"Oh, yes I do."

"Nikki, are you all right?"

"I'm fine. Oh yes. I've never been better." She laughed, and snatched up her purse. "It's time for me to go."

At the door, she paused.

"You know what I love?" Nikki turned, face fierce. "I love that you don't have a boyfriend. I don't think I could confide in you if you had what I don't have right now. Is that awful of me? But it's true. I'm glad you're old and single."

Lorna blinked.

"I love the fact that you don't even like Charlie. Or David. Or anyone. I like David. Maybe I'll make a play for him. But I love it that you don't miss a man. I mean, you've said it over and over, that you honestly don't care, you've had your husband, and you don't want anyone now. You don't even think all that much of David, and he's so good-looking. Of course he's too young for you," she laughed, "but I love that in you. You're independent, and he's of no interest to you at all."

I pattered to the door and scraped against Nikki's leg. Not think that much of him? Lorna thought about him all the time!

15

Late that night I moved to the moonlit window. A bat flew past, a silent blur of black, and deep in the grass came the scurrying of mice and moles. In the distance a garbage can lid fell with a clatter—the work of an urban raccoon. The city was bathed in an amber glow, and with eyes half-closed I settled into the silent cat-space that connected me with Puma across the river, communing mind to mind, until I found myself dreaming what was happening at Nikki's. Here Puma ran to greet her at the door, she bent to stroke him. "Hello, sweetheart." I watched the scene unfold: the red blinking light of the answering machine in the dark room. She noticed, punched the button.

"This is Jerry." His voice hard. "Call me."

She listened again, and then a third time. No emotion softened his voice, no remorse, regret. Did he want his clothes? Well, only today she'd packed those up. They were in a box ready for the dumpster. She paced the floor, twisting her fingers, because of course she wanted to call him back. Tears pricked her eyes. She thought of calling Lorna, but she'd only just left. She refused to become dependent on her friend. She punched the button to hear a fourth time that hard, unyielding voice.

She wished Claire were in town. Her godmother would know how to handle this. But Nikki could not phone her in France, not at four in the morning, Paris time.

She listened a fifth time "This is Jerry. Call me."

"No." She hit the erase button. A shudder washed over her. Her emotions bucked and plunged: horror, pride, self-pity, shame. Everyone knew he'd ditched her. She writhed at the gossip, with everyone pitying or ridiculing her. She hadn't been able to keep her man because. . . and here a bat-pack of images attacked, demolishing what little self-esteem remained. This was the man whom only a few hours earlier she'd claimed to love!

Clipping Puma's toenails took only a few minutes. The ancient cat was so accustomed to it that he luxuriated in her lap, patient, while she guillotined his claws.

"I know why he phoned." She spoke aloud. "He wants to know that I'm missing him." She felt in some cranny of her mind the twisted logic of her reasoning, that she was tipping toward insanity. "Or else he wants to tell me they're getting married." She burrowed in her purse for the one photo that she'd hid, and ripped it into shreds.

"To think I'd wanted to keep his teddy bear! Or maybe he's looking for approval. Like you, Puma, dropping a mouse at my feet, to show me what you've caught. Bringing me Penelope, expecting praise. Well, I *don't* approve."

She paced up and down, wringing her hands. Puma watched her from under half-mast yellow eyes, purring out a calm that she could not receive.

"The fact is—" She spoke out loud into the empty house. "Maybe his leaving is God's way of doing me a favor. What do you think, Puma? Maybe it's a way of giving me exactly what I want—a good man, children—just not by him."

Nonetheless, she put her Spanish *retablo* of St. Anthony upside down in the back of the coat closet. She lit a seven-day candle to St. Jude, and another to the Virgin Mary—and set the two candles on the bookcase before her little altar where they flanked a chunk of pink crystal, two seedpods that erupted like white feathers out of their delicate casement; a laughing Buddha, hands upflung with joy; one tiny, grass-braided bird's nest that she'd found on a walk, a delicate confection of home-building woven miraculously by a single, busy beak. She placed a small china saucer on the altar before her Russian icon of Christ. His huge black eyes bored into hers.

"Don't look at me like that. I know I'm wicked, weak." She turned the icon to the wall. Then she snatched up the torn photo and burned the fragments in St Jude's candle flame. She watched Jeremy's smile crinkle, turn black, and fall as ashes into the china saucer. Then, she lit a match to the proxy toenail clippings and the lock of hair that she'd pulled out of the shower drain, and as they joined the ashes of his photo, she loosed an intention so dark and passionate that even across the city I cringed.

"There. I'm free of you," she said to the empty room.

Puma caterwauled. If we had not known each other so well, I would not have been able to dream the scene or capture what was in Nikki's heart. I mewed in my distress, and leapt up on Lorna's bed, where she lay sleeping. I kneaded the covers, but she was oblivious to the shadows coming over us. I jumped down and trotted the apartment nervously. The moonlight fell through one window. I mewed and licked myself to calm the electric fire that sparked along my fur. But nothing helped.

After laying her curse, Nikki fell face-down across her bed, sick at what she'd done.

16

Well, that was an exhausting night! I can't imagine getting so upset about a male. I mean if one were silly enough to scorn me (it's never happened, but as a case in point), I'd certainly not waste a minute wanting him back. No, I'd wander away without a backward glance, because someone who'd jilt me wouldn't be worth my notice; but that's not the way of the 2-leggeds: they grab at everything, including love, and try to hold on, until the weight of their cargo pulls them under, in peril of drowning. When all they need to do is walk away, let go.

That afternoon I managed to squeeze out through the hole in the window screen again and jump into the corridor outside our door, patter up the stairs where, *yes*! the door to the third floor balcony was open. I slithered through and stopped cold. Goliath was lying in the sun. Even on this neutral territory I felt the hair rise on the back of my neck. He bottle-brushed his tail, and we hissed at each other, then each recoiled to sink down at a mutual boundary, ears twitching, backs politely turned. I licked and licked myself in my nervousness, watching in case he decided to spring.

After a time I relaxed.

==I do think it was cruel of you, I said, extending one delicate white paw, to suggest I jump to my death. In the middle of a storm, too. When I was cold and wet.

==Huh?

Males are not as quick as females. You have to make allowances. Eventually his brain caught up with mine.

==I didn't! I never wanted you to die. His natural voice is rasping, with a gutter accent that I courteously ignore.

==You kept calling to me to jump. But you were standing directly in the way. You knew I would have fallen to my death, never to rise again.

==I was going to move. His astonishment was clear by the tilt of his whiskers. I was concerned for you. I knew you could make it. You're an athlete. You're an acrobat. You're graceful.

I preened. He was so contrite that he flattened his stomach to the balcony floor and crawled toward me. For a second we touched noses before he leapt politely back, careful of intruding on my space. I accepted his apology by grooming myself with indifferent concentration. He did the same.

After that we sat in companionable silence until we both had the same idea of padding downstairs to his apartment, where his door had been accidentally left ajar. His rooms aren't at all like ours on the floor above. His are full of black leather and shiny metal objects, of computers and electric cords snaking everywhere, a certain comfortable jumble and messiness. With the air conditioning on, it was almost cold. I stretched out on a luxurious, thick, white, alpaca rug. There, we began to talk. He told me he hates his name. David gave it to him as a joke.

==A joke? I asked. I don't get it.

==I don't either.

==What a disgrace, I sniffed. Imagine naming a cat for a joke! And not even a good enough one to get.

==I know. He hung his head.

It would have been rude to ask his True Name outright, and a discreet and delicate cat is never rude, though curious.

==But after all, you always have your True Name, I said demurely, examining my claws. I was pleased with my tactfulness. Not everyone can be as tactful as that. I mean, I continued, even if you were a Pound Cat.

==My mother gave it to me. I was a Pound Cat, but I knew my mother for the first six weeks. I'll tell you my name.

==What? I was so excited I shot to my feet. This is the most intimate information that a cat can give.

When he told me, I just blinked. I could imagine him lying on a sun-speckled jungle tree branch, utterly relaxed; and then, perhaps in the soft half-light dusk, as evening merges into night, he would spring down, dark as water, and hit the wet, pungent-smelling loam, sniffing the air to prowl in his silent, night-time, jungle hunt. I mean, he's tame and domesticated, but there's something wild about him, too.

==Wow.

==And yours? he asked, which shows he is not as refined as some cats. Like me, Alba.

==Oh, I was bred, I answered. I'm half-Siamese.

I know it sounds snobbish, especially when speaking to a Pound Cat, but what can one do? Social pretensions are sometimes real, but then, because he'd been so open with me, Pound Cat though he was, I told him.

==Beauty. I closed my eyes with pleasure, speaking my own name.

==Beauty, he repeated, and the way he said it made my fur lie flat.

17

It was surprising how quickly Nikki moved on David. Lorna would come home from work and find her car parked outside the apartment, but it was not Lorna but David she had come to see. After the first embarrassing encounter, Lorna no longer knocked on David's door to look for her. Sometimes Nikki would clatter up the stairs in her enthusiasm and barge in on us. She would fling herself on the sofa or else she'd wander round the living room, picking up objects and putting them down: the cut crystal vase, a Victorian bronze of a racing horse, a tiny ruby-red Japanese cup so fragile that you could see your own hand through the glass when you held it to the light.

"What do you think of David? Do you like him?"

If she only knew. After a long pause Lorna would answer, calling from the kitchen as she chopped vegetables for a stir-fry. "I like him well enough."

"You don't think much of him, do you? But I like him. A lot. I think I like him more than Jerry. He's thoughtful. Why don't you like him? He likes you. He thinks the world of you."

"Does he?"

"We should invite him up for dinner, don't you want to?"

"Sure," Lorna would respond. "Sometime. I'm tired tonight." She always had an excuse.

"He's not too old for me," Nikki plowed on, oblivious to the mood of her friend. "He's only forty-eight. That's ok, don't you think? He's never married. He was engaged once. He told me his fiancé died in a car crash, drunk driver, and he's never met the next right girl. He's not too old to have children, do you think? He likes children. I think he'd make a good father."

The fact was, Lorna saw plenty of David. Often he would invite her down for a drink and sometimes—occasionally—they'd cook a meal at her place. Twice they went to the theater together, events which she neglected to inform Nikki of, as she somehow forgot to mention their evening at the opera, for which they'd both dressed up, he in black tie and she in a shimmering evening gown. They'd come home at midnight, laughing and leaning on each other as they climbed the stairs.

Lorna felt no necessity to tell Nikki about these visits. They weren't "dates." She told herself that David asked her only because he had no one else to invite, but she couldn't deny they had such *fun*! They talked about their jobs, about the opening of the Smithsonian's new Hall of Physics or about politics or David's work or his travels in India and Nepal or Lorna's daughter. Mostly they talked about their lives, ambitions, even the search for God, however that word was understood.

Once, after one such meeting, I saw her close the apartment door and lean against it, eyes closed. Breathing. The next moment she lifted her chin with a shake of her head and strode forth again, out into the world—which was to the kitchen, in this case, to take the garbage out. Sometimes our most valiant acts are very small.

And that's the way things went for several weeks until something happened that changed everything. Nikki's godmother, Claire Boisson, telephoned to say she was coming from Paris to open the Georgetown house.

"In summer!" Lorna exclaimed, laughing, when she heard of it. "Is she mad? Doesn't she know the thermometer in Washington tops one hundred degrees with the humidity of a swamp?"

"She has air conditioning. I don't suppose she'll even go outside," Nikki explained, "except to oversee the installation of her latest sculpture in her garden. We're invited to lunch one day. You have to see her house!"

"I will." Lorna gave a quick laugh. "I'll accept any time. I'd like to see her collection."

18

For David's party Nikki went to one of the designer secondhand stores that dot the Washington streets, looking for something special to wear. She found a dressy little spaghetti-strap shift and a pair of gold sandals. She brought them over to Lorna's to dress for the party.

Lorna, on the other hand, wore a frilly low-cut white blouse with slacks and sandals. She looked fantastic with her dangling turquoise earrings and gold bracelets. One glance and Nikki began to worry.

"Oh god! I'm overdressed. Why didn't you tell me you were wearing pants?"

"Well, he said informal."

"I should go home and change."

"Don't be silly. You look fabulous. You look like Helen of Troy."

"Like a corpse, you mean?" Nikki laughed before turning serious again. "Lorna, promise me something." Her eyes bored into Lorna's.

"What?"

"Promise you'll never betray me."

"Of course I won't," said Lorna, smoothing on makeup. "Not knowingly. What's this about?"

But Nikki was dead serious. "I need to know. You're my best friend in all the world. I just need to know that there's one person in all the world I can count on."

"Well, of course."

"My father," said Nikki, giving in to maudlin self-pity. "Always off at his work. And all his women. My mother."

"Nikki, it wasn't her fault."

"I know, but she wasn't there for me either, drinking too much, running all over the world, so I never even knew what country she was in, while I was sent away to boarding school. God knows how many men she had. Now Jerry." Tears filled her eyes.

"Don't cry. Your mascara will run."

"Sometimes I feel as if I'm hanging out over the edge of a cliff," she said with a brave, bitter laugh. "On a rope. And the rope is fraying."

"You're not, you know," said Lorna, her voice flat. She handed her a tissue.

"I know. I've had enough therapy to know it's just Jerry kicking up my old abandonment issues, and I'm fine, really. I'm really fine." The two friends stared at one another.

"Are you?"

"Yes. Say it." Eyes narrowed, Nikki squinted at Lorna, drilling into her.

"Say what?"

"Say, 'I promise I'll never betray you.'"

"Oh darling. I promise, promise, *promise* I will never betray you. I will protect you and love you and be here for you all my life. I'll never let you down, not intentionally. Okay?"

Nikki looked up with her dazzling smile. "There. Now I feel better. Thank you."

"But I still don't understand. What's going on?"

The story came dribbling out just as I had seen it—the moonlit curse she'd chanted in her rage and jealousy.

Lorna was taken aback. "My god, you did it."

"I'm not sorry. I refuse to be sorry. I'm not a victim. I won't be a victim."

"You certainly aren't. You're the wild card. We know prayer works, the energy of love. I suppose the energy of hate works too." She wasn't completely happy. "What wicked witchery did you cast?"

"What didn't I? First I gave him boils and pustules and then impotence—your idea—that he lose his erection whenever he's with her and that his thoughts turn to me and he can't get me out of his mind. For good measure I cast the intention that he'll lose his job and lose Penelope and lose his self-esteem, and he'll try to crawl back to me, just so I'll have the pleasure of refusing him."

"Goodness," said Lorna, though it hardly seemed the apt word. "I gather you've never heard, 'Vengeance is mine, sayeth the Lord'?"

"Don't criticize me. I don't need any of your negative judgments."

"My judgments?"

"I know what you'll say. That I shouldn't have done it, but I don't think it's real, anyway. It made me feel better, and now I'm going to get over Jerry and get on with my life and find a new man, someone who will love me for myself. And forever and ever. I think it will be David," she finished; then: "Oh, did I tell you? Guess what? Claire says she may have some work for me, too. Which is good. I need a painting to restore. I've got to make some money. The problem with working for yourself is, you spend three-quarters of your time looking for work and maybe one-third doing it."

"Your math stinks." Lorna smiled, already forgiving her.

"The rest is for eating and sleeping and worrying and laying curses. Are you ready to go down to the party? Do I look all right?"

"Let's go. You look like—" Lorna paused, eyeing her.

"Goats running down a hillside? Cassandra, the mad prophetess? Come on."

19

Nikki had hardly stepped out of our apartment when she stopped short. From the floor below came the roar of the party, with guests slamming doors and the drumbeat of music partly drowning out the happy voices. She grabbed Lorna's arm.

"I can't do it."

"Do what?"

"Go in. I can't do it. Lorna, we don't know anyone. Oh god. It'll be awful. You go by yourself. I'm going home."

Lorna inspected her quizzically. "Now Nikki, I'm going to tell you what my father used to say when I was just a young girl beginning to date."

"What?"

"Well first, I never left the house without his coming to the door to look me over. 'You look beautiful,' he'd say."

"Oh, well." Meaning that Nikki's own father had never been around to do that for her and it seemed cruel, actually, for Lorna to rub it in like that.

"Wait. I haven't finished. Then he told me this simple trick. Every woman should know this. It's important. 'Now remember,' he'd say.'Before you enter the party, pause on the threshold, throw up your head and say to yourself: *I am the most beautiful woman here!* And only then go in."

"Oh."

"So that's what you're to do. Right now, before you take another step. Stand there. Let me look at you. Turn around. Nikki, you look beautiful! Now we're going downstairs, and at the door you lift your chin and before your foot crosses the threshold you say *I am the most beautiful woman here.*

"And then you enter. But that's not all. Remember his other wise words: that everyone else in the room is shy and scared. It's your responsibility as a guest to help make the party work. You are to go in and put someone else at ease. Find someone who looks lost and talk to him. Everyone else is scareder than you are."

Nikki tossed her head. "I am the most beautiful woman here," she said.

To me they both looked lovely, Nikki with her thick dark hair rolling down her back and Lorna's golden moonbeams and the easiness of her movements. They both wore sandals that set off their pretty painted toes, and if Nikki only knew how enticing men find a snippet of underwear, she wouldn't have struggled to tug on her strapless bra. Nor worried about her soft, plump body and wide, childbearing hips.

I skittered down the steps ahead of them and slithered through David's open door. Then I slipped out to the garden, looking for Goliath. The din was deafening. Everyone shouting.

"The man's a common crook for god's sake!"

"It's a question for the Supreme Court."

They were all ages, from young men and children to middle-aged couples to one cane-carrying, white-haired, bent-backed man. In the garden David was turning burgers and chicken on the grill. Goliath ran to greet me.

==Wait till you see the food, he said in appreciation.

We went off to explore the party, and I must say it was interesting. At one end of the living room David had set up the crowded bar. On the table opposite stood platters of dips, vegetables, charred chicken and hamburgers and platters of desserts. We sniffed the scraps that fell to the floor. Above our heads two young girls were deep in philosophical discourse:

"Like I said, like *'No-oh.'*"

"Like, *ye-ah.*"

"Like, what was he *thinking* of?"

I find humans endlessly fascinating. Here's another snippet, though baffling: in David's office a woman sat by herself, absorbed and solitary in a black leather chair, patiently covering her arms and shoulders and wrists with white linen napkins. What in the world was she doing? I didn't want to know.

Charlie, meanwhile, had rushed to meet Nikki and Lorna.

"I'm so glad you've come. I don't know a soul."

Charlie was not the only man whose head had swiveled when the two women paused at the door. Nikki was swept away in a little pod of men, while Charlie for the rest of the evening pinned himself to Lorna, carrying plates for her, bringing her wine, bubbling with amusing animation. She was stuck. For a good half-hour she and Charlie joined the group around David, but much of the time he was busy playing host. I saw Lorna glance longingly at Nikki out in the garden, but with Charlie dancing attendance, she didn't stand a chance of talking to anyone else, while the party devolved into a wreckage of plates, cups, forks, glasses, of beer and wine bottles tipped on their sides and corks and crumpled napkins scattered on the ground. They talked to a woman psychiatrist. They talked to various lawyers. They talked to a man who worked for the environment. The hours passed. Lorna never did manage to speak to David again, and Nikki was having such fun that she never circled back to help Lorna out with Charlie.

Slowly the crowd dispersed. Only two or three couples remained. The fireflies came out, flaring in the darkness like fairy lights, and Goliath and I hunted the tiny rustlings in the dry bushes or chased a moth or tasted the scraps of hamburger flung underfoot. The July air was balmy, soft. Soon even the last guests were saying their good-byes, and only the music remained, a singer crooning softly in the background to a slow jazz beat.

In the kitchen, David and Nikki stood side by side, washing platters and laughing in undertones, while Lorna, in the living room, listened to a besotted Charlie rattle on about the war and why he approved—indeed he'd join up himself if he weren't too old.

"I think war is a last resort," said Lorna, turning away. "I think it shows you've failed."

Charlie laughed and poured himself another drink. "War is inevitable," he consoled her. "People are genetically designed to kill. We've been doing it since the first cave man picked up the first rock to bop a stranger."

"Cain and Abel."

"Cain and Abel, exactly!" echoed Charlie, delighted that she got his point.

"It doesn't make it right."

"You're probably opposed to hunting, too," he said, with an indulgent smile.

"No, not if you need to eat the meat. I'm only opposed to unnecessary killing. I'm opposed to hurting people."

"And what about citizens carrying guns?" he challenged. "To protect themselves from criminals. It's our Constitutional right, written in the Second Amendment."

"I'm certainly opposed to their carrying assault weapons, and buying thousands of rounds of ammunition on the internet to use on other people, if that's what you mean," said Lorna stiffly. "Because they certainly aren't going to use them hunting quail. It's another form of terrorism. I don't know why the NRA allows it."

He laughed again, and pushed his glasses up his nose preparing for a harangue on the time-honored right to bear arms. Or arm bears. I felt sorry for Lorna, but it was her own fault. They stood on opposite sides of the spectrum politically, and she knew better than to joust with him; yet there she bravely stood, waving her banner while he waved his back at her.

==Why do you stay? I hissed. Just walk away.

A cat will never do anything she doesn't want to, but generous, kind, decent Lorna couldn't bring herself to hurt his feelings, even if his were blind to hers. She didn't see that the more he drank, the prettier she got.

"You're so cute." He touched the tip of her nose with his finger. She cringed. "Cute."

"And sexy, too. I like your blouse. That plunging neckline. I can't keep my eyes off. Which I guess is your intent. Do you know which is the most peaceful country in the world? Guess."

"England?" she hazarded. "Where the Bobbys don't carry guns?"

"Switzerland!" he trumpeted in triumph. "And you know why? "

"The mountainous geography?"

"No!"

"Because it's the financial center of the world?" she tried again. "And they'd cut off the invaders' line of credit if they attacked?" Lorna is nothing if not quick.

"I'll tell you why. Because every male eighteen to forty-nine is obliged to join the army. They all learn how to handle weapons!"

"Even the mentally ill?"

"I don't know about the mentally ill," Charlie conceded in surprise. "When they get out of the army, every man is required to keep his guns and ammo in his house, in case of attack. That's why! The invaders know that every male would come at them with a gun!"

"That is such a *non sequitur!*" cried Lorna and she stamped her foot in impatience. "I think my reasons are stronger. But if you want all Americans to join the army at age eighteen, I'm all for it. We need the draft. I think a mercenary, volunteer army encourages war. Every child, male and female, should be required, like in Switzerland, to join the armed forces—as a private, too—and that includes the children of the President and every Congressman and Senator and all the military, and maybe then they wouldn't be in such a rush to start to war. If their own children might be killed." Tears of passion filled her eyes.

During this speech Charlie had braced his hands on the wall on either side of her head, effectively trapping her. He was worked up now. I could have told him: *It's the girl who chooses! The male presents, the female selects.* But why bother? He couldn't have heard a 2-legged in his soggy condition, much less a cat. *The male offers; the female accepts,* I wanted to shout at him. *Or NOT!*

"You're adorable." Charlie was besotted with Lorna, first on the grounds of her having listened to his doleful tale of lost love; and now because he had the chance to talk of manly things that women didn't understand too well, like wars and guns and bravery, and hunting, all subjects close to his heart. Charlie shot birds in South Carolina and elk and wild pigs in Texas, where Lorna would hardly have shot them with a camera.

"I understand your position. But you're wrong. Every single citizen should carry a gun and know how to use it, men and women. We'd all feel safer. If anyone tried to invade the United States, they'd have me to contend with," he said, smiling down at her.

"I don't notice so many countries invading us," Lorna tried again.

The next moment I suddenly knew what he would do. I galloped over. I meowed. I scraped myself against her leg. But she paid no mind to me.

Caught at the wall between Charlie's arms, she craned to see around him into the kitchen. "Don't you think we should go help—?"

He kissed her. He grabbed her by the waist and kissed her long and fervently.

David, entering from the kitchen, stopped short. "Oh."

20

Lorna was so startled that she stood, paralyzed, her hands frozen at her side, her position made worse by David's exclamation, which she heard—the way he turned aside. I don't know what she would have done if she'd had her wits about her, but just then the outer door banged open to present a thunder of boots and a clap of laughter as a crowd barged into the room, shouting "Party! Party!" They sent me flying under the table.

There must have been six or seven in all, but the one you noticed was the extraordinarily tall, long-legged woman at the head of the pack, laughing, her head thrown back in delight at the chaos of their unexpected raid. Behind her came Nikki's Jeremy. She stood a moment to survey the room with majestic poise, basking in the startled silence as all eyes turned on her. She emanated heat and sex, excitement, thrills, desire, lust, and she was keenly aware of the impression she made and of her own shivering desirability.

"Oh dear." Both hands went prettily to cover her mouth. "I'm interrupting, aren't I? Charlie? Is that you? Were you kissing her?" She extended one hand, laughing. "I've caught you *kissing* her?"

"Hullo, Penelope." David wiped his hands on a dishtowel as he moved to greet them. "Gate crashing?"

Nikki clung to a chairback as if she were about to swoon. She hadn't expected Jeremy to appear with his latest love.

"We heard there was a party," said Penelope, surveying the pitiful remains of food, not to mention the raking appraisal she gave Lorna, who stood in shock, and of Charlie, who had leapt away from Lorna, then stopped in confusion. But Penelope had one other quality

I should mention, and I (creeping under the table) could see why Jeremy had fallen for her so hard: When she turned her attention on you, you felt she saw right to your core, and that you were the most fascinating person she'd ever met, that she wanted to take you to bed right then and do unspeakable things to you all night. This was the look she cast at Charlie.

"Oh, Charlie." Her sidewise look combined flirtatious amusement and reproof. "Come now, don't be ridiculous. Come over here and give me a proper kiss." He did as commanded, moving as if underwater, his face red. She put one arm around his neck and kissed him deeply on the lips. Almost as tall as he, she moved her hips suggestively against him before breaking away.

Afterwards, she smiled at Lorna over his shoulder. "And won't you introduce me to your friend? I'm Penelope Smith-Henderson," she announced, thrusting out her hand. What could polite Lorna do but mumble her name awkwardly and accept the extended hand that was immediately dropped as Penelope turned her fascination onto David.

"We were just hanging out, being terminally bored, when we remembered you were giving a party, David, but it looks like we're too late. It's not too late, is it? We've brought champagne and pâté and all sorts of goodies, and I knew you wouldn't mind. I've never seen your place before. I was curious." She wound one exquisite arm around his neck in another suggestive hug, then drifted away. Women like her are sensitive to how they are being received. "Oh, what a night it's been," she said, flinging herself onto the couch. "Poor me, poor me, pour me a drink, won't you darling?" This last was addressed to Jeremy with a dazzling smile. He stopped staring at Nikki long enough to swivel his attention back to her.

"Introductions! How rude of me. David, this is Melissa, Emma, Marcus, Tristan—isn't that a delicious name? I love it, it's so medieval—and Jeremy Ball. And this is David Scott, everyone. And

Charlie Pace. Charlie, come sit by me." She patted the sofa cushion beside her. "And you are. . . ?" This to Nikki.

"Nicole Petrelli," she whispered.

Lorna shook herself. "Jerry, I hear you have a Pulitzer-Prize-winning story in the works."

"He does," said Penelope, possessing his hand and shining up into his face. "We do."

"Oh, I didn't realize you were working on it, too," Lorna said sweetly. "I heard it was all Jerry's, except for some minor clerical work."

Penelope pursed her lips and smiled. "Tell them, darling."

"It's true," he said in a strangled voice—the first words he'd spoken so far. "Penelope is my. . . partner." He flushed crimson as he spoke. But the goddess beamed at him and then around the room, while Charlie rose from the couch beside her and took one stumbling drunken step of shock. Meanwhile the groupies, talking noisily, had scrounged up clean plates in these few minutes and set out cheese, pâtés, chocolates, as if the party weren't actually over. Someone popped the cork of a bottle of champagne and started pouring into stray mugs and tumblers, handing them round, while Penelope reclined on the couch, the Odalisque.

Charlie couldn't take his eyes off her.

Neither could Nikki.

"The thing is," said David, still wiping his hands ferociously on the towel, which might have represented more than cloth. "We're just breaking up."

"Oh dear, and I didn't even know you were an item. Nicole, is it?" She laughed at her own joke. "Men are so fickle, aren't they?" I don't think she had any idea who Nikki was. She just liked to create chaos. Fun.

Nikki clung to David's arm, and I think she would have fled to the garden if she thought she could have gotten away.

==Goliath, do something, I whispered. But he only looked at me blankly. He has no imagination.

==What?

== Go jump in her lap. I nudged him.

==Why? I don't like her.

== She's allergic, I hissed.

"Yes, well actually," Lorna intervened, "it really is late. Charlie was just about to take me home." She stepped forward and slipped her arm in his, never taking her eyes off Penelope.

He glanced at her in puzzlement, but before he could speak, Goliath took this moment to leap into Penelope's lap with a thud. She screamed and tried to throw him off. He dug in his claws and peeled his tail across her nose.

"Eeuwww!" She bounded to her feet throwing him to the floor. "Get him away. I'm allergic to cats." Under the table, I curled my tail daintily around my paws and smiled. It's a marvel the way a cat knows which 2-leggeds out of a whole crowd is allergic to us. Penelope was shaking her fingers and screaming.

"My god, he's huge." I sauntered out of the corner then, and pressed against her leg, while she jumped and shrieked some more. Then she sneezed.

"I'll shut him in the other room," said David, grabbing at his cat; but I could see he could barely control a smile. "Come on, Goliath." I noticed that he took his lazy time in strolling out of the room.

Her groupies gathered round Penelope, everyone competing to ask if she was all right, which made her feel a lot better. She put one hand on Jeremy's sleeve and looked up at him appealingly. I realized this was her other attraction: that she could appear so vulnerable, so fragile, that she required a good man's protection. "I'm so sorry. I

suppose we really ought to go. I didn't expect a cat. I'm so allergic."
All this while Nikki stared at the floor, the walls, the ceiling, or back
into the kitchen through the escape-hatch doorway—anywhere
except at Jeremy.

"The party's over."

"We shouldn't have come."

"I think you should take me home," Penelope murmured to Jeremy,
and sneezed. She blew her nose, which is not the sexiest of acts.

Meanwhile, Lorna had grabbed Charlie.

"Listen to me, Charlie," she whispered fiercely. "You are to walk
past her right now. You will not look at her. Look at me. Look in my
eyes. That's right, keep looking in my eyes. Come on. We're going up
to my apartment."

She kept a tight hold on Charlie's arm, because she was afraid he'd
run over to Penelope like a lap dog and start to drool. As she passed
Penelope, she said something about her being a National Treasure.

"Really? Why, what a lovely thing to say. Thank you." Penelope
preened under the compliment, but Lorna later told Nikki she meant
the woman should be locked up in Fort Knox, underground, and
never let out.

At the door, Lorna threw one anguished backward glance at
David who stood beside Nikki. She scooped me up, and the next
moment we were all three climbing the stairs to our place. But why
was Charlie with us? He didn't even like cats.

Later, I heard Lorna describing the scene on the phone to one of
her girlfriends. "It would have been a parody," she exclaimed, "except
it was so real, and it left three people suffering, and who knows,
maybe more."

21

W hen the door closed behind us, Lorna pointed to the sofa. "You can sit here until Penelope leaves, and then you can go."

"Go?" Charlie was as dim as Goliath.

"Well, you're certainly not going to stay the night." She faced him, arms crossed, and her high color and the tilt of her chin showed her pride clearly, for she was hurt and angry with Charlie and also, it must be admitted, with Nikki and David, and most especially with herself.

He flushed, since staying the night was exactly what he'd imagined, given the earlier kiss and Lorna pulling him up to her apartment and the effects of considerable alcohol on a hot night. I could see him pretending the idea had never entered his head.

"Look, Charlie." She leaned forward and touched his hand, which is what tender-hearted people like Lorna do when breaking bad news. Already she'd forgiven him. "There's nothing between us. I mean, we can be friends, perhaps, but that's all. Anyway, you've told me time and again that you're in love with Penelope. I'll help you get her, if you want, but you have to start using your head." She tapped her forehead with one finger. "She probably came to the party expressly to see you."

"You think so?" He perked up.

"Well, it wasn't to meet me," she said a little crossly. "Unless she just likes to crash parties."

"Actually, she—"

"And while we're at it," she continued, "I don't like to be kissed without permission. Okay? That's not allowed." She turned away, hiding her face in both hands. It was embarrassing to say these things out loud. She wanted to run and hide: a grown woman, and she felt like a teenager.

"Oh. I thought—"

"Well, don't. It's offensive. Nonetheless, I've just saved your neck. You were going to run along after her, weren't you? All she has to do is crook her little finger, and you come galloping over. Am I right?"

He looked sheepish.

"Now listen. If you want Penelope, you have to play her. Like a fish."

"I don't fish," he said humbly.

Lorna rolled her eyes. "Well, start. Look. She's a huntress. She's a shark. Actually, she's a bitch, and I don't know why you want her or for that matter why I'm helping you get her. Maybe," she added, eyeing him up and down, "because I don't like her. At any rate, I've just shown her that at least one woman is interested in you, and there's nothing that makes a woman sit up and take notice of a man more than seeing that another woman desires him. You should thank me." She considered what she'd just said, her head cocked to one side. "And not just women," she added. "It's true of men, too. Gays, lesbians. Everyone. It's human nature."

She opened the apartment door, one finger to her lips. From below we could hear the voices in the hallway, everyone talking at once, over and around one another, and the stumbling and laughter, then the metallic hiss and thud of the heavy front door. She moved to the window and, hiding to one side, pulled the curtain aside to peer out. Charlie shot to his feet to join her and take another longing look at his golden girl.

"Good, they've left. In a few minutes, you can go. I strongly advise you to fly back to New York tonight, tomorrow morning at the latest. Whatever you do, *do not phone her.*"

"But isn't that—er?" He stopped, beaten by her look.

"Rude? Absolutely not. If you put yourself in my hands, you'll have Penelope in yours. Ignore what I say and Abandon All Hope." She could be a martinet, my sweet Lorna. "Agreed?" She stared him down. "Agreed?" she repeated.

"Agreed," he said miserably. As if he'd lost a war.

"Right now, what you do is let her stew. Leave her alone. Give her time to think about it. Okay," she finished. "You can go now. . . .Oh, Charlie." She had the grace to blush as she reached out one hand to stop him. "Would you knock on David's door and tell him you are going back to your hotel? To thank him, I mean, for the party."

"I know how to handle myself," he said huffily. "I'm not a child."

"Good-night." She kissed his cheek. But leaning over the railing a few moments later, she saw with a sinking heart that without honoring her request he headed straight for the heavy metal outside door.

Later, she crept down the stairs herself and stood for a moment outside David's apartment, but she didn't have the courage to knock. Upstairs, she undressed, folding her lovely and revealing blouse in its drawer. She put on her old, comfortable, cotton penguin pajamas that had been washed so many times you could hardly make out the penguins anymore, and in the bathroom gave a heartrending, anguished gasp. A sigh. She picked up her toothbrush. I trotted back and forth from the bathroom to the living room, urging her to look, but she didn't even notice the red light of the answering machine blinking in the night. In the end I curled up on the pillow beside her, my head on her arm, and we slept.

The next morning Lorna woke up. . . depleted. She lay in bed, stroking me gently, too despondent to push to her feet, until the doorbell startled us both and forced her to the door.

Nikki stood there, still in her party dress.

"Oh, Lorna, look at you. You're not even up yet," she said, pushing inside. "I hope I didn't wake you up. What did you think of the party? Wasn't it terrific? I had such a good time, even seeing Jerry with Penelope. Which was so-o-o painful! You were right—"

Lorna blinked. "Why are you still dressed up?"

She looked down at herself, then laughing up at her friend: "I spent the night with David. He was wonderful. Will you give me a cup of coffee?" She moved to the kitchen, oblivious of Lorna's expression.

"After Jerry left, I just collapsed, and David took me in his arms and held me and held me while I wept on his shoulder, and then he picked me up and took me to bed. It was wonderful," she repeated. "It was just what I needed."

Lorna put out one hand to steady herself against the kitchen counter. It was then that she noticed the blinking light beside the telephone in the living room.

"I need to get the answering machine," she murmured, as much to change the subject as because of messages. She was reeling. "I didn't see it last night."

"You're the only person I know with an answering machine. Why don't you use voicemail?" Nikki was in high spirits.

"Yes, and I wash the dishes before putting them in the machine," said Lorna acidly, her words covering her confusion, hurt, and dismay.

By then she'd punched the red light button, and what happened next so hurt and upset me that I don't even want to tell about it. In a nutshell, Lorna's mother had been in a car crash. The news spread through the room like wildfire—the car crash, the ER, Lorna's sister, Isabelle, shouting into the phone or pleading with frightened plaintive whines. Isabelle had called once, then twice, then still a third angry and desperate time, demanding that Lorna grab a plane to Santa Fe, because she, Isabelle, couldn't leave Chicago or her family and kids, and Lorna didn't have responsibilities like hers; and in seconds everything in our apartment changed to flurry and hurry, bustle and hustle, to phone calls, schedules for flights to Albuquerque, pencils hovering over Post-its, iPads and computers, and Nikki in her party dress and pretty high-heeled sandals clicking up and down the stairs in her helpless efforts to help.

I think Lorna was glad to leave. I think she was glad for the distraction. I skittered round the apartment watching her throw clothes in a suitcase. She had no place in her thoughts even to pick me up and kiss and hug me, much less worry about Nikki's happiness, which Nikki was concerned about as she followed her friend, still talking about the party and David and how much she despised Jeremy.

"You'll take care of Alba, won't you?" asked Lorna, handing me into Nikki's arms. "She knows your place. She'll love being with you and Puma. I don't know when I'll be back. Thank god for computers. I can work from Santa Fe. God help us, my mother." For a moment she stood in the living room, hands folded in prayer, and burst into tears. A moment later she dashed the back of her hand across her eyes. "No, I'm all right."

David carried Lorna's suitcases stolidly to the car, and the way he looked at her with deep concern so touched her that she burst into tears a second time as she climbed into the passenger seat beside Nikki.

"My plane leaves in two and a half hours. We have to hurry."

"You'll make it."

"I don't know. Security. . . ."

David walked beside the open window. Did she have her computer? What about a book? Did she have a sweater for the plane—it can be cold—here, take his. He thrust his sweater through the window where it fell into her lap. She fingered it, unseeing.

"Good-bye."

She didn't know whether to keep it or throw it back in his face. Or toss it in Nikki's lap—it rightfully belonged to her.

"Good luck," he called again. "Call me."

22

Each day at Nikki's the sun poured through the windows, waking me up to another glorious morning, my heart (and paws) leaping up to sing at the wind and birds and small scurrying insects in the high summer grass. Oh, I love mornings! I love my first stretch. I am a happy cat by nature, and yet I missed Lorna. I missed the water of her laughter. In a way the sun had gone behind the clouds. Moreover, Puma wasn't feeling well. Nikki didn't notice, but I felt the need—the desire—to stay close by, to comfort him and purr him back to health, and this meant slowing myself down. He was old, old in cat years, and his bones stuck out, and he could hardly walk. I hadn't noticed it before, but being with him this time all by myself and without Lorna—it wasn't fun.

I'd only been at Nikki's a few days when she invited David over to dinner, and it didn't take long for her to bring up Penelope; but David had nothing to tell her on that score. Then David brought up Lorna, and Nikki was thrilled to point out how much her friend liked Charlie Pace.

"And why not? He's rich. Sophisticated. I've never known her to invite anyone to her bed before."

That conversation also died, as David became suddenly intent on cutting his lamb chop, and after that they talked about the art world and Nikki's conservation business and David's case at the Justice Department and the war and the price of living and where to buy the best lamb chops—neutral things. When he was leaving, David asked for Lorna's number, but Nikki forgot to give it to him, and anyway it didn't matter because she phoned Lorna almost every night, so she could pass on anything he wanted to say.

David had hardly left when Nikki picked up the phone to Lorna, for with the two hour time difference from Virginia to Santa Fe, she knew she wouldn't wake her up. "I'm fine," she reported, which was odd given the nights she spent weeping into her pillow. "David came over to dinner tonight. He asked about you."

"Did he?"

"He's working like a demon. They're flying in witnesses from all over the world. You know it's a huge case. Bid rigging and collusion, where some construction company ripped off USAID on a one *billion* dollar contract to build sewers in Egypt, can you believe it?"

"He told me." Lorna's voice was cool. I stretched on the pillow at Nikki's ear, listening to Lorna's voice. I nudged the telephone. It didn't smell of her at all.

"So you're seeing a lot of him?" she asked after a pause.

"Well, I won't say a lot," Nikki laughed. "But some, yes. We're going to the movies next week. Are you all right? Lorna, are you crying?"

"No, I'm not crying. Oh, well, okay. A little. It's my mother," she lied. Then nastily: "You've certainly forgotten Jerry quickly."

Nikki was stung. "Isn't that what you told me to do?" she said, but her gates had slammed shut. "To look for someone else? So, I am. Anyway, David is really nice."

For some reason they got off the phone quickly that night. After that, by mutual consent, both David and Jeremy were off limits during these evening phone calls, though Nikki still felt responsible for finding topics to cheer up Lorna, and fortunately her godmother, Claire, sweeping into town on a wave of perfume and money and self-centered egotism, took up residence in her Georgetown mansion with its huge art collection, and a whole new world opened for Nikki to talk about.

23

Nikki says that everywhere you look in Claire's house, you see a work of art, from de Kooning to Chinese pottery. She has a Chagall mosaic in her garden, and every wall is covered with paintings. But Claire doesn't have a cat, and if you ask me, a home without a cat is like a garden without flowers.

When Claire came to see us, she was dressed in stockings and alligator shoes and a pale summer suit that Nikki fingered in admiration, because it was what's called Chanel. She wore a silk scarf at her neck, even though full summer had settled in with blast-furnace heat. She waved her fingers at her cheek as if to bring up a breeze and threw herself into the coolness of the air conditioning.

"Ah *Voilá! C'est toi, la célebre Alba.*" She leaned down to stroke my back. "*Tu vas bien?*" which is French for, *Oh, you're the famous Alba, how are you?* And then she asked after her old friend Puma, and when she saw him she was shocked at how old he'd gotten, and then she patted her own white hair and looked as if she'd swallowed a prune.

Later she kicked off her alligator shoes, which must have been hurting her, and walked through the house in stocking feet, telling Nikki how with a little thought she could do better on the décor. "It needs curtains. I see white voile. Yards and yards of it. It should have a subtle pattern, white on white, and you must hang them in swags. If you can't find the material, come to Paris. I know a place where we can find something, perhaps antique."

Nikki smiled at the idea, knowing she couldn't afford anything like that, but delighted by Claire's attention. Claire is accustomed to ordering other people's lives.

Then they went into Nikki's conservation studio carrying their iced teas and chocolate cookies and talked about restoring paintings, while Nikki showed off her photo album of the work she'd done for the Department of the Treasury and for the Kreeger Museum and the Virginia Museum of Fine Arts and various other institutions and private collectors.

"Most of my customers are just ordinary people," she said. "They have a painting of an ancestor that needs cleaning or of cows where the canvas has ripped. I do a lot of cows. Sometimes, though, I get really good paintings."

I sat on the shelf above Nikki's hot table and listened. I was proud of her. It was then that Claire asked Nikki to return home with her to look at one of her paintings. She said she'd give her dinner. So Nikki accepted and said she'd drive Claire home, which meant Claire's driver could be dismissed and take off his hot uniform and have a cool drink at his home.

Soon they switched to gin and tonics and sat out in the shade on the deck, since the heat was cooling off. There, Claire grew sentimental.

"I've been a terrible godmother," she proclaimed.

"What do you mean?"

"You must come back to Paris with me. Your mother and I were such good friends, but then life has a way of whirling one apart, don't you find? I never gave you any religious training. Well, how could I? I had none myself, but that's what a proper godmother's supposed to do."

"You gave me wonderful Christmas presents though."

"Did I? Yes. When you were small. But I was so self-absorbed. I mean, I've had such an interesting life, always traveling and marrying and divorcing. Goodness, it takes up time! But I adored your mother. She was so much fun. Wild as a wolf. You never knew what she was going to think up next. And generous. I remember... but never mind. Such a dreadful accident. I would have come to the funeral, you know, nothing would have kept me away, except I was in the hospital at the time, bound to a bed. Now tell me about the nice young man you're engaged to."

Oh.

"We broke up," Nikki confessed with a toss of her head, and then she gave a censored version of his betrayal.

"Oh, men are so irritating," Claire scoffed in sympathy. "How childish of him. But men *are* childish, aren't they? I've been married four times (though twice to the same man, so I've only had three husbands, actually), and affairs, lovers, lots of lovers, and I can tell you, Nikki, they're all impossible. Even the ones you love. Especially the ones you love." She peered at Nikki sharply. "Just remember the old adage: 'If you let him go and he comes back, he's yours forever.' "

She took a sip of her drink. "It isn't true," she added.

24

Well, all of this was reported to Lorna in their nightly phone calls, together with news of Claire's big welcome-home party and a description of the designer dress she'd given Nikki to wear to that smash event; but best of all *(Calloo! Callay!)* she'd given Nikki a painting to restore! Which Nikki desperately needed, being short of cash just then. And then the story of Claire's mystery lover came out.

What happened was this. After their drinks on the back deck, Nikki drove Claire back home to Georgetown, and by the time she returned, kicking the door open with one foot, her arms full of packages, full night had fallen, with the pale stars struggling to be seen past the swollen icy moon. This is a favorite time for any cat, but Puma and I were both distraught to find that the first thing Nikki did was go into the kitchen and pour herself a drink. Then she dialed Lorna.

"You should see her house. It's a museum!" Nikki bubbled over with excitement. "She has a Hans Hoffmann and a Matisse and Paul Klee and Picasso and de Kooning and a Childe Hassam seascape that takes your breath away—oh, they all do—and some of the artists gave her paintings out of friendship, and some she and her collector husband bought, but everywhere you look you see 18th century tables and silk rugs that are walked on even with shoes, French Louis XV chairs, of course they're real. She has a Calder mobile in the dining room. A *Calder*!"

I wondered what these names meant and why they were so desirable. Sitting on the back of the sofa listening to Nikki bubbling over the phone to Lorna, I thought how odd it was that one moment Nikki would be weeping, inconsolable (only the night before, wetting our pillow with her tears), and the next, like now, flying high as a lark in the sky. I preferred Lorna's steadiness, but Puma reminded me (later, when we talked about it) that Nikki's emotional storms, these sudden ascents to typhoon heights and plunges into valleys of despair were new, though she'd always been volatile, passionate, what Lorna called "Mediterranean." It was only much later that we made the connection between her mood swings and those tumblers of golden liquid she'd begun to chug. After her visit to Claire that night, I'd say she was walking three inches off the ground.

"Claire took me upstairs to her bedroom," Nikki reported to Lorna, the phone propped on her shoulder while she buffed her nails. Her drink sat on the table next to her and periodically she took a gulp. "I'd never been there before, and oh, Lorna, she's made her bedroom into this big, gracious room by knocking down a wall between two rooms. Hardly anything is in it but a chest of drawers and a four-poster bed with its carved vines and flowers crawling up the posts to the pineapples on top. Pineapples for prosperity, you know. One gorgeous Oushak rug. Claire sat on the foot of the bed and pointed to a little painting on the wall opposite. It was so small I had to walk over to look at it, and you won't believe this."

"What?"

I huddled against Nikki's shoulder, where I could hear Lorna's voice. She didn't sound quite as enthusiastic as Nikki. I mewed into the phone.

"Is that Alba?" she called. "Mew, mew!"

But Nikki was on a rant. "Lorna, it's a horse painting. It's exquisite. Of a bay mare with her long neck draped over her foal, and in the background the darker stallion standing splendid under the trees. I was stunned. All I could think, Lorna, is *Charles Stubbs, 1747-1806*, the finest horse painter the world has ever seen, and there I was looking at it in my godmother's bedroom. That, or an amazing copy. I asked her, 'Is it a Stubbs?' I mean, she has a lot of art, it very likely could be, don't you think?"

"Was it?"

"She didn't answer. Maybe she doesn't know. 'It was given me by a friend,' she said, 'a very close friend,' and then, oh Lorna, to my surprise her eyes grew moist.

" 'You see a picture of three horses, don't you?' she said, her voice catching a little. 'But I see. . .' and she stopped.

" 'What do you see?' I sat down on the bed beside her, and then, Lorna, this beautiful love story comes pouring out.

" 'He was my lover for eight years. In France. You'd know his name if I said it, a former Minister of— No, never mind, I won't say. He was married, of course, and I knew he'd never leave his wife, but we loved each other. Oh, we did. Then I got greedy. I wanted him for holidays, too—never to have him at Christmas or for the August holidays. You know the French take off the entire month of August, everyone, all four weeks, and none of it ever spent with me. . . . Knowing he was with his wife and children. I had a baby by him. We had a baby, but she was stillborn. Maybe it was all for the best, but that's what I see when I look at my painting. I see a family portrait, the mare with her long neck, cradling her foal, and the stallion in the background keeping guard. Our family. The one we never had. He's dead now.'

"Oh, Lorna, I was so moved."

"You sound just like her."

Nikki laughed. " Claire went on. 'I'm very spiritual. The other night I felt him so clearly he could have been in the room with me. Holding me." I thought she was going to cry, but a moment later she gave this lovely smile. 'I know it sounds silly,' (she said), 'but I think he came to say good-bye, that he won't ever come again, and then I started thinking about the picture. I haven't taken care of it. You see the crackling?'

"I said I could fix that, and she said, 'Exactly. That's what I want you to do, and put it back in condition. For him. And for me, of course.' Then we just sat there together looking at this staggeringly beautiful painting.

" 'It was all so long ago. I never had children. I urge you to have children, Nikki, while you can, if for no other reason than it makes your estate planning so much simpler. Without children, I can't tell you how many hours I've spent trying to figure out where to leave my money.'

"I told her she could always leave it to me, teasing, and she laughed and said she'd left me a small inheritance in her will but not to get my hopes up—and of course now I can't stop wondering how much!" Lorna joined in her laughter and remarked how now Claire had better watch her back.

It's interesting what goes on in the mind of the 2-leggeds, because all the while she was relaying this conversation, Nikki was remembering how Jeremy had said the same thing to her—that she could leave all her money to him, and how he'd spend his life making her posthumously famous; and suddenly she missed him so much that the conversation about Claire didn't feel compelling anymore, as she fell into another of her torpors. When the pause drew out so long that Lorna asked, "Are you there?" she gave a start and set in again, talking with animation that was only partially pretend.

"She's leaving everything to art schools for scholarships and to her favorite museums. Wouldn't it be fantastic to be really, really rich?"

"Well, I don't know. Is she happy?"

"Happy? Is anyone happy?" asked Nikki.

"Yes, of course," said Lorna with finality. "You choose to be happy. Or not. Happiness takes a form of courage."

"Well, I suppose," said Nikki without conviction. "Anyway, I have the painting to restore. It's in the studio. And she gave me the most beautiful dress."

"What kind of dress?" Was Lorna interested or merely being polite? I couldn't tell.

"Oh, I can't wait to show you. It's so beautiful. She opened this huge closet, and it was just jammed with clothes. 'I have a dress for you,' she said. 'At my age, your body thickens, nothing to do, mind you, with how much exercise I get.'"

"You're such a good mimic," Lorna murmured.

"Did you know she was a night club dancer once? There's nothing she doesn't seem to have done. She told me, 'I used to have a size twenty-three waist,' she said. 'But eventually, with the pull of gravity, you turn into a tree trunk.'" Then she pulled out the dress. Lorna, it's a Luisa Newland! One of a kind! There is no other like it in the world. I'm going to wear it to her party on Sunday. It's gold with shimmering tiny pleats. It looks fabulous on me."

So, then Nikki announced that she had invited David to the party, to see her new dress, and he said he'd go, and then Lorna had to get off the phone because she didn't have time to talk anymore, even though Nikki yelped that she hadn't even heard any Lorna news, what with jabbering about Claire; but Lorna said there was nothing to tell, all she did was pray. Her mother was better, thank you. Her sister had come out for two days to be with her, and that was nice. They were trying to plan her mother's rehab and how and where she would live in future, because at ninety-one she couldn't stay alone anymore in Santa Fe. It was a problem. Her voice sounded stiff as she expressed the hope that Nikki would have a good time at the party.

I sprang down and went off for a cat nap, which is what you do after an exhausting day with the 2-leggeds, not to mention hunting birds and wasps or rolling in the dust to keep the sun from burning your tender skin. I found Puma and curled up near him. He lifted his head in slow greeting before nodding back to sleep.

The fact is I missed Goliath. He's not the brightest bulb on the block, a great, big, goodhearted lunk, and naïve for the simple reason that he doesn't have the wit to be shrewd.

It makes you want to poke him.

That's what I missed.

Poking him.

I missed Lorna, too, and our cozy apartment. So a nap was hardly out of line, because there's nothing that doesn't look brighter after a little sleep.

25

Nikki wor e her new dress for the party. The golden cloth fell in hundreds of tiny shimmering pleats and glowed against her skin. Her lipstick was shattering red. When David picked her up, he stared so hard that he forgot to greet me until I snagged a thread in his pants with my claw and tore a tiny hole. When they closed the door behind them, Puma and I went outside to listen to the rustlings of things in the night.

It was late when I heard the front door open and crash shut. The clatter of shoes dropping on the floor. I padded down the steps and into the living room. Nikki had taken off her moonbeam dress and draped it across the back of a chair. The light from the streetlamp revealed her sitting on the couch in bra and panties whispering into the phone, and when I jumped up in her lap her naked skin was cool against my fur, but she pushed me down in annoyance, concentrating urgently on the story she poured into the phone.

Apparently, there were a hundred people at the party, including the director of the National Gallery of Art and the Ambassador of France and various diplomats, and journalists, senators and congressmen, and a White House staffer, and it was hard to know who was trying harder, the journalists or the politicians, because they were all buttonholing each other and "working the party." In Washington "working a party" is part of your work.

Nikki felt like a million dollars in her designer dress. Claire introduced her to two museum directors, and told them that she was an absolutely marvelous conservator, whom they should hire for their conservation departments. David drifted off to talk to two lawyers he knew. Some people were talking about the war, of course, including one woman who was so upset that priceless art treasures were being destroyed in the bombing that she had started a Foundation to preserve world heritage sites. She wanted Nikki to join her campaign and lobby the United Nations. But much of the talk was simply social. Lorna has often commented that most people think Washington is all about exciting political and intellectual conversation, when it's really about getting Janie to soccer practice or finding a rental on Martha's Vineyard in August to mingle with the same people you meet at home.

At the party Nikki was having a really nice time when she heard Jeremy's voice behind her.

"Nikki?"

He held out a glass of wine for her. She took it without even thinking, because all she could see was that he'd shaved off his beautiful beard. His face was broken out.

"What's happened to you?" she blurted.

"But Lorna," she whispered into the phone, "I felt a twinge of guilt that the curse had worked. Do you think that's possible? Did I do that?" Sitting in the comfortable dark, where confidences are shared, Nikki poured out her self-reproach. "Lorna, I wanted to reach out and touch him, he looked so whipped. Was it wrong of me to want to comfort him?"

He said he didn't know what was wrong—an allergy or stress, the doctors didn't know. He didn't want to talk about it. He said she looked terrific, and then just as she was about to ask about his big story that still hadn't come out, Penelope came up and slipped her possessive arm through his and beamed up at his scarred, pocked cheeks, laying public claim to him. Her ruffled blouse opened almost to the naval, exposing the swell of impressive breasts. Her smiles were the kind that don't reach the eyes. Nikki admitted that sexy or not, Penelope was a bus she'd want to miss, and why couldn't men see it? She wanted to walk away, but Penelope caught her hand. She adored her dress. She said she was mad with envy and wanted one just like it, which gave Nikki the pleasure of saying, "You can't. It's a Luisa Newland. One of a kind," and then she had looked at Jeremy and said, "Some things are one of a kind." Which she thought quite clever, until she realized he might think she meant *him* being the one instead of alluding to herself.

After that, Penelope asked about Charlie, and Nikki reported that he was intimate now with Lorna. Did Penelope want to pass a message on to him?

"Why did you say that?" Lorna yelped. "There's nothing between us!"

All this while, Jeremy had stood uncomfortably between the two women, saying nothing, until Nikki could have hit him. She asked again about the foster children story, at which Penelope rushed in: "Oh, it's marvelous! It's going to be unbelievable."

"Unbelievable," Nikki repeated. "Which means either it wasn't well researched or well written. But I didn't say that. 'Well, he's a professional,' I said, just to let Penelope know she wasn't."

Penelope must have sensed her distaste, because she hugged Jeremy's arm tighter and beamed at him. 'He's so generous. He's letting me play a teensy-weensy part, and I'm learning so much.' Nikki could have puked. 'I'll have my own by-line,' Penelope rattled on. 'And all because of Jeremy.'

"Lorna, I nearly choked. My god! He's sharing his by-line! If looks could kill, she'd be weeping right now at her own funeral," Nikki spat out at the phone.

Just then Claire came up to thank god carry Nikki off.

All this time Lorna had been listening quietly, and now Nikki noticed the silence. "Are you there? Am I boring you? I just need to tell someone, because it hurts so much. I mean, Jerry just stood there like a post, and he wouldn't even look at me. Are you there?"

"I'm here. Go on."

Later Nikki saw Jeremy deep in conversation with David, and when they split up, she asked David to do her a favor, to make a fuss over her.

"He didn't even ask why. He was right on the button, so that afterwards we were together all evening, and I know Jerry took note. I didn't speak to him again, but Lorna, if I went to the garden or into the dining room, pretty soon Jerry would drift in. I wondered if he were following me. But he was always with *her*. I felt so uncomfortable. Thank god for David. I spent the whole night with him. Have you heard from Charlie?" she asked, finally remembering there was another person across the country on the other end of the line.

I don't know what Lorna said, but Nikki's voice grew hard. "Well, I really like him," she said in a tone that made me creep under the table, shivering. "I know it's hard for you to believe a man can be nice." And after Lorna answered: "Don't use that tone of voice. David is wonderful. He's handsome and smart. And fun. He's observant and respectful. I know you don't want a man, and I'm not judging you. I'm just saying I like him... I'm not asking you to have a *romance* with him, for God's sake. It would be utterly inappropriate. At your age. All I'm saying is—oh, never mind. But I want you to know I plan to know him for a long, long time!"

Silence followed. The kind that cuts like a drill.

After Nikki hung up she finished her whiskey and drifted to the window to watch the cold moon sail across an indifferent sky, and then she heaved a great shuddering sigh and covered her face in both hands. By this time, Puma had climbed painfully downstairs to find her. He brushed against her leg.

"Oh, Puma, I hurt so much. My heart aches."

==Come to bed, he said. I wound myself around her leg, purring her upstairs. Her mood swings were tiring.

That night she dreamt that Jeremy had his arms around her. They were dancing a slow-step, barely rocking to the soaring music of a golden horn, her head in the familiar crook of his neck, his beautiful soft beard against her hair.

She woke up groggy and confused. It was dark. Puma nudged her with his chin to comfort her with his warmth, and she drew him close, then pulled me up from the bottom of the bed: two cats in bed with her.

But she was wide awake. After a while, she turned on the light. "Stupid! Stupid!" she exclaimed, then, feverishly: "No, I will *not* let him destroy my life. I will *not* be put down by one stupid schmuck, so stupid he doesn't even see my worth."

She tugged on her terrycloth bathrobe, pulled her hair back with an elastic band, and carrying her cup of coffee she wandered into her studio.

It was 4:30 in the morning. She set down her cup.

26

I lay on the shelf next to the tubs of chemicals, where I could happily look down on her. A strand of hair curled down her cheek, so that every now and then she tossed her head to flick it back. The quiet was broken by the gentle snoring of Puma sleeping on the tattered, yellow couch in the corner. Pale pearl tinted the windows with the increasing light of dawn as Nikki set the painting upside down on her large work table and carefully removed the nails. She lifted the canvas from its frame and placed it on the table to check for damage.

Her camera flashed repeatedly, as she recorded it. With her jeweler's glass, she examined the painting inch by inch, photographing trouble spots. She put a tiny bit of solvent under the rabbet of the frame to find the true color of the painting, darkened by varnish and time but not discolored underneath the frame.

The phone startled me.

Nikki reached out for it, then pulled back as if it were a snake. She'd seen the Caller ID. A moment later, Jeremy's voice on the answering machine filled the room:

"Hi, Ba—" He didn't finish the affectionate word. Babe was what he used to call Nikki, and my ears twitched, knowing the word had slipped out of his mouth by habit, before he swallowed it.

"Hey, um? I want to talk to you. I was sure I would find you home this early. We have things to discuss. I mean I have things I'd like to talk about. Whatever. I wanted to talk at Claire's party, but you were always surrounded by admirers." A cough was followed by stuttering and muttering. "Maybe you're not there. Fuck."

You'd have thought the phone was an octopus ready to grab Nikki with its tentacles. She stared at it. Then she poked a button and listened all over again. What did he want? And gradually I saw a change fall over her, a shift like the shadow of a cloud darkening the grass, or like the wind rolling across a field of wheat.

Nervously, she yanked her hair down and caught it up again in both hands, tying it back with the elastic.

"Well, why shouldn't he love Penelope?" she announced out loud to the room at large. "Surely Penelope has good qualities, or else he wouldn't be with her." Nikki remembered how Jeremy often stood with his hands thrust fiercely in his pockets, his voice loud with indignation at the injustices of the world. He was idealistic. Intelligent. Hard working. Kind. Why wouldn't Penelope want him? Any woman would.

After a while she walked, hard heels pounding (I jumped from my high perch to trot curiously after her) to the tiny hatch under the stairs, where she crouched down, and pawing through the coats, boots, gloves, scarves, and wire hangers that breed in closets, she backed out, holding a small, square frame. She turned the picture to the light.

"Okay, Anthony." She dusted a cobweb with the tail of her pink wrapper. "Here you are. I give up. I'm bringing you out of prison. Want some milk and cookies?" She set him on the shelf by her altar. "I'm sorry. I don't want his face all scarred and pocked. I don't want him to be unhappy. Or lost. Or unemployed. Even if we got married, he'd probably be creeping to her house on the sly before he came back to me, the bitchy, nagging wife." The image was revolting.

"Undo the spell. Forgive me, St. Anthony, as I forgive Jerry, and please make him happy in the clutches of that conniving big-tit slut."

You see, she hadn't quite gotten the forgiveness part down pat.

Then she went upstairs and dressed in jeans and a tee shirt, and made more coffee and munched some toast and jam while she listened one last time to his voice, and then she erased him.

Afterwards, she went back to bed, curled in the fetal position.

Later she went to the health club and later still, in the afternoon, returned to her studio. None of us knew that this marked a turning point or guessed the unexpected turn events would take, all art and love of beauty commingling in Nikki and enhanced by love itself, and not a quiet maternal caring either but sensual, romantic, erotic passion that spilled over like a river leaping its banks to involve the work itself. But I'm ahead of myself again.

She worked on the painting all the time. She fell in love with it: the brown rocks, the delicate leafy trees, the far-off hills, and in the foreground the mare's arched neck curling tenderly over her foal; the delicate hooves, the glowing eyes. Behind her, the stallion watched with proud possession. Nikki photographed the painting from several angles.

"Chagall compared the colors of painting to music, Alba. What do you think of that? He wrote, 'The pulse of a work of art goes through the eyes and remains within the soul.'"

And then after a long silence: "I wonder who he was, Claire's *very good friend*? I won't forget her face when she spoke about him, her mystery man."

She could not find the painting in the Stubbs catalogues. She extended her research. "It's in the style of Stubbs.... It's the right age, though forgers are clever...."

She put the painting against a black cloth with ultra-violet lights on either side and pored over the canvas one more time to see if it had ever been restored or in-painted. She took more photographs.

Next came the tests on a hidden patch of color, to see how best to clean the work, and as she swiped her cotton Q-tip across a flake of paint, pressing off the yellowed varnish—"I really ought to take this to the National Gallery and ask them to check it." She stopped,

Q-tip in hand.

Ahead of her lay days of work. She would fill any hairline cracks with gelatin, then brush a thin coat of B-72 synthetic acriloid as an isolating coat. She would in-paint using a magnifying glass with a triple 000 series 7 Windsor Newton sable hair brush, and when the in-painting was finished, she would dip the tip of another sable brush into a synthetic, non-yellowing varnish thinned in naphtha, and wipe the excess on a lint-free cloth and brush the painting in smooth, long, even strokes. Not a single ridge or mark allowed, not a speck of lint or dust. No mistake. No mis-stroke.

The more she examined the beautiful horses, the quivering trees, the more hesitant she felt. She lifted the phone and dialed. "May I speak to the Director's office please?"

27

Jeremy called twice more. Each time his voice took on more edge.

"Hi, Nikki. I phoned before. I guess you didn't get the message. Would you call me? I want to talk to you."

And the third time:

"For Christ's sake, Nikki. Pick up the damn phone. Okay, you're not there. I'm sorry. I know you hate me to swear, and I swear I won't swear any more, but will you just pick up the damn phone? Or, if you're not there, will you please just call me back? What are you doing, hanging me out on the line to dry? Can't we talk? Talk is just moving of the jaws up and down, a little tongue motion. Come on. Okay, the truth is, I misah—" (and here the rest of his word was lost in mumbling). "I wanna talk." After rummaging and muttering for another thirty seconds, he clicked off.

Nikki thought he was drunk. If ever she considered phoning back, she remembered the way his eyes had followed Penelope, the fact he'd shared his byline with her.

At this stage in the story I, Alba, am forced to withdraw, for I didn't witness the next events. Puma and I heard about things later from Nikki or Lorna or Claire, and some parts I've pieced together, others guessed at, remembering odd moments, and some I've just made up, which goes to show how wrong the authorities are when they say cats don't have imagination. What nonsense. It shows how little they know. These are the same pet-less, deprived (and maybe depraved) scientists who get grants to study whether animals feel pain or have a sense of humor or know what it is to love or be jealous or frightened or unhappy.

But as I was saying, I never saw what happened next. I'll tell it the best I can.

The first thing that happened, Claire invited Nikki to lunch at the Cosmos Club. Nikki was so excited she couldn't stop talking about it, because although there are numerous social clubs in Washington, only the prestigious Cosmos Club accepts members for accomplishment alone. Its members are all "Distinguished in their Field" or known for "Meritorious Original Work." Claire, as an art collector, fluent in three languages, and recognized for her philanthropy and intellectual salons, was "Known to be Cultivated."

Lunch ended in disaster.

We heard about it in her next phone call to Lorna: how she met Claire in the grand entrance, how she admired the marble floors covered with splashy red Oriental rugs, how she followed Claire on a tour of the baronial library, the 18th century (reproduction) ball room with its real gold gilt and high French windows and ceiling moldings carved with cherubs and dragons. An oval ceiling panel in pink and blue showed gods disporting in the golden clouds.

"Wow."

"It's lovely, isn't it?" Claire had pointed around with proprietorial pride. "Upstairs we have beautiful bedrooms. If you ever want to stay overnight, let me know. Now, come downstairs and I'll show you the photos of the Nobel Laureate members of the club. They line the hallway as we go in to lunch."

They took a window table.

"Claire! Isn't that the Vice President?" Nikki gawped.

Claire looked over disdainfully. "Don't even look at the man. I don't know how they could have let him in."

"Well, but he's the Vice President of the United States!" Nikki laughed.

"I don't care who he is," Claire announced. "My car was held up by his entourage the other day. He was on his way to the Senate, I suppose. First there were seventeen policemen on motorcycles, I counted: seventeen, all with their lights flashing and sirens screaming, in case anyone happened to miss the Vice President driving by. Then about seven jeeps and SUV's, each one with blackened windows, and you know the Swat teams are sitting inside with their machine guns pointed at you; and these were followed by not one but *two* stretch limousines, each with black-tinted windows, so the potential bomber won't know which one holds the Important Man. And the whole cavalcade ended with more screaming police cars, all with sirens blowing and blue lights flashing. Traffic stopped in both directions. When I think of the cost! You'd think people would revolt! In my day the Vice President used to drive his own car to the Senate himself from his own house in Spring Valley. As if anyone would want to assassinate the man! He's not that important. I have a good mind to go over and tell him so." She half-rose from her chair.

"Claire! You wouldn't!"

She sat down, laughing. "No. I can't. This is a social club. It wouldn't be good manners, but I'd certainly *like* to give him a piece of my mind."

"Well, it's probably the Secret Service that insist on all that."

"Oh nonsense! It began with 9/11. Don't get me started. If he wanted to be safe, the best thing in the world for him to do would be to get in a Ford Fiesta and drive like anyone else, stopping at the red lights like an ordinary citizen. No one would pay the slightest attention to him. He could have the windows blackened, if he's particularly paranoid. I'd be happy to give him a driver, so he doesn't have to circle the block looking for a parking place. But imagine! Stopping all the traffic in both directions for twenty or thirty minutes whenever he goes to lunch.

"Oh well. The best thing to do is to ignore the politicians, dear. They're all transients. Of no importance. Oh good, here come the famous popovers."

They examined the menus, and then Claire commanded, "Now, tell me, how are my lovely horses coming?"

At which Nikki reported with pride that she'd taken the canvas down to the National Gallery of Art to be examined by the curatorial staff. "I think it's real."

"Nikki!"

"I think we've found a new Stubbs."

"Oh, you fool! What have you done?" Claire threw down her napkin. "Come on. We have to go. Right now."

"Where?"

"To the National Gallery. To get my picture back."

"But—"

"Don't *but* me. I sent my driver off to lunch. We'll have to take a taxi. Come along. And when you get there," she continued as she bustled onto the black leather seat of the taxi— "To the National Gallery. Main Building. Please. And hurry," (this to the cabbie)— "When we get there you will go inside without me, and go straight to the curator's office and ask for the picture back. Don't even call it a painting. Call it a picture. Tell them you've just discovered it was painted by your great-uncle. And now that you've found the provenance, and it's by no one at all, you're sorry to have bothered them. Do you understand?"

Nikki nodded. She was not at all sure she could get it back. "I'm sorry. I didn't know." Know what? That the painting was stolen? A forgery? Confiscated by Nazis? The owner gassed and the descendants looking for it still?

"Well, just get it back. Dear god, what damage ignorance can do!" Claire stared out the window with a distracted air as the taxi careened down Massachusetts Avenue. Outside, the city lay under a cloud of moist polluted summer heat. "But *really*! You should have asked me first."

The taxi drew up at the entrance circle to the National Gallery. "We will wait," Claire told Nikki, then raising her voice to the driver, as if he hadn't heard: "We'll wait here." Turning to Nikki: "Now don't come back without it. Say whatever you need to. Tell them it's just junk."

By the time Nikki returned to the taxi, holding the canvas on its stretcher and covered in bubble-wrap, Claire was steaming with heat and impatience.

Leaning forward she tapped the glass. "Take me home." She gave the address, then flung herself back against the seat, eyes closed. "I'm tired now. I need to lie down. When the cab drops me off, take it back to the club to get your car. My driver will be waiting for me there. Tell him I've gone home. This has been an exhausting exercise. . . . "

"I'm so sorry, Claire. I thought—"

"Well, don't," she snapped. The older woman's prerogative.

Nikki shifted uncomfortably. "Do you still want me to do the work?" she asked in a tiny voice.

"Of course you'll do the work. You're perfectly capable of that. Just don't go showing the painting off to every Tom, Dick, and Harry."

"The National Gallery of Art is hardly—"

"If I wanted them to know I had the piece, I'd show it to them. Now no more questions. This is between you and me. Do the work. Do a beautiful job. Bring it back to me. How long will it take?"

"A week?" said Nikki tentatively. She was terrified. Apparently the picture was real.

The cab let off the old woman. "Are you all right?" Nikki grabbed

the painting off the seat before walking Claire to her door. She wasn't
going to let it out of her hands.

"I'm fine. Cook will bring me some broth in bed. I'm sorry. I've
been difficult. I love you, darling. We'll have lunch another day. Now,
be careful of that canvas. Don't lose it. It's not insured."

Not insured! Nikki could hardly breathe. Back at the Cosmos
Club, she fumbled for cab fare, Claire having neglected, as rich people
often do, to pay for their outing. It was expensive. She clutched the
painting to her chest as she sent Claire's chauffeur home, then waited
for the parking valet to bring up her own beat-up dented car. It was
only when she had the picture safe once again in her studio, the security system clicked on, that she even partially relaxed.

"Don't you dare come close, do you hear me, Alba? Don't even
sniff at it." I walked away, my tail in the air. As if I wanted to sniff
her old picture.

She lifted the phone to call her insurance company. She took
out an extra million dollars in insurance. That would use up all the
money she earned from Claire's commission, but what other option
did she have?

"What a story!" Lorna exclaimed halfway across the country on
the phone. "Is it a Stubbs? Why doesn't she want to know? I don't
understand."

"Neither do I. By the time I got home I felt like Claire—I wanted
Cook to bring me a bowl of bouillon in bed. Here I am, an established
painting conservator, and I was so shaken I had to check all the doors
and windows, absolutely convinced a thief would break in and grab
the painting." They laughed about it.

"Well, I have news too," said Lorna happily. "I'm coming home. We've finally got my mother settled— "

I nudged the phone in my delight and dashed upstairs to tell Puma, and then I curled up next to him and washed my ears. I was so happy I thought my heart would burst out of my body.

That evening Puma had an attack.

He lay on his side on the bare floorboards. His mouth opened in a silent scream, tongue curled. He panted, panted. I saw his belly ballooning. I was frightened. He couldn't breathe.

==Nikki! I raced through the house. She'd gone out.

==Hold on, hold on. Puma. Don't die.

His eyes rolled at me. He couldn't talk.

I heard her car outside. I ran to the door calling out—

==Yow-l!

She rushed him to the hospital. It was after midnight when they staggered home, Puma dopey on drugs. Nikki threw herself in bed. The house creaked with night sounds. I nestled close to Nikki's back.

==Mer?

She stroked me gently.

"Oh Alba. He's going to die. The vet wanted me to put him down right then. I couldn't do it." Her tears spilled wet onto my fur. "I can't do it. I just can't."

28

Lorna dropped her suitcases in the front hall, hugged Nikki and twirled me in circles until I got dizzy and had to scoot out of her arms to clear my head. She and Nikki sat in the kitchen jabbering at each other, all their differences forgotten— "No, you go," and "No, you," and "What were you—" while I sat on Lorna's lap and let her beautiful fingers stroke me up and down. I was so happy to see her that I didn't even pretend to stand on dignity. Lorna's mother was in a rehabilitation center, learning to walk again. Lorna had had it, she announced, with organizing everything, everyone, and now she had used up all her vacation leave, and moreover her daughter, Nancy, who lived in New York, was having marriage trouble, calling her for advice and sympathy. The bills were piling up. Lorna felt she'd crash, she had so much to do. She'd barely managed to stay on top of the situation at the Hall of Physics, thank god for technology, but she really needed to be physically in the office. There was the question of an exhibit from the Niels Bohr Institute in Copenhagen—Bohr who had won the Nobel Prize in 1922, and whose son Aage won the Atoms for Peace prize in 1969 and his Nobel in 1975: two in the same family! A delegation was going to Denmark to clear the problems up. Nikki, on the other hand, wasn't much interested in nuclear atoms. She shifted her weight and squirmed until she could interrupt to tell her news about rushing Puma to the hospital and her worries, and then later she repeated the story of taking St. Anthony out of the closet and undoing the curse. She thought David was just a darling, though I'm not sure Lorna heard this last because she dropped her spoon just then and ducked under the table to fumble for it, and when she reappeared, a little flushed from being upside down, she switched the conversation.

"Oh, guess who phoned while I was gone."

"Who?"

"Charlie."

"Charlie! I told you he liked you!" Nikki flashed her brilliant smile.

"He called to thank me for the night of the party, and to apologize for his behavior."

"Is that all?"

"And to tell me," said Lorna, "that my advice was right on target, because two days later Penelope had telephoned him."

"She phoned him? She wanted him back?"

"I doubt it. I think she wanted to make sure he didn't swing too far out of her orbit. But he told me that he'd sent her flowers, so I'm pretty sure he's lost her again. Poor guy. He tries too hard."

"He's so serious," Nikki said.

"I guess that's why he's successful. For play he goes out and murders ducks."

Nikki laughed. "Lorna, lots of people like to hunt. Even Jerry went shooting."

"But for skeet!" cried Lorna rising in indignation. "For clay pigeons. Not to kill animals. I know I'm queasy that way. It's just something I don't ever want to do, much as hunters tell me how much fun it is." She paused a moment, glanced at Nikki, then away. "I don't see why you don't call him back."

"Who?"

"Jeremy."

"All he wants to do is trumpet some triumph with Penelope."

"You don't know that. Maybe he wants you back."

"Oh Lorna, you should have seen him at Claire's party, dancing attendance on her."

"I thought you said he was hovering near you, appearing round the corners."

"Well, I did," she admitted. "But on reflection, I think it was wishful thinking. No, I've met David now. I'm over Jerry."

Lorna did not look happy, but she lifted her head. "Show me your painting," she said with a brave smile. "I want to see the beautiful horses."

So then they went into the studio and talked about art. "I used to think it was skill and craft that made a work of art," said Nikki.

"Isn't it?"

"Yes, but it's more than that. It's the artist's very soul. I think a bit of the soul of Michelangelo or Cezanne or Modigliani resides in the work, and it's true of all the arts—music, writing, dance. The soul of Beethoven remains in the music like a resplendent hologram."

"These giants. I agree."

"And I get to work on their paintings. It makes me humble. And grateful. I'm so lucky. I get to repair and restore the damage of the ages on. . . on. . . on works of art," she finished lamely.

I loved Nikki when she exposed herself like that, striving for the highest ideals, for whatever is noble in our shabby world. Lorna felt it too.

They stood before the glowing painting, while Nikki explained why she thought it might really be a Stubbs. Then it was time for Nikki to drive us home.

Only I didn't want to leave Puma. When Lorna takes me someplace she lets me ride freely in the car, but Nikki had brought me in a carrier, and she insisted I go back in one.

"She'll be all right," said Lorna. "She likes to drive."

"I don't feel comfortable even with her sitting in your lap. I'd worry the whole time that she'd get under my feet when I want to smash on the brakes."

I don't like a carry-cage.

When she tried to push me into the carrier, I struggled, both front legs splayed against the door, and I twisted out of her hands and ran upstairs and slunk under the bed to hide.

"Look, she doesn't want to leave. That's so cute." Nikki laughed. Didn't they understand? But Lorna dragged me out by the scruff of my neck, cooing and petting me, while I fought like a tiger, and she walked downstairs holding my front feet in one hand to keep me from clawing her. She forced my head into the cage, my claws scrabbling for purchase against the door and my body arching under her hands.

"Come on, Alba. Don't be like that."

Puma lay under a chair, his head turned away, heart aching. He knew too much to struggle, but I was urgent with youth.

==*Puma!* I called.

He lifted himself from the floor and started toward my cage, but before he could reach me, Lorna clicked the door shut and swung the carrier into the air. I was frantic.

==*Puma! Puma!* I whipped in circles inside the carrier. The mesh hid him. I couldn't see him.

"Come on," I heard Nikki's voice. "I've got your other suitcase. Sorry the car's so messy. Do you think trash breeds in the night when we're not watching?"

==*POOMA!* I howled.

"Don't cry, Alba," said Lorna.

==*Puma!* I saw his face at the window—a flash before my carrier was thrown on the back seat and extinguished the sight of him. I was wild with anxiety. I was so mad I could have peed on her.

"Why is she carrying on like that?"

Sometimes the 2-leggeds understand nothing.

Then we were back in our apartment, and I wandered the fusty, unused rooms, placing my scent back where it belonged, making the apartment comfortable again. Lorna threw mail and papers on the table (glancing through the bills), lugged suitcases into the bedroom and began to unpack.

There was a knock on the door. David and Goliath stood outside. I was surprised at how pleased I was to see Goliath. I rushed to welcome him, bottle-brushing, inviting him in, and trotting after him to see he didn't spray; which was more courtesy than Lorna showed. She took two steps back, her energy field exploding. She leaned down to pick a scrap of paper off the floor, stared at it unseeing, and crumbled it in her hand before glancing up at David. She stood back, then, one hand steadying herself on the table, and you could see her struggling to contain her solar winds. Their eyes locked. David did not enter, but stood, smiling, a hand on each doorpost, scuffing the floor with one foot.

"I just wanted to welcome you home."

"Thank you. And thanks for bringing in the mail."

"Is everything all right?"

"It's fine. It's fine, thank you."

"Your mother's all right?"

"Now it's my daughter I'm worried about," she smiled, shaking her head. "Her marriage. If it's not one thing it's another."

"Well, nice to have you back. Let me know if there's anything I can do."

He hesitated at the doorway, not invited in, yet not quite sent away.

==What's going on? I whispered to Goliath, who trotted to the kitchen. The tension in the room was palpable.

"I'm really tired," said Lorna stiffly. "Will you forgive me? I'm in no shape to talk tonight."

His head jerked. "Of course."

They both stood on distant, formal behavior, and both agreed several times that they'd talk in a few days, though David added that he was working flat-out these days, the trial having begun, and Lorna, fidgeting, said she hoped it was going well for him and to come up when he had a chance (shearing her eyes away). She, too, was working like a beaver. She'd be late at the office all week, because she'd been requisitioned at the last minute to help clinch the Niels Bohr material. David picked up Goliath and they left, and then Lorna, standing at the table, began to riffle valiantly through mail. I don't think she even saw what she was reading.

After a moment I mewed.

==Me?

"Oh, Alba." She turned heavily. "I forgot you. You want something to eat?"

Me? She forgot me? How could she forget me?

29

Sometimes you can only feel sorry for the 2-leggeds. All the other animals know the point of living is to enjoy it. But sometimes I think they don't know *how* to be happy. Maybe it's because they're always Thinking. We cats think too, of course, but most of the time we're in the state of Being. Which is the only way to Love. Or is it the other way round: love, the only way of *Being*?

A cat lives in the present tense, and you can say this isn't true or I wouldn't be telling this story that happened in the past, an observation for which you get full credit. But the 2-leggeds hear voices in their heads all the time, commenting, analyzing, criticizing, remembering, planning, dreaming, scheming, scolding, judging; and worse, reproaching. The ones they reproach most often are themselves, which in itself is odd. The voices are all about what happened long ago (or didn't) or else about a misty future that is sweeping toward them at a sensibly slow pace, not even visible yet, but which they so often foresee as fearful. I think they like being scared. They seek it out. They tell stories or read books or go to movies and come back telling each other how frightening it was and what a good time they had. A cat would never think of doing that.

We try to teach them. We show them how if you stare for a long time at running water, like the little fountain in Nikki's yard, where the water spills and dances and flicks, light-dancing, off the rocks, or if you watch the motes floating in a beam of sunlight, your mind grows still, and for long minutes you exist without a single intruding thought. Just Being.

It's then you feel the connections between all living things; it's then you know intuitively exactly what to do. It's then you see the edges and outlines of the luminous beings who sit sometimes in corners or high up at the ceiling or in the space between the branches of trees or rising in the blue air, always watching and guarding us. The 2-leggeds wonder what we're staring at.

That night Lorna put on a silvery nightgown that she'd bought in Santa Fe. It flowed and swayed around her sensually, very different from her bunny pajamas. I can't say she slept any better for it. She tossed and turned, aching for what she could not have. Which was a waste of the nightgown, too.

The next morning she left when it was hardly dawn, and she came back so late in the evening that she had only time to feed me, undress, and throw herself in bed. She barely spoke to me. The same thing happened the following night, and then the next, until she tottered with exhaustion. If she wasn't at the office, she was on her laptop. When I lay across the keys to remind her to stop, she pushed me off in a distracted way, hardly seeing me at all. She didn't even have time for her daughter Nancy, who suspected her husband was having an affair, or as she put it acidly between her tears, "can't keep his pants zipped up." Lorna reminded Nancy that she had no proof, that the thing to do was talk to him, go together to counseling, and yes of course she could come live with her mother to get some space, but not right now, maybe after the Hall of Physics had opened, because right now Lorna had no time, and she was really sorry, but Nancy was going to have to work this out for herself.

One morning I saw her stand at the window to watch David throw his athletic leg over the bike seat and peddle off to work, and another time when she heard him talking to a neighbor outside, she shifted the curtains, straining to see him without being caught, and afterwards she had to lean against the wall to recover. I think there were moments when she truly disliked Nikki. It took David no time to figure out that Lorna wanted nothing to do with him, and then he, too, withdrew, until they both barely nodded when they met, and I could think of nothing more different than those days when they had run up and down the stairs, laughing and talking and playing like otters.

Hot summer turned into sweet September.

One night, a knock came on the door. It was after ten. Lorna turned off her bath water and snatched up a thin summer robe to cover her nudity.

"David." For a moment they stared at each other. She opened the door wider. "Are you all right?"

"May I come in? Am I disturbing you? I saw your light on and thought. . . " His voice trailed off.

"You look dead on your feet."

He was inside now. "Is it too late? Send me away if you want." He stared at her shadowed shape visible beneath the gauzy robe.

She waved to the couch. "Do you want a drink?"

"No, I have to be in the office at 6:00 tomorrow morning, probably pull another all-nighter. We're down to the wire. We have a good judge, though, and we'll just hope. . . ." His voice faded out again. When he settled on the couch, I jumped in his lovely lap and began to knead his belly while his strong fingers massaged my skin.

"Were you a goddess, Alba, in Ancient Egypt?" Lorna couldn't hear him from the kitchen. "In Alexandria a mob once tore a man limb from limb for killing a cat. Did you know that?"

David is one in a million.

"The cat was the goddess Bast," he finished. "He'd killed a goddess." I thought the punishment made good sense.

Lorna returned with two balloon glasses and a bottle of cognac. "You can also have mint or chamomile tea, if you prefer." She poured him the drink he'd refused and sat in a straight-backed chair, pulling her robe around her legs. She looked very pretty without makeup in a disheveled sleepy slovenly way.

They talked about her mother and David's trial and how after David's party, Penelope had phoned Charlie, just as Lorna had predicted, after which Charlie had sent her two dozen roses and invited her to fly at his expense to attend the theater in London, so of course she'd dropped him again. Lorna said she might be sent to Copenhagen with a delegation for the Physics Hall; it wasn't decided yet, but that would be fun. Then David asked if Lorna had fallen in love while in New Mexico, and she asked why he asked that and he said because she was acting so strangely when he'd thought they were friends, and she fidgeted and fingered the lace on her robe.

"No, no. I've just been busy." She blushed and took a sip of cognac. She didn't even want the drink—just something to occupy her hands, and she noticed that David hadn't touched his at all, but swirled the golden fluid thoughtfully, sniffed it and warmed it in his hands.

She lifted her head. "I gather you're seeing Nikki these days."

It was a flat statement, but his eyes flashed. I slipped off David's lap onto the floor. He'd suddenly become unstable. The next moment he stood up, set down his glass, and in one swift movement lifted her from her chair and kissed her so long and tenderly that it silenced both of them. Lorna pulled away a little shakily. She pushed him away.

"You shouldn't have done that."

"Why?"

"Oh, David. I don't have time for games, all right? You're involved with Nikki. She's my best friend. I don't need a womanizer."

"Womanizer." His face grew black. "Is that what you think I am?"

"I don't know what to think," she said. "I don't really know you. You come up in the middle of the night—well, after ten, anyway, and for what? What did you want? To go to bed with me? One of those men who can't keep his pants zipped? You ought to be ashamed." Was she talking to herself or him? "I'm thirteen, fourteen years older than you, all right? It's not appropriate," she finished, echoing Nikki's charge.

"I don't see that age makes any difference," he said stiffly. He downed his cognac in one swallow. "And I didn't come up here to seduce you."

It took all his self-control to walk to the door. "I won't trouble you again. Forgive me. I thought we shared—" A wave of his hand: He wasn't going to say what he thought they shared.

"Good night." He closed the door behind him.

Lorna stood in the living room, her fingers trembling. She ran her hands over her body, touching her breasts, her belly, her buttocks. She gave a little mew of longing and distress. She squeezed her elbows. Then: "Stop it!" She spoke out loud. She picked up the brandy bottle and glasses and put them, hands shaking, in the kitchen sink, where she stood, both hands on the counter, and burst into tears. Then she sat down at the kitchen table until she stopped shaking.

"Wash the glasses," she ordered herself. Instead of washing David's glass, though, she held it, and for a moment, eyes shut, pressed her lips to the rim where his lips had touched, before plunging the glass fiercely under the hot water, pouring blue liquid soup from its jolly dispenser, and washing away his marks.

30

After that I stayed in the apartment alone, sleeping or padding round and round. The air conditioning worked now, and with all the windows locked and blocked, I couldn't go outside. Loneliness tormented me. For the first time in my life I was bored. Not even my bug-on-a-wire felt interesting.

A few days later a letter slipped under the door. I sniffed it. It smelt of Goliath, soap, and ink, and male. When she got home from work, Lorna turned it in her hands.

"You'd think he'd write an email," she murmured, but she tore open the envelope.

Dear Lorna:

You have made your position very clear, and I respect you enough that I won't intrude again, but one thing that you said the other night offends me. You called me a womanizer. I deny the charge. Given my present state of celibacy, I can only imagine you are referring to Nikki staying overnight at my place some while ago after my party, and while it is not my place to impugn your friend—and I don't know what she told you—you should know the truth from my side: that I felt she was too drunk to drive home. I put her in the guest room. Nothing happened. Which may be more than might be said of you and Charlie. What you do, of course, is your own choice. I am not criticizing. For myself, I admire you. I've enjoyed our friendship, and I am sorry you feel it unpleasant. I will do my best to stay out of your way. However, if you ever need anything, please feel free to call on me. I will not overstep the bounds.

David

She read the letter over and over, tracing his strong handwriting with approving eyes. It didn't change anything. He was still too young for her. Nikki was in love with him, and either she betrayed her friend or betrayed her own convictions; but at least he'd held out the hand of friendship, and when she was ready, she thought perhaps one day she'd be strong enough to take it.

Soon after, Lorna came home from work early, pulled down her suitcase and began to fold and pack up clothes. "I'm off for Copenhagan, Alba," she reported. "I'll only be gone a few days. It's a great honor—to be part of the delegation. If the Boss hadn't gotten sick, I don't suppose. . . ."

I curled up in the suitcase to remind her not to leave me. She picked me up, stroked me, scooped me to floor.

"I'm sorry, Alba. I'll be home Saturday. Can't you stay alone? You'll be all right for a few days. I suppose I could ask David to—?"

==Yes! I shouted at her. Because it would be more fun to play with Goliath than to stay alone in the apartment for days and days all by myself, with my heart breaking, and no one to take care of me or pet me or keep me company or feed me or empty my litter box or even worry about me at all in all that time. How would I be able to stand it? They say that cats are solitary animals, but we're sociable, too. We like the warmth of company, and I thought how sorry she'd be if I peed in the potted plant in my anger or scratched her sofa to shreds.

"I can ask Nikki." But the fact was, she couldn't bear to speak to Nikki just then. She had relinquished the man she loved for her friend. It was an act of nobility, you might say. At least that's how Lorna saw her sacrifice. But it didn't mean she wanted to see or talk to her friend just then. Moreover, she didn't have *time* (she told herself) to call Nikki and listen to her, much less wait for her to cross the river in rush hour to pick me up. In the end she scribbled a note and thrust it under David's door. She read it aloud first to make sure she'd said what she wanted:

David:

My apologies for the other night. The situation is more complex than you may know. But I appreciate your letter, and I apologize if I offended you.

I, too, am sorry to lose a friend who means a lot to me. You say I may call on you. May I take advantage of your offer? May I ask a favor—my way of patching things up? I leave in a minute for Copenhagen and The Hague. I'll be home next Thursday. You still have a key to the apartment. Could you check on Alba to make sure she's got food and water? This is such a short trip that I'm sure she'll be all right, though lonely. I'd be grateful.

L.

It wasn't much of a note, terse and tense, but after the scalding water she'd thrown at him, the best that she could manage in her hurry.

As she heaved the suitcase off the bed, the phone rang. It was time to go, but her hand reached out automatically.

"Lorna. Thank god you're there."

"Nikki?" The last person she wanted to talk to. She glanced at her watch. The taxi would be downstairs any second.

"I've just heard Jerry and Penelope are getting married."

"So, that's what he was calling you about."

"Lorna, the phone hasn't stopped ringing. Lucille, Angela, even Claire, my own godmother—everyone calling, can you believe it?

Because they all know how much I'd want to know. All they want is to be the first to break the news, and see my reaction, so they can cat about it to everyone else." (*Cat* about it? Who thought up that word?)

"I'm so sorry. Listen, Nikki, I'm leaving in a minute for—"

"It's a shock. I mean, it's not unexpected, is it? But I don't know what I feel. I'm numb right now. At least with you I don't have to pretend I don't care, like with the others. I don't have to burble about how happy I am for the two of them: *I'm so happy for them both and isn't it wonderful news!*"

"Nikki, listen—"

"But one thing is sure. Now I can just get on with my life, can't I? You were right, Lorna. You're always right, you are so wise, and I remember when Jerry. . . um, shafted me, and you wouldn't let me slide into self-pity. You said someone else would come along, someone better, and of course you were right, and now that I know they're getting married, I'm completely free to work on this new relationship, aren't I?"

From outside, the taxi had honked.

Nikki laughed, and if it had a slightly hysterical quality, Lorna didn't notice because she'd grasped the nettle and in another moment she would hear the name of David Scott, and then she, too, could be completely free to be happy for her friend.

"Nikki, are you in love with David Scott?" There! She'd asked it.

"Oh, wait, there's someone at the door. Hang on. I'll be right back."

Lorna was left with the phone at her ear. The taxi honked a second time. She heard Nikki's shout: "Wait a minute. I'm coming. Keep your pants on!"

Downstairs the taxi blasted its third impatient call, at the same time that Call Waiting clicked in her ear, the taxi calling her by phone. Lorna picked up her suitcase.

"I have to go." She spoke to the empty phone. "I'm catching a plane. I'll call you in a few days." She was setting down the phone when Nikki came back on:

"I can't talk. Something's happened. Call you back." She hung up.

Lorna ran for the airplane to Copenhagen and The Hague. Leaving me alone.

What happened next was so unexpected, so inconceivable that we were all turned upside down. Only this time it wasn't life dealing a blow out of a clear blue sky—that happens, too—like me, caught as a kitten in a drainpipe. This time it was Nikki acting out of thoughtless impulse, though maybe from the highest ideals. But never would she have given in to anger had she understood the consequences, and the rest of us could only stand by, unable to help. Again, I've had to piece the story together from the flurry of phone calls, hallway whispers and hurried rumors, but Puma watched some of it unfold, and Nikki proclaimed with indignation, to anyone who would listen, her side of the international scandal that rocked the art world and made her famous, or infamous, as it were.

We knew nothing of this. Lorna, running for her taxi, closed the door.

I was alone.

I was alone for days.

I was scared.

I mewed. I scratched the door. I'd been abandoned. I took back everything I ever said about cats living in the present. I ached for company. The phone rang. The antique answering machine took its taped recordings, including one from Nikki, something about police. Another came from her daughter, Nancy, weeping about her broken marriage, and one from her sister, Isabelle, reporting that Mom was fine but it would be nice if Lorna would call and show some interest, and how could she be so selfish, she didn't have to put everything on Isabelle's shoulders and to call her please.

I finished off my food. My litter box was nasty. The water, left in a tin-tasting bowl on the floor, had gone rotten and then disappeared, drunk eventually from burning thirst, and gone. I thought my very ninth life was going before my years. I thought of the feral cats who live without 2-leggeds and forage and hunt and snatch at bugs and chipmunks and birds. I could be a feral, if the windows weren't locked.

David didn't come to check on me.

What was worse, I couldn't bring up Puma across the Continents of our Divide. After a long time, though, Goliath heard me. I think he may be the reason I'm still alive, for late on that Friday night of my abandonment, when David came home, Goliath slithered past him and raced up to our apartment. I heard him snuffling at the door, and I ran back and forth on my side. I meowed and meowed. Heavily, David had followed his cat.

In courtesy he knocked. "Lorna? You there?" He waited a while. "What's going on?" he asked Goliath. "It's after eleven." Then he went back downstairs and got his key and came up again and opened the door, as he should have done days earlier!

I ran to him. I rubbed against his leg, and when he picked me up I looked in his face and told him how glad I was to see him, and how scared I was (climbing, my paws around his neck), and how I'd been left all alone for days and days and Lorna would probably never come back for me, ever, or if she did she'd find a corpse that she would never feed again, and never would she see me again alive.

"Poor little kitty." He walked through the apartment, into the kitchen, where he checked for food (gone) and water (also gone). "Where's Lorna? Did she just leave you here?" He cleaned my disgusting, overflowing litter box, because I hadn't peed or pooped in the potted plant or under the sofa on a corner of the rug.

"Why don't you come downstairs with us? Wouldn't it be easier for you to stay with Goliath and me?" But all I could think was, why hadn't he come upstairs earlier to save me? I sniffed his nose in gratitude. He wrote a note to Lorna and left it under a saltcellar on the kitchen table.

So, I was carried in his comforting strong arms down to his apartment (Goliath trotting at his heels), and given food that he set thoughtfully on the top of the refrigerator to indicate it belonged to me, and he also set out water in a little crockery bowl, not knowing that I always drink from the running water. I had to push him aside when he turned on the bathroom faucet to brush his teeth. Goliath was amazed. That night I slept hard, I was so relieved to be with company again. I know there are feral felines that take care of themselves, but they live in the wild outdoors, not locked in an apartment with only a can opener and an unopened tin. I was simply happy to be with humans, taken care of properly. Twice I woke up to prowl the strange apartment, and each time Goliath thudded after me, but mostly I lay curled on the sofa deep in dreams. Once I dreamt that Lorna, Nikki, and David were living all together in Nikki's house, together with us three cats, but somehow it was filled with footsteps and large boots beating on doors and stairs, a dream filled with tension and anxiety while I hid in the bushes behind some stranger's house.

The next day Goliath told me how he'd accidentally shredded the note that came sliding underneath the door. He'd played with it for fun, and patted the crumpled paper underneath the sofa, where David never found it. Goliath asked forgiveness, and I kindly accepted his apology. I had a more pressing question: why didn't Lorna call David to check about me? We discussed it, and this is what we decided. First, that she didn't think it necessary. She'd left a note. She trusted him. Also, she didn't trust herself. She knew she wanted to hear his voice, so that asking about me was only an excuse, and despising her own weakness, she kept a tight hold on her affections. Finally, it would have been an international call, which always seems more important than lifting the phone to reach your next-door neighbor, and anyway she was working hard in a different time zone.

And so our days passed, and I was content.

Meanwhile, none of us knew what had happened to Nikki—and we weren't to learn for days.

32

Nikki had finished shellacking the painting, each tender green leaf individually restored. She'd applied the final coat of varnish and stepped back to admire the work when the first phone call came through, announcing Jeremy's upcoming marriage to Penelope, followed by a half-dozen other calls, the wires ringing and singing with the news. The information left her reeling, and perhaps if she hadn't just received this blow, she might not have reacted so dramatically when she left Lorna on the phone to answer the doorbell.

"Hang on," she told Lorna. "There's someone at the door." And then she shouted, "I'm coming. Keep your pants on."

Two men in business suits stood before her, eyes hidden behind black glasses. She thought, *Gangsters? Jehovah's Witnesses?* She opened her mouth to say she didn't want any pamphlets, thank you, when the taller older man flashed a badge.

"FBI."

"**F B EYE?**" She craned to read his credentials.

"Are you Nikki Petrelli?"

"I am." She laughed, amused to think she'd get a call from the FBI.

"Painting restorer?"

"Yes."

Brave, aged Puma staggered to the door, concerned that he couldn't guard Nikki. She leaned down to pull him back inside.

"We have a warrant for your arrest."

"My *arrest*?!" She emphasized the last syllable as she had with FBEYE, her voice rising with the indignation of one accustomed to entitlement. It was a joke. By then the two men had pushed past her into the hall as if they owned the house. She was indignant. "Where are you going?"

She had to follow. And that's when she went back to the phone and told Lorna she'd have to call her back. But Lorna had already hung up. The men were looking about suspiciously, one standing in examination of her little altar with the icon of Jesus and the bird nest and crystals and image of St. Anthony and a photo of the Dalai Lama and the laughing fat happy Buddha.

"What do you mean my *arrest*?" She turned on them. "Whatever for?"

"Art theft. Interpol contacted us."

"Are you out of your mind?"

Suddenly she remembered. "Oh, my God!" She poured Puma to the floor because the shorter agent was already moving into her studio, where the Stubbs lay drying on the hot table.

"Is this it?"

"That is NOT a stolen painting," she cried, then seeing the bulkier man move in: ***"DON'T TOUCH THAT!"*** She slung herself in front of him. "I just finished it. The varnish is still wet. *Ohmigod,* don't touch it! Don't even breathe on it!"

"I'm sorry, miss, we have to take it with us. Brad, can you find a paper bag?"

"No, no. Wait. You can take it," she conceded. She was trying to get herself under control, because these two men were moving through her rooms like burglars, without explanation, and she was alone in the house with them. It occurred to her that maybe they weren't government agents at all. Art thieves?

"Look, just tell me what this is about. You want that painting. I can see that. But you can't barge in like this and take other people's property. Are you really with the FBI? Talk to me."

He flashed his badge again. "Out of the way, Miss."

"I'm not saying you can't take it," said Nikki with a gulp. "But right now it needs to dry. You just have to wait for the varnish to dry, that's all, and then use bubble-wrap. **DON'T TOUCH IT!**"

They weren't impressed.

The one named Brad trailed in from the kitchen carrying a used brown paper shopping bag with handles. "Will this do?"

"NO! You can't put it in that bag!" cried Nikki. "Please. Please." She held out both hands dramatically. "Handcuff me. Take me to jail. I'll give you the keys to the house, you can come back later and get the painting, but do not touch it until it's dry. I beg of you. You'll regret it all your lives long. You'll dream about it at night." The art professional more concerned for Art and Excellence than for her life. There was something comic in the scene—or would have been, had the two agents shown the slightest sense of humor. She said later what a good movie it would make, but at the time she saw nothing funny in it. Only frightening.

"We shouldn't even be in here," she continued. "Please. Come into the living room. I don't want so much as a speck of dust to land on the surface of the painting, not an infinitesimal hair, not a germ from expelled breaths. Please. We're stirring up the air."

"Let go my sleeve."

"You want to put it in the bag?" asked Brad again.

"Don't you dare touch that!" growled Nikki through gritted teeth, and she flailed at his bulldog face with both furious fists, then in one swift motion lunged for her nearby toolbox and snatched up a blade. She stood with her back to the hot table, weaving side to side, watching the two agents.

"Don't come any closer." She was Horatio at the Bridge. She was the mother wolf protecting her whelp.

"Are you threatening us?

"No, I'm just telling you to leave the room. Right now. The painting has to dry. It only takes twenty-four hours. Then, if you have a warrant, you can take it away. But I will not let you hurt it." She stood before the painting, knife raised. "If you have a warrant. Does Claire know about this? You have to have a warrant."

"Who's Claire? An accomplice?"

The tall agent removed his glasses. His eyes were slits, his mouth a downward cutting curve.

"What did you do to it?" The other agent jerked his head at the picture.

"I restored it. It's delicate, painstaking work. Conservation. It's what I do."

"Painted over it?"

"No, no. You can't repaint. That would destroy the work. You. . . you. . . restore it." How could she explain what a conservator does to preserve a torn canvas or old and crackled paint, how she brings back colors that have dulled or yellowed under layers of dirt and varnish? "You only add in paint where it's rubbed off, wherever there isn't any, where it's down to bare canvas. You never paint over the artist's paint. Conservation is an art form. All the materials we use are reversible, everything you do," she jabbered, still holding the two agents at bay. "And when you finish, you put a layer of isolating varnish between the artist's paint and whatever you've touched up, because the paint put on by the conservator has to be able to be removed without removing the original art, so you can't overlap on the original paint at all. The point is to *preserve* the original. I just finished it an hour ago. Look, I'll give you a cup of coffee. Let's just sit down for a day or two while the varnish dries, and you tell me what this is about."

But she knew what it was about. The National Gallery having

seen the work, had decided it was stolen and called Interpol.

"Are you putting us on? We don't even have five minutes. Put down that knife."

"Not until you back off. Go away."

"Are you threatening us?" His voice was hard, and for the first time a current of fear ran through her.

"No, no. I'm not threatening. I'm just protecting my painting." An unfortunate use of pronoun, since it wasn't legally hers.

"Talk to me," she said, desperately. "I'm not going anywhere."

"Actually, you're coming with us." Her eyes flew to his face in shock.

"Oh." This was the first she'd thought of that. She'd imagined they would confiscate the painting, but nothing more.

Quick as a snake, he hit her wrist a downward blow that sent searing pain along her arm. She dropped the knife. He twisted her arm behind her back, spinning her around, and before she could cry aloud, he'd cuffed both wrists behind her back with professional agility.

"Ow. That hurts."

"Get the picture," he ordered Brad.

"It's still wet." She pleaded, and tears welled up in her eyes. "The varnish will pick up dirt. Lint, grit, fingerprints. You're going to be in real trouble when you deliver this to your boss with the wet varnish smudged. They're not going to be happy about that at headquarters."

"Will you shut up?"

Puma paced at the door, helpless to intervene.

"At least call your boss. Let me talk to him," said Nikki, who would have reached bravely for the phone herself had her hands not been pinned behind her back by the hard white plastic bands that cut painfully into her wrists. "It has to be kept under climate-controlled conditions. It has to dry for a full night. If the varnish hasn't set,

I'll have to take off all the layers and do the entire job all over again. Don't you understand?"

He was not impressed.

She watched Brad pick up the painting. "No!" she cried. "Don't tip it. At least carry the painting flat. Here. Put it on a tray. There's a tray over there. Carry it on the tray. How long will we be gone?" She still didn't understand the seriousness of her position.

"Come on. In the car."

"What about my cat?"

"He'll be all right."

"He's old. He's sick."

But they hustled her out the front door before them. "We'll take care of him."

"My keys. Wait. I have to lock the door. My purse. I need to put on the security system." Puma watched in consternation as they picked up Nikki's purse, found the house keys, and keeping one hand always on Nikki's back, as if she might at any moment disappear, they reset the alarm and shut the door and locks. He jumped to the window to watch the two agents escort her, hands cuffed behind her back, through the gate of the white picket fence and out to their waiting car—to the amazement of the couple gardening next door, who peered over the privet hedge, mouths agape, at Nikki, wrists shackled behind her back and flanked by two men in their dark suits and ties, their eyes hidden by the terrifying black reflecting lenses, like mirrored eye-holes; the one with Nikki's purse dangling from his wrist, the other carrying before him a painting placed on a flat tray, like a butler bringing tea. Puma paced the window with increasing anxiety, back and forth, as the SUV swallowed Nikki and drove away.

33

Looking back, I wonder if Lorna had been there whether Nikki would have found herself in so much trouble. Lorna would have worked things out, but she was sleeping on a flight to Copenhagen and glad to be away. The trip would be interesting, fun.

On the other hand, if Nikki had simply admitted that the Stubbs belonged to Claire, she might not have been thrown in jail. That she refused to say anything without a lawyer present, that she resisted arrest, assaulted an officer, insisted on her rights to make a phone call and impeded in every possible way the appropriation of the painting—all worked against her, as David explained to Lorna after she returned home, because the police have wide latitude in the performance of their duties. The arrest took place on a Friday evening, after the courts had closed. The FBI chose to arraign her across the river in the District of Columbia rather than in the Arlington, Virginia, courts, and they had that right. Nikki wouldn't go before a judge in the Federal Court before Monday, the FBI agents decided, and they were perfectly within their rights, given her behavior, to take their time with the paperwork. They were mad at her. Moreover, it was possible Nikki was part of an international art ring.

They delivered her to the police and left her in the D.C. jail. She was put in a holding tank with two other women. And now she made things worse. The scene became a parody, laughable except for her dismay; but that's what the 2-leggeds do sometimes, create trouble—instead of going off to take a nap and think things out.

Nikki beat on the bars. "I want to make a call." The police

ignored her. "I have a right to a lawyer," she yelled. "It's my constitutional right to make a phone call." She'd watched enough TV to know how things worked, no matter that the Constitution was written long before the invention of the telephone.

"No point yelling," said one of the women, in a languid Southern drawl. Nikki turned and did a kind of double-take, because her cellmate was dressed in the skimpiest possible open lacey blouse over black leather shorts and black, knee-high, leather boots. The other woman had on a gossamer skirt that barely covered her buttocks, and on her feet were four-inch stiletto heels (she was in the act of taking them off, even though the floor was none too clean, in order to rub her sore feet); and then Nikki realized she hadn't quite taken stock of the place before, and it smelled of urine and stale bodies.

"They took my purse," she said. "My cell phone. My money. They took everything. It's all a mistake," she said. "I'm not supposed to be here."

"What are you in for?"

"I really don't know. I think they think I'm an art thief, and they put these plastic handcuffs on me, and they really hurt."

A burst of mocking laughter greeted her.

"Well, it's all a mistake." She rubbed her wrists.

"Honey, it's always a mistake. There's no point yelling. You ain' goin' nowhere till you see the judge, and this is nighttime now. They caught us the first night of a weekend, just for spite. We'll all be here till Monday afternoon for sure."

Nikki was shocked. "Oh no, I'll be out tonight. Or tomorrow morning at the very latest. They can't hold me." Then, irrelevantly: "I don't even have a toothbrush."

Later they even took away her clothes. They issued her an orange jumpsuit.

The police have their own subtle ways of handling difficult cases. Eventually a guard escorted her down a long and dingy corridor to a pay phone and stood back to let her make the call.

"But I don't have any money." She stared at him in surprise. He shrugged.

"I have money in my purse," she said, and by now she was on her best behavior. "May I please have my purse just for a few minutes, to get some money out? I'll pay you. I'll give you ten dollars," she said, not realizing it was tantamount to a bribe.

"No, I can't do that," he said. "Your possessions have all been catalogued. You'll get everything back when you're let out. If something's missing after the cataloguing, we're in trouble."

"But how can I make my call? I don't even have my credit card with me. My cell phone."

He shrugged again.

"Can I borrow fifty cents?"

When he escorted her back to the holding tank, she was humbled. Later, one of the girls loaned her fifty cents.

"You learns to hide your money," she said, taking it from the heel of her boot. "You owe me."

"I owe you," Nikki agreed with relief. "I'll pay you back. I promise."

The girls were the ones to describe procedure. She'd have a court-appointed lawyer.

"I won't need a lawyer." Nikki still couldn't believe her situation. "This is all a mistake. When I explain to the judge. . . "

Her one call to Lorna was picked up by the machine. I was the only one to hear it, and I didn't know what to make of it.

"Lorna, hi, oh Lord, I wish you were there. Listen, I'm in trouble. I'm allowed this one phone call. It's just a minor mix-up, I'm sure, but I'm in the D.C. jail, and I don't even have a comb. They took away my cell phone, my purse, everything. I don't know why they brought me here and not to the police station in Virginia. But right now I need you to do two things for me. First, is Puma. Could you please go over and feed him and make sure he's all right? They tell me I won't go before a judge before Monday morning, but I'm sure that can't be true. I'll probably be out tonight, but just in case—about Puma, I mean. You can't have people just walking into your house and taking things away. The second thing is to call David and—" But the tape clicked off.

She didn't have another fifty cents.

Lorna was in the air at the time, eating her plastic economy-class meal and thrilled to be flying to Copenhagen. She didn't get home for several days, and then her first act on entering the apartment was not to listen to messages on the machine (from her daughter, her mother, her sister, from Nikki and two friends, from a theater pleading for money, a tele-ad offering a last chance, from her bank reporting an overdraft), but to find me.

She went downstairs to knock on David's door.

I was so glad to see her that I turned away, tail high, pretending indifference.

But she trotted after me, caught me, picked me up. "Oh, David, I can't thank you enough. Was she much trouble? "

"No problem. I hope you don't mind that I brought her down here."

"Of course not. No. I asked you to."

"What?"

"In the note I pushed under your door."

The tension was still there, the unacknowledged longings, but they were glancing at each other, never meeting each other's eyes. Lorna accepted a glass of sparkling water and told about her trip and how she'd just heard that the President himself would speak at the Opening, which news had sent everyone swooping and diving like a flight of birds. David was deep in the midst of his trial.

She didn't stay long. As she left, she blushed bright red and bravely met his eyes.

"I'm sorry about the other night," she said. "It means a lot that I can call on you. Friends?"

"Friends." He grinned. They shook hands. Lorna carried me upstairs, and only then did she listen to her machine and learn that Nikki was in jail.

By then the police had turned Nikki's house upside down, looking for evidence and finding instead one aged and unhappy, wailing, lonely and incontinent cat. It was after midnight when Lorna tried to enter the house to feed and care for Puma, or even better, to bring him home with her. The street lamp illuminated the yellow police streamers that marked the property off-limits even to a woman in summer skirt and sandals. Lorna entered with her key, wondering if her action constituted breaking and entering. But the house was empty, echoing and forlorn. By then the cat had been taken by bureaucratic blundering to an animal shelter somewhere and put in a cage just like Nikki.

Meanwhile, the FBI had contacted Interpol at its Paris headquarters to say they had the missing Stubbs.

34

That Monday Nikki went before a judge in Federal court. She turned down the court-appointed lawyer, who approached her with a pad in one hand.

"I'm sure I won't need you." She flashed her luminous smile. "It's so simple. I can talk to the judge myself."

"It's always best to have a lawyer. Tell me quick what happened. They'll call your case in a few minutes." He was a pudgy man in mussed and wrinkled clothing. His oily hair fell over his collar. If he had made a better impression on her, if he'd used the adverb *quickly* instead of the adjective *quick*, if his hair hadn't looked dirty and his eyes too close together, would she have been so dismissive? Nikki had always been a snob.

"I can speak for myself. I'm not a dunce."

"Listen. You don't say anything. You just sit there and look pretty."

She had borrowed a comb, but in her orange jumpsuit she couldn't compete in respectability against the FBI agents in their crisp suits and white shirts and striped ties, and when the agents told their version of what happened, she shot to her feet.

"It wasn't like that at all! Your honor, they burst into my house. Like. . . like terrorists!"

Her lawyer cringed.

"Sit down, Miss Petrelli," said the judge.

"It was just a *little* paring knife!" She was taken aback at how the story sounded. "And yes, I hit him, but they were going to damage my painting."

"Did you assault them?"

"No. All I did was— You see, if—"

"Your Honor." The lawyer rose respectfully; then sternly to Nikki: "Sit down."

"No!" she cried. "I can explain. You weren't even there! I was." The two agents smiled at each other and shook their heads.

The more she explained, the worse things got. Her lawyer rolled his eyes. In the end she was charged with disorderly conduct, resisting arrest, and assault of a police officer. Interpol's interest in the painting and their emails presented to the judge did nothing to help her cause. Not to mention her use of the possessive pronoun when she called it "my painting."

Then came a flurry of activity at the Bench, which is a word for the Judge, and a lot of whispering between the lawyers and ruffling of papers and hurried glances at Nikki, and it took a while for her to understand that a computer search of her name had pulled up the fact that years before, when she was in college, she'd racked up $450 in Michigan traffic tickets, still unpaid. She was not eligible for release.

"What's a painting by this artist worth?" the judge inquired, as he examined the photos on the bench before him. "Aren't there Stubbs paintings at the Yale Museum of Art?"

Nikki answered with open ease, always ready to talk about art. "Yes, from the Mellon collection. They're worth millions. He was the most brilliant animal painter of the 18th century. Maybe of any century."

"Released on bond." The judge pounded his gavel, and Nikki shot her lawyer a triumphant smile. "One and a half million dollars."

She blinked.

"And I'm prohibiting you from traveling more than fifty miles from this courthouse." Her jaw dropped. Her case finished, the opposing lawyers collected papers, stuffed them in their briefcases, and, talking amiably, clapped each other on the back as they hurried off.

"Let me know if you want more help," said her lawyer as he bustled out.

"Come along." The policewoman led her away.

"One and a half million dollars," murmured Nikki, somewhat shaken. "What does that mean?"

"That means you raise one and a half million dollars, and you can get out of jail." To Nikki it sounded like a Monopoly game.

"One and a half million dollars!" She was hustled into the wire-screened green bus and driven back to jail.

Again, it was the girls who explained the system to her, because they'd all been arrested lots of times and even knew the guards by name. "You should have let the lawyer talk," said one indifferently. "That was your mistake."

The others agreed (for there were five girls now, and the cell was filling up with women whose crime mostly was to lead willing men astray). They told stories of friends without lawyers who'd been sent up the river for years, and of friends with lawyers who got sent up anyway.

"But I don't understand what I'm supposed to do." She was trembling now, for she understood in a way she never had before how frightened she was and how out of control.

"A bail bondsman puts up the money for you," explained one. "You raise ten percent, and when the case is closed he gets his money back, plus your ten percent."

"Ten percent! That's a hundred and fifty thousand dollars!" Nikki knew math. For the first time she began to recognize her dilemma. The girls looked at her with curiosity. A million dollars was a lot of money. Usually the bondsman put up a few hundred, or if someone was in serious trouble maybe a couple thousand.

Nikki was a big-time crook.

"What have you got as collateral?"

"I don't know. A car? My house?"

"Well, that's collateral."

"But they're mortgaged to the hilt. I probably can't raise more than fifty thousand dollars." Which made the girls hoot and cat-call, and clap their palms against each other, high-fiving, because she might as well have said she could pull down the moon on a string, it sounded like so much money. But Nikki sank into a corner with her back to the group and wept. She wondered what she'd done in a previous lifetime to bring such misery on herself. It was no joke being accused of stealing, when she knew herself innocent, and no one to believe her, and no one there to help.

Eventually she got through to Lorna, now back at the Smithsonian. "I've got to have some things—toothbrush, comb, make-up, hairbrush. And they don't even allow visitors. So, you can't even bring me anything. But maybe David can find a way to get them to me. He's a lawyer. You did call him, didn't you? Your answering machine went off just as I was asking you to call him."

"Yes, he knows. How much can you put up?"

"With my house and car, maybe fifty thousand dollars. All my inheritance is in trust. It's not that much, and anyway I can't touch principle."

"What about Claire? Won't she put up the money?"

"But you don't understand. You lose it *all*! You give the bondsman a hundred and fifty thousand dollars!"

"You have to ask her, Nikki. Shall I call her for you?"

"No, please! She has such strong opinions. I'm already in her bad graces. Let me get out of this, and then I'll tell her myself when it's all over, when it will make an amusing story. The only thing is, I think maybe I really do need a lawyer."

"You've got one," said Lorna. "David's in court for the next ten weeks. But he's found a lawyer for you. I have her name here. Where?

Where did I put it? Here. Natasha Parrish. She'll see you in the morning. You're wrong about Claire, though. Nikki, you *have* to tell her. It's *her* painting."

"Let me talk to the lawyer first. Let's see what she says."

"I'm still trying to find Puma," Lorna reported miserably. "No one knows where they put him."

And then Nikki's time was up. That night she wept silently into her own balled fist, wept for Jeremy's betrayal and for false accusations and jail and helplessness such as she had never known before.

35

The next morning was Tuesday. Nikki was moved to a pen in Jessup, Maryland, because the D.C. jail was getting overcrowded; but the paperwork didn't move as fast as the person— which is not unusual for the D.C. jail, they say, but it meant that no one could find her, including the lawyer. The good news was that in Jessup, Nikki could use the telephone and receive visitors, and once she got her purse back she could buy toiletries in the lockup store and also phone Lorna, which meant that we learnt what was happening to her more or less all the time, but mostly more, since she called several times a day and whenever she was upset or bored, until Lorna finally had to tell her not to interrupt her at work because she was unbelievably busy with the Opening, what with the President having decided to come, sending everyone into conniption fits—but to call at night after she got home; and that's how I know what happened to Nikki in prison.

The women's quarters opened onto a courtyard, where the prisoners, all in orange jumpsuits, lounged in bored groups. Nikki says she spotted the visitor in her pinstripe suit striding briskly across the glass bridge above the courtyard, and right away she knew. *That's Natasha*, she thought, and sure enough, a guard pointed his index finger at her and thumbed her toward the interview room.

She was shown into a long narrow room. Along one wall was a row of little booths, each provided with an intercom and a flat shelf for resting an elbow or a notepad on. Nikki settled into her booth and pondered the window between them that was so thick it had wire imbedded between its double panes, in case she tried to escape. A moment later the pinstriped lady appeared on the other side of the wired window and picked up her phone. She wore her grey hair pinned back in a bun. With her glasses, she looked intensely competent.

"Hi, Nikki. I'm Natasha Parrish. David Scott asked me to represent you. Is that all right?" She was all business and intellect, fumbling with papers from her briefcase.

"Thank you," said a chastened Nikki. "That's so nice of you."

"Oh, I'll be paid." She flashed a smile. "But David is a friend. I'd do anything for him. Here's my card." She held her calling card up to the wire-meshed window. "Can you read it?"

"Yes, thank you," Nikki repeated. "Can you get me out of here? This place is horrible. I know I sound like a spoiled brat, but I'm really shaken. And I don't know what they've done with the painting. It doesn't belong to me. And they've lost my cat."

"Don't worry. I'll get you out. Now, tell me what you know."

Nikki poured out the story of the painting, the gift to her godmother, the intrusion of the FBI, the charges of assault.

"They think I've stolen it. I've never stolen anything. Why do they even say it was stolen? It was *given* to Claire."

So then Natasha told her what she'd learnt from Interpol: that the picture belonged to the wife of a French politician, Etienne de Gramont. The wife had inherited it from her English grandmother, and it had hung in the library of their French country house until one day, when the wife and children were on vacation in Brittany, professional burglars had broken in, stripped the house, and piled their loot in the living room: jewels, rare coins, silverware, paintings, tapestries, a Fabergé egg inset with rubies and diamonds. At the last minute de Gramont had returned home unexpectedly and frightened the burglars off with his pistol. The only thing they managed to snatch was the small Stubbs painting—not even the most valuable thing in the house, because they could have grabbed the Fabergé egg or a handful of gems and coins instead of a framed picture, but some people just don't have financial smarts. The painting was never recovered.

"I don't understand," cried Nikki in shock. "I heard her lover gave the painting to Claire. Are you saying he manufactured a burglary and stole his own wife's painting? To give to Claire? Could that be true?"

"We don't know," said Natasha cautiously. "It's not at all clear that the family's story is true. Perhaps the wife sold the picture to pay off debts. Perhaps she orchestrated a burglary for the insurance money. Perhaps she never owned it. It's just her word against your godmother's. I'm sure the matter will go to court. The defendant—that's your godmother—will countersue. But right now the important thing is to get you out on bail." Then the lawyer gave Nikki a quick rundown on the illegal trafficking in art, which is on the scale of the trade in drugs or arms, and which gave Nikki a sense of her own impotence.

"In your case, Interpol is involved." Natasha's voice crackled in Nikki's ear. "Also the International Council of Museums, the International Institute for the Unification of Private Law, and UNESCO. They're emphasizing prevention now, since it's nearly impossible to recover stolen work." She looked up from her notes. "What do you know about art theft?" she asked.

"Nothing."

Then Natasha told her how in 1988, a Corot had been taken from the Louvre in Paris during peak hours, right under the noses of the guards, and in 2004 two masked gunmen pulled Edvard Munch's *The Scream* and a *Madonna* worth nineteen million dollars off the wall of his museum in Norway—again right in front of visitors. And Nikki said she thought *The Scream* had been recovered.

"Yes, but the *Madonna* has never been seen again."

In 2006 two Picassos were stolen from the Paris apartment of his daughter, and not long ago a Cezanne and a Van Gogh worth thirty-four million dollars were taken from the National Gallery of Modern Art in Rome."

Late that night all this was reported to Lorna over the phone.

"Lorna, the size of the thefts is staggering. A lot of the information is out of date. We don't even have recent figures, but listen to this: in one year alone—in 1997—2,476 art works were stolen in Germany; almost 3,000 in Russia; in the Czech Republic 2,244; in France 5,569. I wrote it all down. Imagine! Five *thousand* five *hundred* works of art stolen from one country in only one year! In one *year* in Italy *thirty thousand* art objects were stolen—that's the size of an average museum. And I'm not even talking about plunder and pillaging from Africa or Cambodia or pre-Columbian objects or the destruction and thefts that take place in wars."

"But who buys them?" Lorna asked. "A collector wouldn't want a famous painting. He can't sell it, he can't show it to anyone. Everyone knows it's stolen."

"Did you know the entire staff at Interpol consists of only *two people*? It's a scandal!" Nikki was getting worked up. "Moreover, there are always people willing to put something in storage for fifty or a hundred years. But usually the works aren't all that well-known. The collector says it came from his grandfather's estate before the time when provenance wasn't as strictly catalogued as today. Occasionally a stolen work turns up at a dealer's or at auction, but when it does, what's an honest professional to do? If he buys it, he's trafficking in stolen art, and also encouraging the theft; and in addition to its purchase price, he may end up with huge legal fees if the original owners try to recover their property, or else he has to pay transportation to send the art back to some foreign country, all properly packed and insured out of his own pocket," Nikki said. "I had no idea."

"But if it never turns up again in the open market, what use is the theft? The art has no value," Lorna insisted.

"Lorna! We're talking millions! Sometimes a painting is held for ransom. Sometimes it's recycled into arms or drugs. Anyway, all this is to say, I'm in the middle of a very big and very dangerous gangster business. Natasha says that's why I was tossed in the slammer—while they figure out who I am and what I know. Except I don't know anything."

"What happens now? Have you called Claire?"

"Natasha's going to call her. Also, she's making a motion to lower my bail. But she says I may be here for quite some time."

"Oh dear."

"I liked her," said Nikki. "When she left, she put one hand up against the glass to touch mine through the pane. I wish that you could come see me; I know it's a long way and you're busy now."

"I'll try."

"I'd like that. I really would. Oh, Lorna—poor Claire. What if it's true? How is she going to feel when she hears that her one true love, the man she considered her soul mate, stole her painting from his own wife to give to her? The painting represented their lost baby, their perfect love!"

"Maybe it's not true."

"Yes. Maybe it's not the same painting. Maybe he bought it legitimately for her. Maybe the wife is lying."

"Maybe," said Lorna, "the story isn't over yet."

36

When Natasha phoned Claire that Tuesday evening after meeting with Nikki, she found the older woman out to dinner. She left a message saying she'd call again in the morning, but before she reached her, Claire read the story in the papers. Claire never rose before a leisurely nine. Her maid, Charlotte, woke her with the paper neatly folded on her breakfast tray beside a single pink rose in a vase. Charlotte set down the tray, threw open the heavy curtains to let in the light of day and carefully placed the four-legged tray across Claire's knees. She poured coffee into Claire's dainty Limoges cup and left. Without even a kitten to share her milk with, Claire settled her glasses on her nose, opened the paper, and spotted in the lower left-hand corner of the front page the appalling story— *Art Conservator Arrested*, underscored by the lesser type font: *Snitched Stubbs Snatched in Suburban Studio.*

Later we heard every move she made and every thought she had while reading about her painting, and how she leapt out of bed to shower and dress, intending right then to accost the Director of the FBI, how she had snatched up her alligator purse and paused to glance at herself at the front hall mirror in her yellow summer suit when the doorbell rang, and there stood Natasha, just the person to accompany her on her self-appointed round.

Meanwhile, Nikki was calling Lorna who, already late for work, jiggled from foot to foot.

"Nicole, I can't talk now," she explained. "You'll have to call later."

But Nikki has her own sense of time. "Lorna, I've just seen Jerry. You have to help. When I heard I had a visitor— I thought it was you!

And I was so glad. I dashed to the visiting room to talk behind the wire-caged window, when who should appear but Jerry in blue jeans and a lavender shirt. I just stared. I wanted to hide, because there I was in my hideous orange jump-suit. His beard has grown back. He sat down in the cubicle, and he looked so handsome, I couldn't even look at him.

" I said, 'What are you doing here?' And he said, 'I came to see you. I was worried.' And then he asked if there was anything he could bring me, and I said sure, how about a hundred fifty thousand dollars. Which took him down a peg. But he said he had fifty thousand in bonds from his retirement that I could use, if that would help."

"Well, that was nice of him. Nikki, I—"

"I said I wouldn't dream of taking his retirement, but if he had nothing better to do maybe he could find Puma, because they've taken him somewhere, and who knows where he is? So he said he'd look for him."

"Nikki, I have to get to work."

"But that's not all," Nikki overrode her. "He said he thought I looked wonderful and I said, 'I do?' and he grinned and said, 'To me.'"

"Maybe he wants you back," said Lorna sitting down. It suddenly dawned on her that maybe getting to work wasn't so important after all.

"Well, I wasn't having any of his charm. I said, 'Oh, really?' and rolled my eyes. But he didn't notice. He looked around and said, 'You know, you ought to keep notes. You could write a great article after you get out, what it's like to be in a D.C. jail.'

"I said that really wasn't my highest priority. And then I remembered what was, and spat it out. 'Oh, by the way, congratulations.'

" 'For what?'

" 'On your change of life.' I couldn't bring myself, Lorna, to use the word *marriage*.

"He said, 'Oh yeah. Well,' and he shrugged and jerked his head in smug humility, but I could see he was really happy, and Lorna, it tore my heart out. I don't know how I had the courage to sit there on the other side of the filthy, dirty, smutty, grey window talking on the phone to him. I said, 'I hope you'll be very happy.'

"And he said, 'Thank you. So do I.'

"Oh, Nikki," murmured Lorna. "I'm so sorry." She lay back on the couch, realizing this was going to take a while. I leapt lightly up on the back of the sofa and lay down near the phone where I could purr in Nikki's ear to comfort her.

"I said, 'Well, you don't sound very excited,'" Nikki plowed on.

"'No, no,' he said. 'It's good. I mean, I was sick of—' And then— oh, Lorna, he waved his hand in this dismissive gesture. 'I was sick of everything anyway. Before. You know. I don't think I could have stood another minute.'

"I thought I'd faint. Had our relationship really been that bad?

"'So when is it?' I asked, and I do think it was brave of me to ask when I could hardly speak. My heart was in my throat. It took all my courage to keep from crying or to force myself to sit there in front of him in my orange jumpsuit.

"'It's already happened,' he said. 'Two days ago.'"

"He's already married?" cried Lorna.

"My stomach turned over. 'Two days ago,' I murmured. 'So fast.'

"And he said, 'Well, it was pretty sudden. Spur of the moment, you might say.' And he gave this awkward, embarrassed laugh.

"Oh, Nikki, I'm so sorry," Lorna said.

"I pulled myself together. You'd have been proud of me. 'I hope you'll be very happy,' I said again, and he said, 'I fully intend to be. This is one of the best things I've ever done.'

"Lorna, I just stared at him. I couldn't believe he'd say such an awful thing to me. Then he said, 'I left that afternoon,' and I said, 'Left what?' and he said, 'The paper,' and I said, 'You left the paper!'"

"He left the paper?" Lorna repeated in surprise.

"Yes, and my mind just log-jammed. I couldn't think of anything. Was Penelope an heiress? He has so much money now he doesn't even *need* to work? If so, he could have offered more than fifty thousand, I thought, and then I wondered if he'd married her for her money. Do you know? Does Penelope have money? But then I thought, no, that wasn't like him. Money's not that important to Jerry. He's married her for love. So I said, 'Whatever for?' and he said, 'What do you mean, Whatever for?' and I said, 'Leave the paper,' and he said, 'I wasn't going to stay there after that.'

"And then there was this silence while I searched his face through the filthy, wire-meshed glass. Because it's really dirty.

"I said 'I'm missing something. What are we talking about?' And he said, 'I'm talking about leaving the paper. What are you talking about?' and I said, 'I'm talking about you marrying Penelope.' And he said, 'I'm not marrying Penelope.'

" And I said, 'You're not?' and he said, 'I wouldn't dream of marrying Penelope.'

"Lorna, I couldn't believe it! He said, he wouldn't dream of marrying her!

"He said, 'I know in the beginning I was a real fool. It was as if she'd bewitched me.'

"I said I'd heard he was engaged, and that the Big Story was finally coming out. A five-part serial. And he gave this brittle laugh. He said, 'I know. She's marrying Joe Hirsch. The managing editor. He gave the story to her.'"

"You mean, he's not marrying Penelope?" Lorna's spirits lifted again. This might turn into a nice day after all.

"I was outraged!" cried Nikki into our ears. "I said, 'He gave her *your* story?' And he said, 'I know. It's absurd, isn't it? I can't believe how stupid I was, taken in completely.' And I said, 'So you're not getting married?' And he said, 'I'm not getting married to *her,* thank heavens. And neither am I employed. In fact, I'm *un*employed.'

"I said, 'Wow,' and he said, 'Which is why I came to see you.'

"'Because you want a story about what it's like behind bars?' I was offended. 'I don't want to do that,' I said.

"He looked puzzled. 'Well, it's not important. It was just an idea. No, I came to see if there's anything you need.' Then he said the paper wrote a story about me and it's in this morning's paper. He said he was sorry he hadn't been the one to write it because he could have done it better. But that's how he heard I was here. And then we talked about how all the newspapers are folding, no one reads them anymore and they're losing advertising, and there's no place for an investigative reporter because it costs too much to pay someone to do the digging and research."

"Nikki, I have to go," said Lorna, impatient that the story was going on too long.

"Just listen. I'll be brief. Well, I said I have a lawyer who's getting me out. I said David Scott had found her for me, and that soon I'd be out, and then Jerry asked if I'd have dinner with him when I'm out. But I said I didn't know, and after a moment I asked, 'So, what are your plans? What are you thinking about now?'

"Nikki—"

"Well, he grinned and stretched one arm up above his head because he's holding the phone to his ear in the other hand, and he said, 'Well, I'm not ready for a commitment, if that's what you mean.'

"I was so mad. 'I wasn't thinking about a commitment,' I said. 'There's nothing between you and me. We've split up. We're finished. I wasn't asking for a commitment, for god's sake. I was talking about your *life*.' He just stared at me, Lorna, surprised, I suppose, that I'd stand up to him. 'What are you going to do with the rest of your life? Why do you think I'd ask you for a commitment? I'm going,' I said, and I hung up and stalked away without looking back and went off to join the other women who are waiting for their court cases or parole or for their time to be up. And then I phoned you, because I knew you'd want to hear it, and I have to talk to someone. I never want to see him again. Never! David wouldn't do that, would he? I can't imagine David treating anyone like that. David is kind, sensitive, considerate. David, he'd never say a thing like that!"

A long silence followed while Lorna held her breath. The day had turned dark again. Then we heard Nikki's voice on the phone, through her tears:

"Lorna, I'm miserable. I'm so unhappy. When are you coming to visit?" she said. "Can't you come see me?"

By the time Lorna left for work, her emotions leaping about like my toy bug-on-a-wire, I was ready for my morning nap. Humans can be exhausting.

37

Taking a nap is not easy with the phone ringing. It's enough to make you wish the 2-leggeds would stop inventing things and just lie down. I think half the city must have felt obliged to phone that morning to tell Lorna's machine how they'd read or heard the juicy details about Nicole Petrelli, each recording the same thrills and chills of surprise. Imagine! A professional art theft ring right in Arlington, Virginia! And by Nikki Petrelli! How daring! How clever! What better cover than through an art conservator, who could paint over a known picture, disguise it as some ugly, ordinary daub, and mail it out of the country where the over-paint could be easily removed to reveal the shining work of art. Some people were amazed that Nikki could have been so bold, and others admired her imagination, and still others called to express their indignation at her lack of ethics, for which they held Lorna accountable as well, for wasn't she Nikki's best friend?

I wished I could go downstairs and sleep in Goliath's apartment to escape the fuss. But later that evening when Lorna came home (the downstairs outer door closing with its usual hiss and resounding thud), and after she had straggled up the stairs and opened our apartment door, David called up the stairwell to invite her downstairs to meet Natasha, the lawyer. I trotted along behind.

Natasha was older than I expected, with grey hair and startling blue eyes. Lorna's eyes fixed on her gold wedding ring before she caught herself. So then everyone had drinks (except Lorna, who chose tonic water), while Natasha told the story of how Claire had stormed the offices of the FBI. Lorna had always marveled at Nikki's sense of entitlement, but listening to Natasha, she laughed that now she understood where she got it from: through her godmother, learnt at the knees of Genghis Kahn.

Claire's driver had delivered the two women to the massive, sandstone fortress on Pennsylvania Avenue that holds the FBI. It is a brooding, hulking, secretive presence that Claire dismisses as simply vulgar. "Mussolini-architecture," she pronounced with a toss of her patrician head. Once inside, Claire had bullied her way past ranks of guards and secretaries and into the spacious, blue-carpeted, high-windowed, corner office of the Director of the FBI, moving with a force that impressed Natasha.

"I've come to see you about my painting," she informed the man, seating herself with regal self-possession. The director is not famous like J. Edgar Vacuum Cleaner. Natasha said he was short and bald with sharp eyes glittering under shaggy brows. But no one underrates his intelligence or lightning intuition. On the walls hung his honorary plaques and autographed photos of himself with Presidents.

"That painting," said Claire, "which you have taken away—stolen, I might say—was given to me forty years ago by a friend, a very *dear* friend, if you understand my meaning."

"And who might that have been?" The director steepled his fingers under his chin, armored against her attack.

"No one you know," she answered haughtily. "A former minister of France, Etienne de Gramont." She sat ramrod straight on the edge of her chair, staring him down.

"I gave it to my goddaughter to restore. She's a brilliant conservator. It is absolutely *not* stolen. The whole thing is a vast mistake, and you will find yourself with a lawsuit if she is not out of jail and this whole business straightened out immediately."

Natasha cringed.

The director buzzed a button on his desk and spoke into the intercom. A few moments later, his secretary entered with a manila envelope. He pushed a photo across his desk to Claire.

"Is this the painting?"

"Yes. But it looks awful! What have you done? The paint's all smeared! Look at it! You've destroyed it!"

"Do you have any provenance? Any proof it's yours?"

"Of course I have no proof. It was a gift. What do you get when you receive a gift? A bill of sale?" Her scorn was a fleshing knife. The director curbed his irritation.

"Sometimes you do. When the painting is important. Why did you give it to Nikki Petrelli instead of to the National Gallery of Art to restore?" He stared at the photo. "Or to one of the conservators in New York or London, a painting of such value?"

"Nikki's my goddaughter. It's her profession. She's restored dozens of paintings—a Gilbert Stewart, among others, *all* the paintings at the Treasury, the Kreeger Museum, the Walters in Baltimore, collections at Yale, and I don't know what-all. Then too," her eyes grew milky with memories, "I didn't want a lot of people looking at it—"

"Aha!"

"It was private. For my eyes alone. Now it's public. But it is *not* stolen, of that I can assure you."

In the car Natasha had told Claire the story of the bungled burglary, and the wife's claim that she owned the painting. Claire was indignant. ("A lie! An out-and-out lie!") Now here was the director repeating the same outlandish tale.

"I will not give it up. I will sue the woman in court!" Claire announced. But her face went white. She remembered now, hearing the story for the second time—that, yes, there had been a break-in. She remembered laughing over it with Etienne during one of their meetings, the *cinq-à-sept.* . . imagining the burglars' shock at his unexpected appearance, his daring as he snatched the pistol from the drawing room desk, their hurried flight through the open French windows; but the burglary—she'd forgotten all about it. What was it but a single instant, one laughing conversation over a glass of wine at the sidewalk café, one moment of concern for him amongst the years and years of their affection? Months later he had given her the painting for her birthday.

Listening to the director, she felt woozy. Was it possible Etienne had orchestrated the whole affair? Yet even as she declared his innocence, she remembered his politician's charm, the ruthless ambition that she had found so fascinating. The attempted burglary had happened long ago, and to think that all these years his wife and daughter had been looking for the painting. . . . After he died, Claire had remarried (twice, actually, the last when she was only a youthful sixty-one), but Etienne had been her one passionate, true love.

She twisted her arthritic fingers, then glanced up, head high. "I want to see the theft report. I want to read it with my own eyes. If the Paris family can prove its claim, I will return the painting. Yes." Her mouth twitched. "It meant a great deal to me. . . . But if they can prove it. . . . I have one request, however. I'd like Nikki to finish the conservation work. I'd like her to recoup her reputation. I understand your *stupid* FBI agents grabbed the painting before the varnish had dried, and now *look* at what you've done! It's a *disgrace*! You should be ashamed of yourselves, destroying a work of art like that. It needs to be *totally* restored all over again from step one. I want it back. I want Nikki out of jail and doing the work. I want the Government to pay for it. I will *not* have it go to France in the condition you have put it in. I have that much pride." She rose to her commanding feet.

"We'll see," said the director. "First we have to establish that this is not an art theft ring, and that that woman is not in the business of laundering looted art."

"Oh, for god's sweet sake!"

Claire left the FBI building chastened. She leaned on Natasha's arm for support. She felt old. They went to a nearby restaurant for lunch.

"What will happen to Nikki?"

"That depends on you," said Natasha softly. "I'm filing motions to have her bail reduced. Otherwise we need to raise $150,000 to get her out immediately."

"That's a lot of money to give away to the bondsmen," said Claire, who knew, like all rich people, how to hold onto hers. "Do you think you can get it reduced?"

"I think so. Depends on the judge. But meanwhile, you understand she stays in jail."

"Well, let me know what happens," said Claire cruelly, business being business. "I don't suppose we could put up her Trust as a pledge and avoid the bondsmen entirely?"

So they talked about money, which is always a consuming subject for the 2-leggeds.

"She still faces charges as an accessory to stolen art."

"Oh, that's such nonsense!" cried Claire. "How could she have known?"

"She knew something. She was researching the painting. That's why she took it to the National Gallery."

"Only to help me," Claire snapped. "And to me? What happens to me?"

"We'll see what the family wants to do. It helps that you are willing to return the painting to them, if they can prove ownership. Do you want me to fly to Paris and talk to them?"

She heaved a sigh. "Perhaps you'd better. Do you speak French?"

"I'm fairly fluent."

"Well, that's a help. But on reflection, no, I'll talk to my Paris lawyers. Let them talk to hers. You'll have to be involved, but no point in paying plane fares and hotel fees when a computer and a phone will serve. I'll want proof of the burglary. I'll want proof of their ownership of the painting and proof it was taken in that insane burglary. But if it truly belongs to her. . . Oh, the *malin*." She shook her head.

Natasha raised one eyebrow. "Crafty?" she translated.

"Such a cunning trick," Claire whispered. "To steal his wife's picture and give it to me."

Her mouth and chin were working. Natasha reached across the white tablecloth and covered Claire's hand with hers.

38

M eanwhile, Lorna was wild with anxiety.
She whipped around the apartment like a hummingbird, poking the buttons on the phone, the computer, the stove, the texting pad on her cell. She couldn't sit still. When her worry wasn't about work, or David, or Nikki, or me, it was about her daughter, or her mother in rehab, and finally about Puma, whom no one could find.

"Oh, Alba, do you suppose he's dead?" she asked me. "I wouldn't put it past the agents to hide the fact they killed him—accidentally or on purpose. That's their business, secrecy. Tell me where to look, Alba. Can't you find Puma?"

==Me? I mewed.

The fact was I'd already tried. I couldn't find him with my instinctive mind. But while I was saying that, Lorna's mind was already churning other questions. Like, why the FBI had questioned her? Two agents had come to the door. They had interrogated her like a terrorist. Had she given the wrong answers? They thought she was part of the art ring, while she knew only what any cultivated person knew about art, only what she'd seen in museums or at a gallery, only what Nikki had taught her. Weren't you innocent until proven guilty? Wasn't that the American way? Why did the agents make her feel guilty? The way they'd glared at her, she'd almost been ready to confess. Except she didn't know her crime.

She talked to David about it—hurried, whispered conversations by phone, or an occasional chance encounter in the hall. For she didn't trust herself to be long in his presence. Despite her best intentions, after hearing his voice on the phone or fleeing his touch (though his efforts at contact happened infrequently now), she was filled with conflicted feelings, confusion, impotence—she who had always been lighthearted, free. He was almost young enough to be her son. Her sleep brought restless dreams.

A cat can only do so much. I curled close to her at night, my head beside hers on the pillow, but I couldn't comfort her.

One evening we were both surprised by the squawk of the downstairs intercom. It was Jeremy.

"I have something for you," he shouted into the intercom. "Can I come up?"

Lorna put down her book. She didn't want to see him. Did they have anything to say?

==Let him in, I said, and twined myself around her legs. You have to let him in.

I think she blamed him for her difficulties. If he had married Nikki as planned, then she and David. . . but she left the treasonous thought unfinished, for it wasn't true: he was too young for her; she was too old for him.

"What is it? It's late."

"I have something for you," he repeated.

She rang him in, resentment boiling in every move. She allowed him time to climb the stairs, then opened the apartment door, her face expressionless.

In his arms lay Puma.

"Oh, my god!" She broke into her glorious watery laugh. "Oh, Jerry!"

"I found him," he said with an engaging grin. "It's my present for Nikki."

"Oh, wow!" She gathered the old cat in her arms. "Where did you find him?" But she did not stand back from the door to allow him in. I mewed and stood on my hind legs against his knees in greeting. I was so excited to see Puma again!

"In Clifton, Virginia. At a shelter. God knows how he got there. I paid his bills. I started to bring him home with me when I realized I don't even have a litter box—well, I could get one, I suppose, but I thought he'd be happier with you and Alba. Is it all right to bring him here?"

"Of course. We're all on one floor here. He won't have stairs to climb. I can't wait to tell Nikki."

"May I come in?"

She gave him a searching look. Under his new growth of beard she couldn't see the scars that Nikki had mentioned, but he saw her look, and one hand crept in embarrassment to his cheek. "I know. I've been really sick. I'm better now. I had to cut my beard. It'll never look the same. Is it coming in straggly? I was sorry to hear about your mother. Is she all right?"

"She's better, thank you."

She stood back reluctantly, motioning Jeremy inside, then set Puma tenderly on the floor, careful to place him on all four feet. Puma stepped into the living room, sniffing daintily and asking courteous permission to explore. He'd never been in our apartment before, and he was shy. I trotted over to him. We touched noses, in joy.

==Look around. The litter box is in the bathroom in case you want to know. But you can't use it. It's mine. I could hardly contain my delight. I thought I'd never see him again, and here he was exploring my own place.

"This is nice," said Jeremy, casting an appreciative eye at the flowered chintz, the vase of delphiniums, roses, and daisies on the coffee table.

"I gather you left the paper." She stood arms crossed, offering nothing.

"News travels fast."

"I heard Penelope's getting married, too," she said, but her eyes were hard. If he was unhappy, he deserved it. Make your bed, you lie in it; lie down with dogs, get fleas. Jeremy wandered the living room, seemingly impervious to her disdain. It was all she could do to be kind to the man who'd hurt her friend, even if he had found Nikki's cat.

"Yes, she's getting married. Did you hear? Charlie flew down from New York, hoping to dissuade her."

"Oh, how like him! Poor Charlie."

"He's well out of it," said Jeremy cruelly. "She's a bitch. She told him she wanted him to know she's going to be very, very happy. 'We will be very, very happy. I will always love you, Charles. At one time I thought we'd get together. We were perfect together, weren't we, both of us being English, but now it's time for me to think of higher aspirations.'"

"She said that?" Lorna was shocked.

"She likes to talk about her conquests. 'I don't think of myself as particularly pretty,' she told me one day, 'but somehow men find me beautiful.' The thing is," he added with a shrug, "when a woman tells this to a man, he suddenly notices that she *is*. Beautiful, I mean. Other men find her beautiful, and suddenly you do too. At one time she told me that she and Charlie had been an item. And then they had an argument, she didn't say what about, and they split up. She'd planned to marry him because he was rich and they had the same background and cultural references. 'You know Mountbatten was a great uncle. He's almost royalty, she told me.' Oh, Penelope was a number."

Jeremy stood at the window now, examining the view. I trotted over and rubbed against his leg.

"Hello, Alba." He leaned down and picked me up, and I nuzzled his ear. "Well, here's one person who will welcome me," he said, glancing at Lorna with a teasing smile. "I'm *persona non grata* with everyone, and I deserve it. I've really messed up." He gave a deprecating shrug.

"I'd offer you something, but it's late and I'm busy."

Goodness! And I'd been praising her for being sweet. I hopped to the floor and ran over to her, then back to Jeremy, trotting between the two, while Puma moved arthritically across the floor to sniff his shoe. I looked at Lorna and mewed.

==Mer?

"What's going on with you two?" she asked in surprise.

"They're trying to tell you something."

"What is it, Alba?" She reached for me, but I pulled away and ran back to Jeremy, and since she was so dense I swung up into his arms. Puma brushed against his legs. She stared in disbelief. "Anyone would think you all know what you're doing."

Which really is annoying, when after all, she lives with us.

"May I sit down?" he asked politely.

She tossed her head. "It looks as if the cats have invited you." A moment later he was seated in a chair by the cold fireplace with me in his lap.

"So, what's the request?" She stood over him, arms crossed. She wasn't going to give him the time of day. This was the man who'd hurt Nikki, and whose actions had impacted her.

"I want to return Puma myself. Don't tell Nikki he's been found. I want to be the one to bring the news."

"Don't you think it's a little late for that?"

"It may be," he answered calmly. "But I can try."

She sank into the chair opposite him. "You want Nikki back? Now that you can't have Penelope?"

He grew grave at that. "I don't know if she'll have me. First things first. All I know is that at the moment I want to be the one to give Puma back to her. After she gets out. It will give us a chance to talk. Right now she wants nothing to do with me. Meanwhile, I'm asking you to hold Puma for me, but only until Nikki's released."

I mewed again and stood on his lap to sniff his lips. "Alba agrees," he smiled. "All right? A deal?"

"I don't know," said Lorna. "She's worried about him. Shouldn't she know that he's all right?"

"When we get the news she's been released, I'll come pick him up. You say nothing, that's all I ask. Say you haven't found him."

"But I have."

"No, you haven't. I found him. It won't be a lie."

"Oh, you are devious."

"I don't think she'll see me otherwise. She won't answer my phone calls."

Lorna stared at the floor, pensive, then looked up. "Tell you what. Leave Puma here. I'll take care of him. I'll tell her that you found him and I'll urge her to see you. She owes you that much. I'll push it. Is that a compromise? I don't want to lie. Also, she's got enough on her mind without thinking her cat has died."

"I shouldn't have brought him to you."

"Yes, you should have." Then, roughly: "You know she's in love with another man."

He grimaced. "Is she? Well, she has that right." His hands rested flat on his knees. "I really fucked up. Who is it?"

Lorna turned away. "I don't feel comfortable saying more than that. Just to warn you, though. She may not care to see you."

He went still, a wash of red spilling over his face. "I know that." After a pause, he looked up. "You don't have to be so possessive."

"What do you mean?"

"You're a righteous woman, Lorna. You can stop controlling. Just let things rise and fall away in their own time. We all have far less control than we think. Just let go. Let go and let God."

"I don't know what you mean."

"Nikki's a grown woman. She's quite capable of making decisions. Why do you feel you have to take care of her? As if she's made of porcelain. If she gets in trouble, well, that's how people learn, isn't it? By making mistakes. That's what mistakes are for, our teaching tools."

"I don't protect her," Lorna defended herself.

"You're protecting her from me right now." His candor took her breath away. "Look, I'm not happy with my behavior," he continued, running his hand through his hair. "All I want is a chance."

"Is it right to keep the good news from her?"

"I don't know." He rose. "I leave it to you. You do what you think best. I'm glad I found Puma. I'm glad I could do that much for her. All I want to do is talk to her."

She nodded. "Okay."

"Good-bye, Puma." He leaned down to scratch the sweet spot just above his tail. "Stay well, Alba." He rubbed my ears. "Don't think too badly of me, Lorna. I think badly enough of myself as it is."

She closed the door behind him. He'd given her a lot to think about. Was she really righteous? Controlling? All she wanted was to hurt nothing, no one, that's all, not ever, not by thoughts or acts or words.

39

And then one day Nikki was sitting at our kitchen table with Puma in her lap. She'd lost weight. Her hands shook when she lifted her mug to her lips. She seemed to tremble inside, too, with a kind of fragility we hadn't seen before.

Outside a cold rain clattered against the window panes. "We're so lucky, Lorna," she said, looking round the cozy kitchen with enormous brown eyes. "You have no idea what it feels like to be locked up. Not to hear rain on the roof," she whispered. A peal of thunder rocked the room and made the electric lights flicker.

Lorna rose to check that the bedroom windows were closed.

"Or children." Even her voice held a tremor. "The voices of children."

"Well, you're out now. Don't think about it."

"No privacy. Never to be quiet or alone. It's so crowded. And people coming in and out all day. The TV blaring. The noise."

"The worst is the way they screen the visitors," Lorna said, adding to the list.

"No, but they have to do that. They'd be taking prisoners up and down to the interview room all the time. They do that anyway, but then, too, they don't want cases influenced by people agreeing to alibis. It's just bureaucracy."

"You don't sound angry about it."

"No. I've had the stuffing kicked out of me." She smiled a little sadly. "I've also had a lot of time to think. I've not lived my life very well so far, and I'm hoping I can do better in future."

"In what way?"

"To begin with, I want to be more loving."

"Nikki! You're very—"

"My Nonna was wrong," Nikki overrode her. "Taking vengeance, holding onto resentment, wallowing in self-pity—it doesn't make you happy. I've spent so long being sorry for myself. And selfish. And ungrateful. You tried to tell me that, but I couldn't hear you, could I? I was angry, comparing myself to others, especially to Penelope. In jail I began to think about forgiveness. Christ said it: 'Pray for those who hurt you.' He was very clear. I'm not quoting it, but something like, 'If you come to the altar to pray and remember your brother, who offended you, go reconcile with him first and then come back and pray.' Something like that. I think it's in *Matthew*. But what it means is that we can't be happy as long as we're full of malice and hate and resentment. Then we're just filled with hate. We feel awful. We're supposed to forgive each other all the time. And you don't just do it once. You have to forgive the person over and over again. And then again, because no sooner do you think you've finished, than you find yourself annoyed once more. I cast a spell on Jerry and Penelope, and I desperately hope that spells don't work," she added with an uneasy laugh, "except there's some superstitious part of me that believes that thoughts have power. Maybe what you think is what you get, in which case curses work. Except it's against the one who lays it. That's the irony. What goes around comes around. Maybe that's what got me arrested, the scorpion's tail swinging around to sting me in the back." She glanced at Lorna. "Well, I mean, I've had a lot of time to think in jail, and I'm not proud of myself."

"Well, I am."

"No, I was childish and romantic. I don't know how I could have been so blind. In prison— Oh, Lorna, there's so much suffering in this world."

They were silent. "I told you, I had a talk with Jerry," said Lorna after a moment. "He wants to see you. I think you should."

"I don't want to see Jerry," said Nikki. "I'm glad he found Puma. It was good of him to make the effort, but—"

"But what?"

"Listen, Lorna. They say there are only two emotions, fear and love. But it's not true. There's anger, violence, hatred, guilt, loneliness, shame. How can I see him after what I did? I wasn't thinking about *him*. I wanted to punish him. For what? For being truthful with me? I'm so self-centered that I think I should experience no pain? No, I have nothing to say to Jerry, not after the way I've behaved."

She drew a breath and gave her luminous smile: "Tell me about David. I'm so sorry he's in Court today. He'll be working till midnight, I suppose. I can't wait to see him. How's his trial going?"

"He's fine."

Lorna took the time to pour herself another cup of tea. "Do you want more?" Nikki shook her head, and Lorna settled again at the kitchen table.

"Nikki, I have a question."

"Shoot."

"Are you—? What do you feel for David?"

"Oh, I love David," Nikki exclaimed. Her eyes went soft. "I really love him."

"Are you in love with him?"

Nikki glanced up in surprise. "Oh, Lorna, you still dislike him, don't you? I know you didn't like him when you first met. But I was hoping you'd come to appreciate him. David is—why, he's wonderful. I'm not ever again going to use exaggerated words like 'in love with.' I did that with Jerry, didn't I? And look where it got me. I'm going to be more like you, slow and steady in my affections. And cautious. Reserved. I've been too impetuous in the past, and now I'm going to be more careful. But I'll say this. If there were one man left on earth, it should be someone like David. I want David in my life all my whole life long. I never want a time when I don't know him. That's how special he is to me."

I notice that the humans hear what they expect to hear. They even hear what they don't want to.

"Oh," said Lorna. "All right then."

"No, not all right. What's the matter? Is he hurt?" she asked, voice rising in concern. "What's wrong? Has something happened to David? Tell me!"

"No, no. He's fine. Everything's fine." Which patently wasn't true, but Lorna changed the subject, talking with courageous animation, first of her mother, then Claire, then of her concern for her daughter, Nancy. Puma struggled from Nikki's lap and moved to the living room to stretch out on the sofa. Which brought Lorna back to Jeremy.

But Nikki skidded off the subject instantly.

"You know it was David who found Natasha Parrish for me. He's been such a help. Did I tell you that she's defending me *pro bono*. Though maybe Claire is paying her. Do you suppose I'll have to pay her back? Natasha's in Paris now, talking with the French family. The wife—Mme. de Gramont—she's an old, old lady now, in a nursing home, losing her memory, apparently. Who knows how it will all come out?" Nikki was hard pressed to keep her mind on one subject at a time.

Lorna's eyes drifted to the wet leaves outside, the steady, pouring rain, with its dark, chill hint of autumn in the air.

Later, when Puma and I were alone together, he started to lick my face. He caught my jaw in his teeth and shook his head from side to side, affectionately, but also with a hint of scolding me.

==What? I asked when he released me. What is it?

==You have to do something about the 2-leggeds, he said. They need your help. You'll have to get Goliath to help you.

==Help me do what?

He stared at me with yellow eyes, the pupils narrowed into thin slits of reproof, and then he lectured me on a cat's responsibilities to her human, and how I should know these things at my age without his telling me, and then he stung me by comparing me to Penelope. I cringed. That's what David had accused me of, as well. I stared into the middle distance, hurt, ashamed. Puma was quiet then, allowing me time to recover before he came over and nosed my cheek, purring to comfort me,

He ended by telling me that it was up to us to unravel the ball of our 2-legged's yarn, since they were incapable of doing it for themselves; and then he laid out his plan.

==I have to do that? I sank back on my haunches. It was a big job.

==This may be the last thing I can do for them, he said. I can come up with the strategy. But you're the ones who have to execute the plan, and you should act soon. You don't have as much time as you think.

I went away, thinking over what he'd said, and thinking, too (after his lecture), how much I admired the 2-leggeds, how goodhearted they are, how courageous, how rich in complexity, and how I hadn't given them credit for trying so hard to do what is kind, even when it devolved to their disadvantage. Nikki. . . Lorna. . . I saw that Puma was correct. It was up to us to sort things out! We cats! We lovely, brilliant cats. We animals, I thought, extending my gratitude to the whole animal kingdom. To dogs! (For I felt generous just then and included the dogs who love their humans too, although I've never been fond of that species; and yet they have their place, and I'd seen men who would have died for their dogs, as the dogs would have done for their 2-leggeds, and then I felt how noble we animals are as well! How generous! How forgiving we are! How hard we try—as hard as humans probably.)

My heart swelled with love and happiness. I could have exploded with humility because Lorna belonged to me. And I to her.

After dinner, Lorna drove Nikki and Puma back to Virginia. When she returned, she lay down fully clothed on the bed. I jumped up on the bed to nose her ear, and she hugged me to her. I could sense how sad she felt. She was certain now that Nikki was in love with David, and with all that had happened to Nikki—jilted, jailed, her reputation ruined—Lorna could only hope that David loved her in return. She remembered the promise made months earlier, never to betray or hurt her friend.

Later that night, while brushing her teeth, she spoke to the face in the mirror: "You feel you can't live without him," she told her image. "But you will. Abraham Lincoln said it: A person is only as happy as she decides to be. Life goes on. You don't need another person to make you happy."

So, she put in ten and twelve hour days at work, including weekends. That's all she did. She went to work; she came home. Sometimes when she heard David's footsteps in the downstairs hall (for often our apartment door was left open for reasons she would not admit even to herself), she balled her fists so tight that her fingernails made half-moon indentations on her palms. They had come to a kind of neutral balance—just friends; and both were careful of the boundaries, for David had been infected with the virus of her restraint, her silence having answered his suit. There was a certain nobility to this denial, the way they avoided each other in the hallway—with only their energy bodies lunging out to merge. But such meetings were rare, for David also worked late every night. That's what the 2-leggeds do in Washington, D.C. They work. Goliath and I sunned amiably. I told him of the plan.

40

One Friday night, well after ten o'clock, we heard his heavy footsteps in the hallway as he put his bike away. Lorna stood at our apartment door to listen to his tired tread. Even his footsteps were dear to her.

==Invite him up.

I dashed down the stairs to demonstrate. I can't say that she heard, but impulsively she leaned over the banisters.

"David? Is that you? Want to come up for a nightcap?"

He looked up with surprise. "Now?" His voice was tired. "Isn't it too late?"

Would he come? She found she was holding her breath. I rubbed against his legs.

"All right, but just for a few minutes. I'm not much company." He was already climbing the steps, carrying me in his arms.

==Bring Goliath, I purred to him.

"Bring Goliath," Lorna called, having actually listened for once. He slipped me down onto the stairs, went back three steps and opened his apartment door.

"Coming, Goliath? Want to visit your friend?" His voice sounded strained.

Lorna turned her back to the banisters and hid her face in both horrified hands. What was she doing? she asked herself; then remembered it was just a friendly invitation to a neighbor. All she wanted was to hear his voice. Be near him. Nothing had to *happen*. That's how people in love delude themselves.

The next moment I saw her toss her chin, stiffen her resolve. Good friends. Neighbors. That's what they were.

Goliath galloped up the stairs ahead of David and slipped in the door. We were both on the alert.

He did not try to kiss or hug her, not when she hung back, elbows clasped defensively.

Goliath prowled the apartment, nervous and anxious.

"What would you like?" she asked. "I can offer herbal tea. Coffee. Wine. A cognac, if you'd like." So much did she ache for him that her voice came out harsh and hoarse.

"A glass of wine, that would be nice." He rubbed his eyes between thumb and forefinger.

"Tell me about the trial." She poured herself a Perrier, and wine for him, then sank into an armchair nearby. I lay across her lap, purring her into serenity.

David, meantime, drink in hand, rose to pace the carpet. His eyes roamed the walls, the darkness outside the windows, the flowers and books on the coffee table; but he was so abstracted, so consumed by his own words that he saw only the courtroom. There were twenty lawyers in all. The government prosecution consisted of three lawyers, including himself, plus the whistleblower responder. They sat at one long table, with the opposing ten or twelve defense lawyers at another. The jury, off to one side, seemed almost incidental to the proceedings.

The trial concerned bidding for the construction of fifty miles of sewer lines in Egypt funded by USAID. The prosecution had called in witnesses from around the world: construction experts, economists, accountants, bankers, and the USAID officer who had opened the bids and registered with horror the outrageous tenders, three times higher than anticipated.

Lorna's eyes never left David's face. "How much is a normal profit?"

"Good question. I must remember to tell the jury that. We lawyers get so involved," he laughed, "that we forget the simple things the jury needs to know. A normal profit is fifteen to twenty-five percent. These companies were making fifty to sixty percent. You wouldn't mind, if it weren't for fraud. Collusion and bid-rigging."

Goliath prowled impatiently, but I pretended to nap. We had time. David returned to his chair, sipped his wine, flushed and happy.

"And after the defense has finished?"

"Then come summations," said David.

"Do you give a summation? What will you say?" Her eyes were shining with admiration.

"You really want to know?" He threw back his head, smiling. Suddenly he felt ten feet tall, and why not? Wasn't she beaming all her light at him?

"I do."

"I'm still working on it. Tell me what you think." He rose to his feet and began an impassioned speech about the meaning of the words *collusion* and *conspiracy*. Another word for it is *stealing*. This company stole from the US Government. They stole from the American citizens, snatching the tax dollars we trustingly pay. They stole the good name of the United States of America—our reputation. They stole from the Egyptians. Members of the jury—they stole from you. Eighteen miles of sewer pipes were cut from the project due to inflated bids."

He went on eloquently, passionately, about the importance of water, and how the jury could declare the defendants guilty or innocent; but no matter their decision, he hoped that every time they flushed a toilet or washed a cup, they would remember the mothers in Cairo living along those eighteen sewerless miles who have no running water in their kitchens because of this bid-rigging, who must trudge to an outdoor pump to carry water back inside in buckets; of the little children who play in streets with open sewage running in the gutters—maybe to pick up their soccer ball and wipe the dirt off with their sleeves, maybe to contract typhus or typhoid or cholera, diseases wiped out in America long ago. Why? Because a few greedy businessmen colluded to deprive them of pipes.

When he finished, Lorna shot to her feet, applauding. They were both exalted, inspired.

== Goliath! I whispered. Ready?

"What do you think?" David asked humbly. "Is that all right?"

"Oh, yes!"

They stood only two feet apart. They did not touch, but their eyes locked.

"I have to leave," he murmured.

"Yes," she said.

But he made no move to go. For a long moment he stood, his glass in one hand, held captive by her eyes. He shook himself. He set down the wineglass and reached for his cat. "Come on, Goliath."

==Now! I shouted, and Goliath shot out of his grasp, into the bedroom and under the bed.

"Come here, cat." David followed him, trailed by Lorna.

Goliath slid deeper under the bed, and as David fell awkwardly to his knees reaching for him, he slithered out the other side, then jumped up onto the gorgeous Indian bedspread, teasingly out of reach. David dove across the bed to catch him as Goliath dropped back to the floor, and now Lorna dodged in to catch him in both hands.

"Come here!"

I tangled between her feet at the same time that Goliath wound himself around her leg.

"Oh," she lost her balance. "Oh!"

She fell on the bed, sprawling on top of David. The next moment his arms were around her, and his mouth was on hers, their legs and arms entwined, and neither one was thinking of David leaving or of Goliath or of betraying Nikki, but only of their mutual desire as they rolled on the huge, wide, comfortable bed, pulling at each other's clothes.

Goliath and I trotted delicately into the living room to clean ourselves with nervous modesty. Afterwards I lay down and curled my little paws under my chest, and then I smiled my ate-a-canary smile.

The next morning Lorna brought David coffee in bed and a cup of tea for herself, and they lay together, her head on his shoulder and talked with silly smiles on their faces. They kissed, they touched each other's skin, exploring, and sometimes one or the other would give a little moan and at other times a sharp intake of breath. Sometimes there would be only heavy breathing on the rocking bed.

In addition, they chattered like birds. They hardly stopped talking. They talked about Nikki, who had to be told. At one point Lorna rolled over on her back.

"Why do you love me? I'd like to know."

"Why does anyone love one person and not another? It's a mystery." He was grinning, teasing her, then seeing her expression, he grew grave. "You really want to know? You don't know? First you have many qualities I like, and I could name them for an eternity. In addition, we're friends. I like being with you. In your company I feel I'm whole. It's hard to explain. I'm at peace. That's nice. But maybe another reason is, I see in you a vulnerable young girl. I don't imagine many people see this. They see a competent, adventurous, exciting woman, generous, giving, open, confident. You take the dare to live. Also you take care of everyone. . . except yourself." He stroked her cheek. "But underneath all those protective layers is a scared little girl. So, I feel protective of you also. I want to take care of you."

A shiver ran through her. When had anyone wanted to take care of her? Wordless, she nuzzled his neck and pressed closer into the hook of David's arm. He was wrong, of course, but that's because the 2-leggeds can't see that it all comes down to the way their vibrations harmonize.

Later still, David lifted himself on one elbow to look down at her.

"What did you mean when you said this would be inappropriate? Wasn't that your word?"

"I'm so much older than you. When I'm seventy, you'll be a handsome, vital, virile fifty-something."

"It only means we'll live together for a long time, because women live longer than men, so you'll have me longer than you would if I were older than you. You'll be magnificent at seventy!

> *There was a young woman named Lorna*
> *Who worried her years marked her Fate*
> *Along came a lover*
> *Who told her 'Move over,'*
> *And thus she learnt age not to hate.*"

Lorna laughed. "Did you just make that up?"

"Hush. Move over... there, like that. Very good. You know, I'm serious. Why is it that it's considered perfectly all right for a young woman to fall in love with an older man, twenty, thirty years older, and wrong for a man to love a woman older than he?"

"Cultural conditioning?"

"I can step outside the apartment today and get run over by a truck. Or have a heart attack. We can't worry about the future, Lorna. One day at a time."

After a while, she came up for air. "You really don't care?"

"I've loved you from the first moment I saw you. But just to ease your heart, remember Colette, the writer?" he asked, nibbling her ear. "She was in her sixties (how old are you?) when she met her third husband, Maurice Goudeket, and he was seventeen years younger. How many did I say? Seven-*teen*! He was mad about her. He pursued her. 'And I did so,' he wrote, 'with the firm determination of proving to her that fidelity was not an empty word.' "

"And?"

"They married and lived happily together for thirty more years."

"Goodness."

"Or, here's a better example: Fanny Vandegrift Osbourne. You ever hear of her? She was a grandniece of Daniel Boone, born in the 1840s, I believe. She married a man ten years older, who went off to make his fortune in the silver mines of Nevada. They had a daughter, Isobel. No, no, don't interrupt, this is a wonderful story. (Put your hand here, like that. Hmm. Yes. Like that.) Later, Fanny followed him. She took the sea route from New York, got off in Panama, discovered the canal wasn't built yet, and walked, *walked, mind you,* across the Isthmus, carrying her baby in her arms. Somehow she not only managed to get to Nevada, but found her husband—"

"Is this about an age difference? He's ten years older than she."

"Shh. Don't be impatient. She soon decided she hated Nevada, not to mention her philandering husband. So she went off to Paris with her three children (they had three by then) to study painting. It's now 1875. There she fell in love with a Scotsman eleven years younger than she. He was in his twenties and she in her late thirties. He wanted to be a writer. She decided the relationship couldn't work, returned to her husband at the Nevada mine (you can feel her distress, going back and forth, sort of indecisive, like you, trying to work out the right thing to do). Well, for three years the young Scotsman, poor as a church mouse, saved his money to follow her. That's how much he wanted her. He finally caught up with her in San Francisco, where she divorced her husband and married him. By then she had a son, too, by the first husband. One day her son asked his stepfather to write him a story without a girl in it, and he wrote one. It's called *Treasure Island*."

"No! He was Robert Louis Stevenson?!"

"He was."

"Is this true?"

"Cross my heart. Later they moved to Samoa, where he died. But that was not the end of Fanny's effect on men. She must have been an extraordinary woman! For the last five years of her life, when she was in her seventies (didn't you tell me you'd be doddering in your seventies?), she had an adoring, live-in companion who was. . . get this, *forty years younger* than she."

"No!"

"Ned Field. Later, he became a well-known playwright and film script writer. He described her as 'the only woman in the world worth dying for.'"

"She must have been very special."

"So are you."

He kissed her. For a long time neither one spoke except through lips and hands and skin.

"Now what does it take to get invited as your boyfriend to your black-tie bash to see the President open the Hall of Physics?"

"Oh, so that's what you're after?" They set off teasing and laughing with each other again. Most of their time together seemed to be spent laughing.

41

The next day, Sunday, was a holiday. Lorna drove to Virginia to talk to Nikki. She was not happy about it. It was not what she wanted to do.

"Happiness is a form of courage." She spoke between gritted teeth as she snatched up her keys. It was the second time she'd used the line, though I don't for the life of me see why happiness is all that difficult. If you're fed and kept warm and have people to clean your litter box and do what you want them to and leave you alone when you want, then anyone can be happy, I say.

I heard about her visit when she whispered the story in David's ear as they lay in bed together that night. Lorna knows how to stretch out a tale, describing every detail. The two friends sat on the wooden deck overlooking Nikki's autumn asters and watching the bees that hummed in the shrubbery in determined, late September, foraging before the cold of winter. Two shining green hummingbirds attacked each other at the feeder, swooping and swinging in the air, driving each other away from the treasured sugar-water and returning only to defend their claims again or buzz the two friends sitting below with their coffee and iced tea.

Lorna took a breath. "Nikki, I—" but Nikki interrupted gaily. "Guess who called me!"

"Jeremy?"

"Charlie Pace!"

"Charlie called you?" Lorna was shocked.

"I hope you're not hurt. Are you? He asked me to fly to London with him when this is all over. He'd pay my way."

"Charlie?"

"Well, you mustn't say it in *quite* that astonished tone of voice." Nikki laughed. "It's not all that preposterous, is it? Except that originally he was interested in you. But you didn't give him any encouragement, and now that he's truly lost Penelope he's casting around for a woman to hang on his arm. He wants me to go with him to the opera."

Lorna leaned forward, laughing. "Do you like opera? But you should go! It would be fun. He's rich, sophisticated. Imagine, London. Theater. Royalty. Isn't he related to royalty?" Who knows the complexities of motives in the human heart? Was this her reprieve?

"I probably should."

"But?" Lorna prompted during Nikki's fidgety, lengthening pause.

"Well, first I'm not allowed to travel more than fifty miles from the Federal Court, remember?"

"He said when this was over."

"And second, I'm not in love with him."

"I thought you weren't going to use those words again," Lorna teased.

"You're right. I won't."

"Does that matter? Sometimes caring comes later, doesn't it?" said Lorna, ever hopeful. "Maybe you'll learn to love him. You don't know him all that well." She'd already forgotten (or forgiven) his conservative politics, his hunting trophy animals.

"We'll talk no more about it," Nikki said with finality, and smiled at her friend. "It was flattering to be asked. I told him no. That I have other things on my mind just now."

"Well, he never asked me!" cried Lorna, laughing. "And after all I did to keep him company at that dreadful party! First he ruins the party for me and then he never even asks me to New York, much less to London."

"Life is unfair. Your turn. What were you going to tell me?"

"Yes. I do have something to talk to you about." Lorna grew quiet. "But it's not easy."

"You look serious. Is your mother all right?"

"Yes, she's fine. It's not about her."

"Nancy?"

"She's ok. They're in therapy together. Everything's working out."

"Well?"

"Nikki, I'm so sorry—I didn't want—I would never, never hurt you. You know that, don't you? Promise you forgive me." Lorna was never good at breaking news. Nikki grew grave.

"What is it?"

"Oh, I wish I didn't have to tell you this! I'm so, so sorry." She squirmed with shame.

"Spit it out." Nikki narrowed her eyes.

"I'm afraid you'll never speak to me again."

"What is it?"

"It's about David. It's about David and me."

"What about him." Nikki's voice was cold.

"I mean, we've—I've—how can I—?" she stammered. Nikki waited, searching her face.

"Oh, Nikki, I know he means the world to you. But we've—we're—I've—I mean. . . " She took a big breath. "We'vefalleninlove." The words came out in a gulp.

Nikki stared at her in disbelief.

"Say something," said Lorna miserably.

"You've fallen in love with David?"

"Yes."

"He's in love with you?"

"Yes."

"You're in love with each other?"

Lorna covered her face with both hands. "Yes."

"And he's told you so? He said it to your face?"

"Yes."

"You've made love to him."

Lorna nodded, staring at the ground.

Nikki was silent for a long heartbeat. She stared out at the garden, head turned, as if she'd lost her train of thought, and Lorna, in panic, could hardly breathe. She searched the edge of Nikki's ear and cheek, for her expression.

"It's sudden." Lorna rushed to fill the silence. "It's happened suddenly."

What was Nikki thinking?

"I know it's inappropriate. You've told me so. Right to my face. He's younger than me. He's young enough to be my son. I know, I know. Look at my neck, my underarms! I know. And god knows what I'll tell my daughter, it's so humiliating, an old woman thinking—what will people think, but—but he loves me and—"

Nikki turned back with a wide, sweet smile. "I'm so surprised. You've caught me off guard."

"I am so sorry!"

"Sorry! Don't be silly. Why would you be sorry?"

"Because you're in love with him, and I'm betraying you," cried Lorna, rising to her feet, and now she burst into sobs. She threw herself on her knees, and the tears poured down her cheeks. "I wouldn't hurt you for the world. Oh, Nikki!"

"No, no. I think it's wonderful."

"But if I didn't tell you, it would be a greater betrayal. I know you care for him. Oh, Nikki, forgive me."

"Of course I forgive you."

"You do? The way you looked just now. . . "

"I was thinking about me," said Nikki, "and everything that's happened this summer." Her face lit up with her luminous smile. "I was thinking how happy I am for you. And for David. It's beautiful."

"It is?"

"Aren't you happy? And all this time I thought you didn't like him."

"You're not mad?"

"Why should I be mad?"

"Because you're in love with—"

"Lorna, listen. I think the world of David. I adore him. He's like my brother. But no, I'm not *in love* with him. And what are you doing, worrying about what other people think of you? What people think of you is none of your business. Isn't that what you've always told me? What do you care what people think of you, anyway? Nancy will be overjoyed. And if she's not—screw her!"

"Ohmygod, and all these weeks. . . ." They were both on their feet now, hugging and kissing each other, and holding hands, and throwing their arms around each other, and laughing as they kissed and kissed. "There were moments I hated you," Lorna confessed. "For being so beautiful. And young. I hated myself. I was so jealous."

So then the story poured out about how she and David had fallen in love, and how out of loyalty and love for Nikki, Lorna had resisted him, her secret burning into her.

"Oh you poor girl! Oh, Lorna!"

"I told him I couldn't betray you. Remember my promise? I've been so concerned—"

"But that was—"

"David said the betrayal would be if I did *not* tell you, even if you were hurt and never spoke to me again, that good friends always tell the truth. I was trying to protect you."

Nikki was laughing with open pleasure. "Where is David now? Let's all go out to lunch. And celebrate."

Was it real, this generosity of Nikki? Was she hurt and had decided not to show it?

"I only wish that you could be in love," said Lorna.

"Someday maybe," said Nikki with a sad, gentle smile. "But right now I have everything anyone could want. I have my freedom— from jail, I mean, and you have no idea how sweet that is until you've been locked up. I have my house. And my cat. I have two hummingbirds fighting at my feeder on this lovely day, and my garden is filled with bees dipping into the nectar of the flowers. I have my conservation work and enough money if I'm careful to get by. And I have my best friend," she added, gripping Lorna's hand, "who is in love with a man I adore. What more could anyone want?"

"So you see, all your worries were for naught." David laughed softly, holding her captive against the pillows. "They usually are."

I didn't listen any longer, but pattered to the living room window. Something was happening with Puma, and all my senses reached out to touch him.

42

It was Puma's cry that woke Nikki. You'll say that a cat is a night-hunter, always prowling in the middle of the night, but Puma couldn't move. His mouth opened and closed. He panted, sides heaving—as I'd seen in that earlier attack. He meowed, a strangled cry.

Instantly Nikki was awake, reaching for him on the bed. She was terrified.

"Don't die. I'm here. You need a doctor." She slung herself out of bed, began to throw on clothes.

Puma lay on his side, struggling for breath against each wave of pain that surged across and through him.

"Hang on, darling. I'm taking you to the hospital now." Gathering him gently in her arms, she started downstairs. She never gave a thought to whether she was breaking parole, whether she could reach the all-night animal hospital in time, whether rushing was the smartest thing to do. Then she did something so uncharacteristic I could only marvel.

She stopped. She crumpled to the floor in the hallway and settled Puma on her lap. She sat with her back to the door, petting him, crooning and singing to him, as she rocked him in her arms.

"Oh, Puma, forgive me," she whispered. "The only hospital open at this hour is miles away. It will take an hour to get there. I don't think there's time. Do you want me to?" And surely she heard him, for she did not doubt that what he wanted was to lie there in her arms. "I love you so much. Oh, my beautiful cat, my best friend." She prayed over him. She called on angels to be with him, to heal him, to make him well, to love and keep him, and the tears rolled down her cheeks and dripped onto his tawny fur, dry and clotted with age.

218

He sank into her embrace; and I, watching from far away, my four feet tucked under me, my tail coiled, and my chin pressed onto my chest—I purred and purred, purring his soul on its way. I saw him tip his face to hers, look into her eyes before closing his own, already withdrawing. He drew in another breath, let it out, and he was gone.

Nikki did not recognize it for a time. She continued to rock and sing to him, comforting him, and in doing so her light field grew enormous, gleaming so bright I think she could have read a book in that dark hallway by the light of her being, the light of love.

After a time she felt how stiff he'd gone. Weeping, she laid him on a thick white towel on the couch and pulled the end of the towel over him like a blanket, and then she sat on the floor beside him, one hand resting on his cold body in blessing and in sorrow. She wandered the house restlessly. She made a cup of tea, and forgot to drink it. She picked up his toy stuffed weasel and placed it near his head. Finally she dragged herself upstairs and threw herself fully clothed onto the bed.

And I? I sat in the window, listening.

In the east, a silver rim of light opened up the edge of darkness. Dawn was creeping on little cat feet to pounce joyfully on the coming day.

From the bedroom I heard the sound of Lorna breathing lightly in her sleep, David beside her, breathing more heavily. From outside came the *coo-cooing* of a dove, as first light tinted the dark to pearl. A clock ticked. I stretched my senses out. I'd seen his last breath followed by nothing. Eighteen years of breathing in and out had stopped. Like that.

You are padding unseen through the house. Your empty body lies on the couch. Nikki has slung herself across the bed, drowned by grief and sleep. Now you leap silently up on the bed and curl beside her, touching her. Cleaning yourself. You lie, invisible, beside her sleeping form. She doesn't even know you're come to say good-bye. And now you hop down and stalk the familiar rooms. Young again. You can jump great distances, play with your toy ball, twist round in the air. Lithe and lean as an athlete, you leap to the windowsill. You can catch a mouse again, scare a bird. Daybreak has come, the light increasing steadily. In a moment the world will explode into pink and golden streamers that spread like water before the fireball of sun, and you are sitting on the bed, watching Nikki in the soft dawn light, loving Nikki before you go. She doesn't know you're there.

Suddenly I am hit by light. I can't see. When my eyes focus again, you have gone.

43

Nikki buried Puma in her garden. The house felt empty. She wandered through the desolate rooms, grief-stricken. Late that afternoon, when the doorbell rang, she moved dully to open it.

"Oh. Jerry."

"May I come in? I just heard about Puma. Lorna called me. I'm so sorry, Nikki."

She stood back to let him pass.

"Is there anything I can do?"

"No. I buried him this morning. In the garden."

"I wish you'd called me. I could have helped. May I see?" He was so courteous, so gentle in his regard for her that she felt as if he were a different man than the aggressive newsman of before.

She led him around to the back of the house and pointed to the freshly dug earth.

"He was a wonderful cat," said Jeremy with feeling. "I'm going to miss him."

She looked at him sharply.

"I think when I found him, he knew."

"Knew what?"

"Knew everything. Knew he was dying. Knew I'd come to take him back to you."

"A little romantic?" she asked, but tears filled her eyes, for she, too, felt Puma knew everything.

"There should be more of a ceremony. Would you mind if I—?"

"What?"

"I don't know. We should plant a flower. Say a prayer. Sprinkle some offering on the grave. Give him ceremony—unless you already did. I want to remember him."

I'm not sure what they did, the two of them, but I think they stood a long time at the grave, telling stories, remembering him, and then they sat on the wooden deck overlooking the grave. By now evening was falling, the grass glazed golden in the light of a fading day. They talked of trifles. At one point, Jeremy went to the kitchen and returned with a tray of hot tea and cakes and butter and a pot of jam, and they sat on the deck and waved the bees away from the sweets. Somehow the cakes and jam made Nikki feel better, or perhaps it was having unexpected company.

"Nikki, I have a suggestion." He waited respectfully for her nod. "I've been a real bastard. I want you to know I know it. I apologize. But listen— No, don't interrupt. I've been thinking. I've rented a place on Mt. Desert Island."

"In Maine?"

"My lease begins next week. I'd like you to come up with me. We can fly up and rent a car at the Bar Harbor airport."

"Jerry." She looked away. "I don't think we should take a trip together."

"Just for a week, a few days. What are you going to do here?"

"Well, for one thing," she said with a weak smile, "not jump bail."

"Oh. I forgot. You're not allowed to leave the area, are you?"

"I can't go beyond a radius of fifty miles from the D.C. Courthouse. And did you forget that we're not a couple? Whatever did you have in mind?" She heard the tears of irritation in her voice.

"I just wanted to give you a good time," he said simply. "I've wanted to ask you for a long time. But especially now, with Puma's death. You might like to get away. The house is on the water. It's beautiful up there now. Well, actually," he took her hand. "I'll tell you what

I imagined. And I'll describe it to you, everything that would have happened. Since now it won't."

She took back her hand. "It's all right, Jerry. Maybe there's no point. I was very hurt when you. . . left. But I'm pretty well over it now. You don't need to worry about me."

"I'm not worried about you. You're a strong woman. You're a survivor. I'm sorry you can't come to Maine, and I accept the reasons why—your two reasons. First, that you're on probation and can't leave the area, and second, that you don't want to be with me. I understand that. I deserve it. But I'll tell you what I'd imagined. It was a kind of dream. Will you listen?"

He waited for her nod. "I thought we'd fly up in the same plane, but you wouldn't have had to sit beside me," he said. "God knows, I'm perfectly well aware we're not a couple now. I messed that up. The rental car is already reserved. We'd drive over to the house. It's a very pretty Cape Cod, with weathered shingles and a big hedge for privacy. You'd have your own room. It's got flowered wallpaper and dormer windows that overlook the water. From your bedroom you can hear the waves grinding and growling against the stones of the beach. They wash up on the stones and roll them over each other and suck back out again; and the air is fresh and salty, and every now and again you hear the bellow of a boat's horn as it passes by, and when the wind is right you can hear the solitary mournful bonging of the buoy far out in the bay."

"It sounds lovely," Nikki said. "You've been there before?"

"To Maine. Not to this house, but I've seen pictures of it. I think we would eat lobster and walk in the woods and maybe one day we'd charter a sailboat and go out sailing. It's the best sailing on the East Coast. The water's too cold to swim in, but you'd spend your days, Nikki, lying on a window seat reading. It's covered in rich brown corduroy. Or maybe you'd do some painting."

"And you?"

He smiled and shook his head. "Oh, I'd have my projects. I'd cook us grilled salmon on the barbecue. I'd read and think about how to make a living with the newspapers going bust.

"And then I think on the third morning, really early, maybe four thirty, when it was still dark, you'd hear a knock on your bedroom door. It would be me with a cup of coffee. 'Get up,' I'd say. And you'd dive deep under the covers and complain, because you don't like to get up early, but I'd make you put on your socks and sneakers and warm pants and a heavy sweater and maybe a jacket and hat, and we'd go out to the car."

"Whatever for?"

"That's just what you'd ask me, 'Whatever for?'" He smiled. "And I'd tell you I had a surprise for you. We'd drive up Cadillac Mountain in the dark, up the winding road, until we couldn't go any farther, and then we'd get out, you and me, shivering in the chilly air. I'd have brought a flashlight, but the moon and stars would be up and we could probably see in the dark, and we'd start to climb."

"I wouldn't," she laughed. "You wouldn't get me out there in the middle of the night."

"It's not the middle of the night," he said as if it were happening right in front of their eyes. "It's about five-thirty now. And you'd do it just out of curiosity. You'd want the surprise."

"Walking in the dark up the mountain?"

"Yes, past the pine trees, onto the open rocks above the trees. We have flashlights. And there's no one on the mountain except us. And then we get to the top with a light wind, perhaps, playing in your hair; and the pale light beginning to crawl over the stars in a soft grey, misty way. I think you're shivering with cold. I have a thermos of coffee and I pour you a cup, and you drink it, still complaining and nagging about why you were there, but also intrigued, because by now you're fully awake, and also you see how beautiful it is up there on the bare rocks, with the dark sea spread out below us. You can hear the beat of the breakers down below, and you can just begin to pick out the islands as the light creeps across the sky."

"You make it sound—"

"Shh." He held up one finger to her lips. "I tell you to hush, because in a moment you're going to see something so spectacular that you'll remember it all your life."

His eyes were shining, and his hands formed pictures as if to mold the rocky mountain on which they stood, the trees below, the chain of dark islands that extended like long forested fingers into the black sea, and the sky now shooting ribbons of color across the blue.

"And then—here it comes! Here it comes!" He shot to his feet on the deck. "The sun! It rises like a great golden globe of hope, shining in our eyes and declaring a whole new beautiful golden day! All across America it's still black night, and here we are watching the sun rise at one of the most eastern points of the United States, standing together. You turn to me and say, 'That's splendid,' and I drop to my knees, like this—"

He fell to the floor before her. "And I say, 'No, you're splendid, and I want to live with you all my life. I want to eat breakfast with you every day for the rest of my life, and I want to be buried beside you when I die. Will you marry me, Nikki?'"

He opened his hand to display to her astonishment the ring flashing on his palm.

"Will you?"

And that's how the story should have ended, except that Nikki turned him down.

44

S he gave a wail of dismay and burst into tears.

No, she couldn't marry him because his proposal wasn't real.

"What do you mean it's not real?" he said, climbing off his knees. He was left helpless. Her mouth worked. Her hands hung helplessly at her sides.

"I know I'm a jerk," he said. "I've behaved badly. The weeks before my birthday, do you remember? When you made me that special dinner? I was planning to ask you to marry me, only I got all bent out of shape by Penelope. But now I'm myself again. Why can't we get married? You don't trust me?"

"Because I laid a curse on you," she said, turning away, "and you're only proposing because of that and not of your own free will. I cast a spell to make you hate Penelope and want to be with me. I was so angry. I— I can't lie to you. I know it was wrong, but I was hurt, and—"

Jeremy took her hand in his and turned the palm over and laid his ring on her palm and closed her fingers around it while he held her fist in his.

"When did you do it?"

They had to get the calendar to figure out the date.

His face lit up. "No problem then. Because I'd already broken off with her. I broke up with her on that Thursday before. Whatever was left to break."

"You did?"

"She came over to my house with her guitar and her flirting, and all of a sudden I couldn't imagine being in her presence for more than two hours at a time. All I could think of, as she stood on one foot and presented herself, singing for me, was you. I had this daydream that in a minute you'd ring the doorbell and save me. You always tell me when I'm acting like a dope. You don't have all that pretentiousness. After that evening Penelope and I remained business colleagues, nothing more. Working on the story together."

"Oh."

"And even that was a farce." He paused. "Listen, Nikki. I know I'm not much of a catch. I have no job and no prospects. But sometime I will. I want children with you. I can't imagine being with any other woman. I'll try to be a good husband. And anyway I count on you to keep me in line."

"On one condition," said Nikki.

"What?"

"You have to get back down on your knees," she ordered.

Without a word, he dropped in front of her.

"Is that it?"

"No, there's more."

"What?"

"Okay, my condition is this. As soon as my probation is over and I'm allowed to leave the area, you take me to Cadillac Mountain on Mt. Desert Island, Maine, to see the sun bound up out of the ocean like that, and you have to propose all over again a second time, as the sun leaps over the horizon while it's still dark everywhere else in America, to announce the new day."

That's what she started to say, though actually she didn't finish the last sentence because he was kissing her, and it didn't matter if he proposed again or not.

And that's how it all ended. It took a lot of effort on our part. I don't see how the 2-leggeds would have managed without us cats.

Jeremy and Nikki bought a small newspaper in Virginia, down

in the country, where Nikki has plenty of conservation work now that she's become internationally renowned. She was pregnant within the year, and now they have two children and live in messy, noisy improvidence with two cats and a leaping, barking dog, and seemingly endless trains of friends, who move in and out for play-dates or dinners or child-swaps or to work on Nikki's numerous charities and Jeremy's politics. Nikki also has two black goats, because she wants to see them rippling like hair down a hillside. She makes goat cheese and sells it in the local co-op. Who would think she'd milk a goat? She's never had occasion to wear her designer dress again.

Claire counter-sued the French family for possession of the horse painting, and the court case threatened to go on for so long (like *Jaundice and Jaundice*, complained Natasha) that the lawyers finally mediated an agreement, whereby the Stubbs divided its time between Washington D.C. and Paris, with the understanding that on the death of Mme. Gramont, the wife, the painting would belong exclusively to Claire. She left it in her will to Nikki.

Charlie married an English girl and continues to work in London, Paris, Tokyo, and New York, though he bought a house in Surrey, England, and has two children who are in Pony Club. Penelope divorced Joe Hirsch, the managing editor of the newspaper after only four months and took up with the publisher of a New York paper, and then switched to the owner of a TV station, who promised to give her her own show, but hasn't yet.

Lorna took David to meet Mrs. Pullet, who was so delighted by their news that she pushed out of her stiff armchair, and with her withered arms raised high above her head, performed a tiny, slow-step circle-dance of joy. Then she sat down breathlessly, laughing and hooting and petting Lorna's hands, and then holding David's in her loving fingers, she blessed them and told the two of them to be careful of each other, and always give the other person the benefit of the doubt, and never to go to bed angry but to make up any disagreement before they got in bed so that resentment didn't have a chance to fester overnight, and to remember that we all make mistakes, and then she told Lorna she was utterly thrilled (as if her voice and body didn't show it), because Lorna was always doing for others and it was time she had a good man who would care for and do for her, reminding her how beautiful she was.

Lorna's daughter, Nancy, phoned to say she and Philip were back together, and by the way, she was pregnant. Lorna would be a grandma. Lorna refused to marry David (a fact that relieved Nancy). She said she was too independent to navigate another marriage. But they've redesigned their two condos into one large unit with an inner curving stairwell that joins the bedrooms up and down, and so they have moved in together anyway. She's still sure he'll fall one day for a younger woman, and she hopes she'll be big enough to support his need. Meanwhile she wears his ring on her left hand, third finger.

Goliath and I have the run, therefore, of all the floors and rooms and hallways of both apartments, including the garden, where we hunt chipmunks, birds, mice, bugs, lizards, and anything else we can find.

One day Lorna noticed my stomach was dragging, that I slept more. I tried to tell her it wasn't serious, but she took me to the vet. He laughed. A few weeks later I had six kittens, three black ones and two black-and-whites, and one adorable, smoky female with gold ears and white twinkle-toes. I think they are almost prettier than me. We've given first choice to Nikki and Jeremy.

Goliath has long been neutered, but he doesn't know that matters. He's proud as punch. And so am I. That's all I have to say for now. Except the reminder that everything always works out for the best, if you let a cat take charge.

Love,

Alba

ACKNOWLEDGEMENTS

The work of so many people goes into creating a book, any book, even a bit of froth and fun, as this one is intended to be, that it's impossible to acknowledge everyone. So many friends read the novel at various stages, and when I despaired, picked me up, brushed me off, and encouraged me to forge on, that I can recognize only a few: Ellen Perkins, Eileen Davis (cat lover and cat savior), Elizabeth Waugaman (herself a brilliant writer), two assistants, Lori Stuardi and Melanie Kwon Duch, Joelle Delbourgo (my former editor at Ballantine, who gave me the title), Balinda Fiebiger, Laurie Anderson, and, of course, my two daughters, who would each break into laughter whenever I announced that I was never writing again. Let's not forget Jane Vessels, whose letter to my cat, Alba, from her cat, Puma, started the entire project.

My friend Judith Tartt, a paintings conservator and founder of the lovely website, Art-Care, brought inspiration and read the art and conservation sections for accuracy. Patrick Hyde approved the court and prison sections. Anne Marzin, my sister, found numerous mistakes and with her unconditional approval lifted my heart. Bloom Beloved arrived out of the blue to direct me to Annie Elizabeth Porter, editor at River Sanctuary Publishing. Emily Johnson proofed the manuscript. You think you know how to write—have spent years learning the craft—and discover that creating a book is a collaborative effort.

Love, Alba draws on a lifetime of observation and on the research of two earlier books—*The Art Crowd* and *The Landed Gentry*.

For information on cats, I had only to consider my own beloved Alba, who was the best cat any owner could have served: who always drank from a spigot of running water, who loved to be washed each night with a warm washcloth (thus calming my allergies), and whose quiet dignity never muted her curiosity, her wit, or the generosity of the love of a cat.

Praise for Sophy Burnham's books

A Book of Angels

Like all good books, it exceeds the subject and illuminates the tough, tiring, and sometimes miraculous business of living, where angels sometimes help out. . .. The visibile and invisible dance with each other continually and as far as angels are concerned, now you see them, now you don't. **A Book of Angels** *gives us a lovely, sustained glimpse.*

>—*Chicago Tribune*

Charming, eclectic.

>—*The Washington Post*

A compelling book.

>—*The Baltimore Sun*

Revelations

Spiritual transcendence, sexual passion, and tragic betrayal make for powerful brew in a New Testament-inspired melodrama. Compelling.

>*Kirkus Reviews*

Ms. Burnham is a contemporary Jane Austen.

>Lee Smith, author of *The Devil's Dream*

She is a gorgeous writer. . . the full palette, dark and light, good and evil, no wishy-washy pastels. . . A passionate book—and a richly erotic one. She deserves a readership as broad as her talent—and as discerning.

>*The Los Angeles Times*

The Path of Prayer

Sophy Burnham is a radiant writer. Her consciousness illumines the dark corridors of the soul. She brings peace, hope, humor and inspiration to the subject of prayer. This book, one of her very best, must rank with **The Road Less Travelled** *in its luminous humanity.*

>Julia Cameron, author of *The Artist's Way*

The Path of Prayer by Sophy Burnham, is a vessel of inspiration and hope. In every sense of the word, this book is a loving companion.

—Caroline Myss, bestselling author of *Sacred Contracts, Anatomy of the Spirit*, and *Why People Don't Heal and How They Can*

The Ecstatic Journey

Passionate, comprehensive, and beautifully written, *The Ecstatic Journey* is a feast of fact and myth, knowledge and wisdom that will nourish and enlighten every spiritual voyager.

—*New Woman Magazine*

Sophy Burnham has written an inspiring book about the most majestic dimension of human experience: the mystical realm. Mystics, it is said, swim in the sea in which the unwise drown. Learn to swim: Read this book.

—Larry Dossey, M.D. Author of *Prayer is Good Medicine* and *Healing Words*

The Treasure of Montségur

Her characters leave no good tale untold. . . In matters of the soul, Burnham is as surefooted as those mysterious mountaineers of Montségur.

—*Washington Post Book World*

Burnham paints a vivid picture of the Cathars' struggles. . . haunting.

—*The Washingtonian*

The Art of Intuition

I devoured this book. Wow!... perfectly executed, saturated with light, love, inspiration, and truth!

—Summer Bacon, spiritual teacher and trance medium

Burnham is a seeker, a storyteller, and a writer of such skill and conversational ease that you find yourself halfway through the book before you know it.

—Phyllis Theroux, author, *The Journal Keeper, a memoir*

About the Author

Sophy Burnham has written novels, award-winning plays, investigative journalism, articles, essays and short stories. Three of her books appeared on the *New York Times* (and other) bestseller lists. Her work has been translated into twenty-six languages.

Apart from travel and writing, she says she's doing everything she did as a child: rides her horse, plays chess, takes classes, laughs, loves people, and is delighted by life, her family, and four grandchildren.

Visit her blogs and website at **www. sophyburnham.com**

To Arrange a Talk or Workshop

Sophy Burnham has appeared on scores of TV and radio shows and speaks on a variety of topics concerning her books, including intuition, angels, mysticism, forgiveness, writing and creativity. To contact her, visit:

www.sophyburnham.com

Hearing Sophy Burnham speak is nothing less than life changing. . .

    —Tami Simon, founder of *Sounds True*

They wished you could have continued for hours.

    —Mary Lynn Kotz, The Arts Club of Washington

I hope you never stop being with people in this way. Your presence is so loving and so vibrant it fills the room when you enter and points beyond, to the nature of our God.

    —Anita Ogden, Church of the Good Shepherd, Washington DC

Delightful and immensely engaging. She speaks from the heart.

    —Susan C. O'Connor, National Storytelling Association

When one listens to Sophy Burnham it's like a light in one's life. She is absolutely magnetic.

    —Marie-Monique Steckel, President, French Institute Alliance Française